THE

Leftover

Brooke Williams

BQB

Published in the United States by BQB Publishing
(an imprint of Boutique of Quality Books Publishing, Inc.)
www.bqbpublishing.com

978-1-945448-04-1 (p)
978-1-945448-05-8 (e)

Library of Congress Control Number: 2017935302
Book design by Robin Krauss, www.bookformatters.com
Cover design by Marla Thompson, www.edgeofwater.com

First editor: Olivia Swenson
Second editor: Pearlie Tan

Don't wait until everything is just right. It will never be perfect. There will always be challenges, obstacles, and less than perfect conditions. So what? Get started now. With each step you take, you will grow stronger and stronger, more and more skilled, more and more self-confident, and more and more successful.

– Mark Victor Hansen

Author's Note

Thank you to all the people who have believed in me over the years—you know who you are. Without your constant support and kind words, I would not be the person I am today. I would never have had the gumption to follow my dreams and keep at it even when I felt as though there was no purpose. I write because I love to write. I can't imagine a day without writing. I am grateful that the characters keep coming to me, bugging me to tell their stories. They are persistent and resistance is futile. If you get even half as much enjoyment from my work as I get writing it, I have done my job.

Other Books by Brooke Williams

Chapter One

"You want me to do what?" Megan Malone tilted her head as she pressed her ear against the cell phone. She needed to hear every word.

"Take my place on the show."

Her sister Molly wasn't asking. It was more of a demand. But that was how Molly operated.

"You're kidding, right? I'm not what they're looking for." Megan paced circles around her couch. She loved her sister and there wasn't much she wouldn't do for her, but go on a reality TV show in her place? *Not happening.*

Megan could imagine her sister biting her lip. People often thought they were twins. Fraternal twins, of course, since they looked nothing alike. Their hair was the same shade of sandy blonde, but Molly's hair was sleek and straight while Megan's was "wavy"—the hairdresser's nice way of saying "frizzy mess." Megan sported wire-rimmed glasses, which partially hid her blue-gray eyes, especially because her head was usually tilted down. Megan didn't like making eye contact with people. Molly had perfect vision and ocean blue eyes that sparkled even in dim light. Occasional sparks of envy flared when Megan compared her own short stature with Molly's tall, toned one, but Megan wasn't one to hold grudges. Her sister was the most important person in her world.

"Why can't you do it, anyway?" Megan frowned. Being on the

local Nebraska version of *Survivor* was nearly all her sister had talked about for the last month.

Molly sighed. "I wanted to tell you in person . . ."

"Come on, Molly, what gives? You've wanted to go on this show since KETO announced they were doing it. Why would you back out now?" Molly had a minor obsession with *Survivor*, so much so that she had auditioned for the actual show three months ago. Megan remembered how devastated she was after getting cut in the final round of auditions. Luckily, two weeks later the local TV station had announced they were doing a version of *Survivor* that would feature contestants from their city. Molly had been gushing about it ever since.

"I know, I know, you're right," Molly admitted. "When I auditioned at KETO, all I wanted was a chance to prove I could compete—you know, show those *Survivor* people what they missed."

"And you got onto the local show. So what's the problem?" Molly was stalling and Megan was ready to get to the bottom of the issue.

"It's not about wanting it or not wanting it. The medic that works for the show . . . found something."

Megan stopped pacing and clutched the phone. As much as she complained about her sister, she loved her more than life. Their mother had Megan when Molly was just thirteen months old. They hadn't gotten along in their early years, but when they were twelve and thirteen years old, their mother left their father for a younger man and they were forced to shuttle back and forth between two houses. The sisters began to rely on each other as constants. Megan sometimes felt like she was living in the shadow of her outgoing, beautiful, genuine sister, but she had accepted long ago that being jealous was exhausting. Megan was who she was and while she wasn't always okay with that, the fact that Molly loved her anyway made her sister all that much more special.

"What did he find?"

Silence.

"Molly, come on. You *have* to tell me." Megan sat on the arm of the couch. The news had to be huge. She needed to prepare for the worst. There was no way Molly would back out of the show without a grim diagnosis of some sort.

Megan tried to imagine Molly, full of life and energy, reduced to a sickbed, gaunt and hairless like their grandmother had been in the final stages of breast cancer. She shook the thought away.

"Molly, tell me this—"

"I'm pregnant." Molly whimpered.

"Pr–pregnant?" Megan stood, her voice almost squeaking at the end of the word. Her heart pounded in her chest, but relief flooded through her. Pregnancy wasn't the end of the world. In fact, it was the beginning of another life. "How can that be? You and Derek have been married for less than a year!"

"It doesn't take a year to make a baby."

Megan giggled. "Of course not, but weren't you, you know, *on* anything?"

"Geez, Megan, lay it all out there why don't you."

"Sorry." Megan laced her fingers into her knotted hair, where they stuck in a tangle.

Molly sighed. "It's okay. Yes, I was on the pill. But apparently it's not foolproof."

Megan's mind was buzzing. "Are you okay? How do you feel? How far along are you? Is it a boy or a girl? What will you name him . . . or her? What if you have twins?"

"Simmer down, Meg. I just found out myself. I'm still trying to take it in."

Megan's feet moved automatically beneath her as she paced around the couch. The path was already worn and she wasn't doing it any justice. "What can I do to help? Do you need some crackers? Saltines are best for nausea, right?"

"You see? This is why I wanted to tell you in person."

Megan frowned. "What do you mean?"

"I knew you'd freak out and I really wanted to see it. You're circling the couch, aren't you?"

Megan stopped in her tracks. "No. I'm standing perfectly still, thank you very much." She squinted through the window across from the couch to make sure Molly wasn't sitting out front in her car. The street was empty. She resumed pacing.

"I know you, Megan Malone, and I know you'll be the best aunt in the world—just like you are the best sister. I'm sure I'll be calling for a lot of favors during this pregnancy, but for now I only have one thing to ask."

"What is it? Anything at all."

"The show."

"Right . . . the show." Megan had almost forgotten the original topic of their phone call. The big baby news had eclipsed their earlier conversation.

"So? Will you do it?"

The hope in Molly's voice was palpable. Megan sighed and flopped over onto the couch, nearly rolling to the floor on the other side. She was nothing if not graceful.

"Tell me the details." She owed it to her sister to at least hear her out.

"You remember *Accept this Dandelion*?"

Megan rolled her eyes. "Of course. We watched it together every week!" Watching each episode of the reality show with Molly had been the highlight of her week. In the first season, a local party boy had chosen from twelve women, like on *The Bachelor*. In the second season, the station switched to *The Bachelorette* and starred Eva, the woman who came in third on the first season. She was presented with twelve local suitors to date and consider.

Seeing the dates in places she recognized made love seem more attainable to Megan. Attainable and yet oh-so-unlikely. Finding the right man would mean actually leaving her house from time to time.

"Our girl nights were so much fun." Molly giggled. "Anyway, you know the show is like *Survivor*. KETO picks local people to compete and vote each other out until there is only one person left."

"So there are challenges involved?" Megan winced. She liked *The Bachelor* because watching people fall in love was easy. *Survivor* was different. Megan knew plenty about the show since her sister, its number one fan, often spoke of it. But she'd managed to avoid watching it herself. It seemed like the contestants did things she could never even dream of doing.

"You got it. But they won't be as big or hard as the national show. I'm not sure what the exact format will be, but it'll be a blast."

Megan groaned internally. There was a distinct lack of facts in Molly's information. "Maybe it would have been for you. Are you sure you can't go on? You'd be better than me in any challenge, even with an extra person on board."

Molly giggled. "I'm positive. Once the medic got my blood work back and realized I was pregnant, I was out. I don't know what they have planned, but it is too big of a risk for someone with a bun in the oven."

"I still can't believe you're going to be a mom." Megan's excitement for her sister overshadowed her nervousness about the show.

"It hasn't sunk in for me either. I always thought I'd be married for five years or more before a baby came along."

"But you're happy, right?" All Megan really wanted was for Molly to be happy.

"I'm happy," Molly reassured her. "Derek and I are more in love now than we were the day we got married. I guess our love created a whole new person."

"Gag me." Megan rolled her eyes. Megan didn't want *all* the details. She sometimes found herself wishing for the fairytale her sister had, but she knew it was a pointless desire. The most interaction she had with the opposite sex was when the pizza boy—pimple faced and barely legal to drive—delivered food to her house. Guys had never paid attention to her in school, and now that she worked from home with her voice-over business, there was no obligation to endure social embarrassment.

"One day you'll have to get over your aversion to the birds and the bees, Megan." Megan could almost hear her sister's wink through the phone. "Anyway, back to the show. Listen up. I'm about to give you the rundown."

Megan nodded and pressed the phone against her ear.

"There will be twelve contestants, including you, and they're taping the show over a week and a half. Each day, you'll have some kind of competition and each night there will be an elimination. So to get to the end, you'll have to last nine days. That's all!"

She made it sound so short, but a week and a half was an eternity to Megan.

"There will be individual or group competitions every day. Whoever wins is protected from being voted out that night. There's also a twist."

Megan's head was already spinning. The deluge of information was giving her a headache. Who came up with this game?

"For this local version, there's going to be a special item hidden somewhere around the shooting location. It's called the Protection Piece. Whoever finds it will get a place in the final four, no matter what. Say you find it the second night but get voted out on night three—you will come back when there are three people left. Understand?"

"I guess so." Megan wondered if Molly understood just how slim her chances were, with or without the Protection Piece.

"After I talked with the medic, the producer came in and said he was sorry to see me go and they would choose another contestant from the auditions. I know it's not my job, but I offered to find my own replacement since it's such short notice."

"And why did you do that exactly?" Megan shifted onto her side and felt the couch groan beneath her. This whole situation could have disappeared if Molly hadn't felt some insane urge to be helpful.

"I can't explain it, but when the producer told me they'd choose someone else, I got an image of you standing alone on a podium, your arms raised above your head. You were victorious, Megan. You looked like a champion."

Megan closed her eyes and tried to imagine standing on a winner's podium, but the base was too small and when she raised her hands above her head, she went tumbling backward. *Yep, that's about right.* "You know I'd get kicked out in the first round, right?"

"But what if you didn't?"

"Then I'd probably drown in the first water-related competition."

Molly chuckled. "Maybe they'd let you use water wings."

"And a nose plug." Megan joined her in a fit of giggles.

When Molly caught her breath, she said, "Do you think you'd be able to get away from work?"

Megan answered without thinking. "I could put in a few extra hours before the show starts and clear the deck. I just wrapped a big audio book deal so I'm okay to take a break." She suddenly realized what she'd done and slapped her palm against her forehead. *There goes that excuse.* Megan knew Molly was circling. It was decision time.

"So . . . what do you say?" Molly's melodic voice was wheedling.

For once, Megan was glad her sister wasn't sitting across from her—seeing her pleading eyes would only make matters worse. It had been hard when Molly got married and moved across town. Only a twenty-minute drive separated them, but sometimes that was enough to make phone calls necessary instead of visits.

"I only have until the end of the day to find a contestant to replace me before they go back to the audition pool and pull someone else."

"Why me, Molly? There's really no one else?" Megan asked. *Someone more like you?* Megan had her own talents, but they didn't involve grace and athleticism and . . . being easy on the eyes. If the competitions were anything like gym class in grade school, she was done for. Plus, Molly could talk to a total stranger for five minutes and end up with a new best friend. Megan avoided people she didn't know.

"You know you're my go-to girl. And why *not* you? You're always putting yourself down, Megan, and I don't like it. I think the show would be good for you. You might surprise yourself. Plus, it's an adventure. If I can't have it, I want the person closest to me to enjoy it."

Megan took a deep breath. Her sister was pregnant. She was going to be an aunt. Auntly duties didn't usually require local TV appearances on *Survivor*-style shows. But she wasn't going to be just any aunt. Maybe the show could be a small way of showing her sister how much she cared about her new niece or nephew.

Molly had done so much for her over the years. When their mother seemed to care more about her young boyfriend than either of them, Molly had packed Megan's school lunches and made mac and cheese for dinner. When Megan was miserable working at a local radio station, Molly was the only one to encourage her to follow her passion and talents to start a freelance voice-over business. Molly believed in her no matter what Megan thought of herself.

This silly show meant the world to Molly. The last thing Megan wanted to do was let her down.

"Okay," Megan muttered.

"What?" Molly asked. "Did you say what I think you said?"

"You know I did. I can't say no to you, much less your child."

Molly squealed. "Oh, Meg, you aren't going to regret this!"

"Calm down, you'll hurt my niece . . . or nephew. And I'm fairly certain I will be regretting this. Daily. On TV." She groaned.

"It'll be great. I'll text you the studio address. Go see the medic and get all the necessary tests to get clearance for the show. He's available this afternoon. You'll be surprised when you meet him. Don't ask for details because I'm not saying any more. Meet me at our spot for dinner. I'll help you prepare," Molly rambled.

"When do the tapings begin?" Megan's nerves appeared as the idea became real. She had been caught up in her sister's excitement at first, but now that Molly was talking about actual details, her pulse raced and her hands shook.

"Next week."

Megan gasped involuntarily. "That soon?"

"I know. We have a lot to do, but you're up for it, I promise. I wouldn't put you in this situation if I didn't think you were capable."

Megan smiled. "You've always believed in me. Thanks for that." Maybe other parts of her life could be different if she listened to Molly more often. The show could be the start of a whole new world. *Or a completely embarrassing disaster.*

Megan leaned her head back against the couch and closed her eyes as Molly said, "And I always will. I'm so excited—almost as much as when I was the one going on the show."

"Yeah, but now you get to sit back on the couch, eat pickles and ice cream, and watch me make a fool out of myself."

"That's right!"

"Hey, you're supposed to be supportive. Look what I'm doing for you." Megan stood from the couch and resumed pacing.

Molly laughed. "Gotcha. You'll be great. We both know it."

"Um, I can't say that we do."

"Well, I know and that's enough for now. Go get ready and I'll see you tonight."

"Okay, okay." Megan drew the phone from her ear to hang up, then brought it back up. "Wait," she called before Molly could hang up. "What's the surprise you mentioned before?"

Molly laughed. "I told you, you'll find out when you get to the studio."

"Fine, have it your way." Megan rolled her eyes. "One last thing. What are they calling the show?"

"Are you ready for this?" Molly asked. "*The Leftover.*"

Chapter Two

Cane Trevino surveyed the items in the back corner sales office. It was a makeshift exam room, but as a paramedic, he was used to doing exams on the fly. In fact, the medium-sized office was better than most in the field. He still wasn't sure what possessed him to take the side job when KETO called him.

Maybe this will help me forget about—

Mike, the show's producer, stuck his head in the door. "She's on her way up."

"I'm ready whenever." Cane raised a hand and smiled as he caught a glimpse of Mike's ever-present clipboard through the closing door.

He consulted the cast list. "Molly," he whispered as he crossed her off the list. "Sorry about that." She had fire in her eyes and true enthusiasm for the show. She would have gone far and loved every second. "Megan Malone." He scribbled the new name at the bottom of the list as a light knock sounded at the door.

Cane stuffed the list under the medical charts. "Come on in."

A head of sandy blonde hair poked through the slight opening. "Are you the medic?" the woman asked. Her voice was surprisingly smooth given her frazzled appearance.

Cane threw his stethoscope around his neck and stood. "That's me. Please, come in."

The woman eased around the corner and hesitantly closed the door behind her. Her eyes widened as she inspected his face.

"Megan?" he asked. "Megan Malone, right?"

Megan dropped her eyes to her hands and nodded, adjusting the wire-rimmed glasses on her nose.

"I'm Cane."

"I know." Megan blushed.

Cane made a face. She recognized him from *Accept this Dandelion*, just like everyone else in the city. So she knew all about his romantic history, his heartbreak, and his embarrassment. It was nothing new, but he wished he could get away from it all.

Forcing a smile, he gestured to the plastic chair at the side of the room. "Have a seat."

Megan obeyed silently and Cane noticed she had yet to meet his eyes.

"I think congratulations are in order." He sat on a nearby stool and wheeled closer to her. It was easier to move past his local fame and act as if he were an everyday professional. Unless she pushed him to talk about the show, he would prefer to ignore the fact that she knew who he was and what he'd been through.

Megan shrugged.

Cane frowned. "You aren't happy about being an aunt?"

"Oh. Sorry, I thought you were talking about the show."

"It should be an interesting venture." Cane was just glad his part in the process was on the sidelines and not in front of the camera this time.

Megan nodded and Cane wondered if she would talk more once she was a contestant.

"How did Molly convince you to take her place?" Cane could tell she hadn't volunteered.

Megan shrugged again, an almost pained expression on her face.

"Sometimes we have to do things for our siblings. I get it." He leaned over to try to catch her eye. *Was she ever going to look at him?* "I take it you're not excited."

"I'm not doing cartwheels, if that's what you're asking."

"I might ask that as part of the exam." Cane kept his expression serious.

"Really?" Megan's blue-gray eyes finally met his as a look of sheer panic crossed her features. "I haven't done a cartwheel in years. I'd probably hurt myself. Or you."

Cane raised his hands. "Relax, just a joke." He had finally gotten her to talk, and he liked the melodic tone of her voice.

Megan chuckled and took a deep breath, seeming to relax a bit. "Funny."

Cane shuffled some papers on the nearby counter and handed the stack to Megan. "Look these over and fill out the medical history sheet if you would. When you're through, we'll start the exam."

Megan nodded and grabbed the pen he offered. She bent over the questionnaires and got to work.

Cane took a moment to study the woman before him. Her hair was a cross between brown and blonde, a color one only got the natural way. It was shoved into a messy ponytail and the light brought out different shades every time she moved her head. Her bluish-gray eyes were intriguing, especially now as they focused on the paperwork. Her glasses were slightly askew on her small nose, giving her a cute, distracted look. Her jeans had holes in the knees, but not the fashionable kind. These holes were from hard use, not from scissors. Her faded maroon t-shirt was plain, without any designs or words.

She couldn't have been more different from the woman who haunted his dreams, yet . . .

Ever since Eva, Cane found himself comparing every woman to her and no one measured up. But the fact that he found himself even slightly attracted to Megan was a big step forward. He smiled as she bit her lip in concentration—probably thinking about when her last immunizations were. Maybe he could finally get past Eva.

He absently stroked his chin. Eva was Megan's polar opposite, at least in the looks department. Eva had dark, shiny hair, chocolate brown eyes, and a petite stature. Her smile could light up any room and . . .

Cane made himself stop. He still ached every time he thought of her. He had come very close to what he thought was love, and when he had made it to the final two on the second season of *Accept this Dandelion*, he had thought Eva felt the same way. In the end, Eva chose neither of the remaining contestants and instead ran off with the show's host.

Unfortunately, Eva wasn't the first woman to break Cane's heart, although losing her was by far the most painful incident. Cane always got the "friend" card. He was every woman's best friend and no woman's soul mate. He fell for women hard and fast only to be told that he made a great friend, but nothing more.

Eva had been different; he'd been sure of it. The way she looked at him made him feel like she could see past his faults and into the depths of his soul. She was beautiful, no doubt, but her beauty ran deeper than her appearance. He'd been sure she was the one and had been completely blindsided to learn he wasn't for her. The last year had been tough as he avoided women and tried to pick up the pieces of his heart. He no longer trusted his instincts when it came to the opposite gender.

Cane shook his head. The thin silver lining of being on the local dating show was that Mike, the producer, had called him for this program. Cane had saved one of the other bachelors from choking on *Accept this Dandelion*, and the station knew about his occupation as a paramedic. Whatever the reason, it was a much-needed change of pace and he was grateful for the opportunity.

"All finished." Megan's voice broke into his thoughts.

"What?" Cane focused on Megan. *What a cute nose.*

"With the papers. I'm done."

"Oh, yes, of course. That was fast."

"Not a lot of illnesses in my family." Megan held the papers in Cane's direction.

"That's never a bad thing." Cane looked into her light eyes, Eva's dark brown ones fading into his past. He glanced over the paperwork, noting she marked only headaches as an issue, as well as eyesight. "Do you plan to wear your glasses on the show?"

"Do they want me to be able to see?" Megan cocked her head to the side.

Cane chuckled. "I think that would be best, yes."

"Then I'd say where I go, they go." A smirk flashed across her face before her eyes dropped to her hands again.

"How long have you had them?" The question wasn't on any chart. Now that Megan was finally talking, he just wanted to hear more.

"Grade school. And yes, I've heard it all . . . four eyes and such."

"I think they look nice on you." Cane tried to catch her eyes again but failed.

A startled look passed over her features. "Th–thanks."

Cane rolled his stool closer. "Let's get to work." He swung his stethoscope from around his neck and stuck the ends in his ears. He pressed the metal side to her chest and listened to her heart. It was beating rapidly, but the rhythm wasn't abnormal. He moved his arm around her back and pressed it to one side. "Take a deep breath for me." Megan inhaled. Cane moved the instrument. "And another one." She inhaled again and he felt her breath on his neck as he brought the stethoscope back around her side. "Sounds good."

Megan folded and unfolded her hands as Cane reviewed the paperwork again. "No history of trouble with running or swimming?" he asked.

"Medically? No."

Cane frowned. He was curious as to whether there was a story behind that comment, but it wasn't his place to ask. "I'd like to take your blood pressure now." He removed the cuff from the counter and wrapped the band around her arm. As he squeezed it tighter, Megan seemed to be holding her breath.

"120 over 80. That's very good."

"It's usually lower. White coat syndrome."

"I'm not wearing white or a coat," Cane quipped.

"Maybe that's why it's not higher." Megan glanced up and smiled before resuming the examination of her cuticles.

Cane sat back, scribbling down some notes, and realized he was grinning. He found her charming. She was a little shy to do well in the social part of the game, but she had a subtle sarcasm that would gain fans within the city. People might identify with her in some way. She was an underdog, for sure, but who didn't like to root for the dark horse?

"I need to take some blood and then you can fill this up." He placed a cup on the table next to her chair and prepared the needle to withdraw her blood. When he swiveled back in her direction, he noticed the stricken look on her face.

"I'm supposed to fill that with . . ."

"A urine sample," Cane supplied.

Megan blushed crimson. "Of course."

Had she never peed in a cup for a doctor before? "Are you right handed?"

Megan nodded.

"Great. I'll check the veins on your left arm. That way you won't overuse your arm later and form a bruise."

"How thoughtful."

Cane detected a hint of sarcasm as he pulled a latex glove over each hand. He ran his finger up her arm to look for a good spot. Megan shivered.

"Sorry."

She shook her head.

"You have nice veins." He grabbed the needle and swabbed her arm with alcohol before inserting it and beginning to draw the blood.

"If I had a nickel for every man who said that to me."

Cane snorted. "You get that a lot, huh?"

Megan nodded, more animated than before. "Only from every cute doctor this side of I-80." She clapped her free hand over her mouth, and he caught her wide eyes as she ducked her head.

Cane bit his tongue, holding in his laughter. He didn't need to enhance her embarrassment. She obviously hadn't meant what she said to be so personal—more of a passing thought that she accidentally said out loud. He let the silence settle between them as he finished drawing blood. Once the vials were secure and she had a bandage, he removed his gloves.

"Okay, fill the cup for me, bring it back and then you're good to go."

"That's it?"

"Relatively painless, huh?" Cane winked at her.

Megan glanced at the cup. "Are there any red flags?"

Cane leaned back on the counter next to his stool. "Do you want there to be?"

"No. Yes. I mean, I don't know."

Cane stroked his chin. "I don't see any reasons why you wouldn't be able to compete on the show at this stage."

"Great," Megan muttered.

Cane's heart went out to her. She was about to embark upon an experience that was obviously out of her comfort zone. He knew what it was like to make a fool of himself on TV, and he had an inkling that she expected to do the same.

"Just do your best, Megan."

Megan half-smiled at her hands.

Cane let a few beats pass as he studied her unusual eyes. Her glasses almost framed them and set them off in a deeper way. She would add an element to the show. He wasn't certain what, but definitely something.

"Now, about that urine . . ."

Chapter Three

Megan closed the door behind her and slapped her forehead. Her cheeks were still fiery hot from delivering the cup to the cute medic, who just happened to be former local TV star Cane Trevino. If she was going to make it past the first day on The Leftover, she was going to have to get over her embarrassment . . . fast. She'd had a crush on Cane when she'd watched the second season of *Accept this Dandelion* with her sister.

"Megan." Mike, the producer, appeared with a large clipboard extending before him. "Everything all set?"

Megan looked down. "I . . . I think so."

"I'm sure the medical tests will be fine, but we have to jump through all the hoops. Are you ready for your screen test?"

"My what?" Megan's eyes widened and she self-consciously smoothed her hair back into its lopsided ponytail.

"It won't take much time. We just need to see you on camera for a few minutes so we can get a read on how to shoot you during the show."

Megan frowned. Molly hadn't mentioned any on camera tests. But she probably knew Megan wouldn't have come if she had.

"I, uh—sure." She was fairly certain Mike wouldn't take no for an answer by the way he turned on his heel and barreled across the studio before she could say more. Megan stuffed her hands into her pockets, ducked her head, and followed.

"Sit here." Mike tossed his clipboard in the direction of a soft interview chair Megan recognized from the local news program. "Our camera crew will ask a few questions, adjust lighting, things like that. We'll be filming outside, but it's good to get an idea how you look on screen."

"If you're looking for my best side, I'm pretty sure it's the back of my head," Megan muttered under her breath. She tried to control her breathing—in two counts, out two counts.

"I'll give you a call as soon as the tests are in and get you details about the taping." He turned to the nearby camera operator. "We good here?"

"Ready to roll, boss."

Mike disappeared into the dark part of the set. Megan shifted her eyes back and forth and crossed one leg over the other. She leaned back into the chair and then scooted forward and crossed the other leg. She was all nerves and every second that passed made it worse. At least there weren't any people that she had to make eye contact with. Maybe she could pretend she was talking to Molly. She could get through this.

"So," said a voice from the other side of the camera, "tell us what it was like when you heard you were going to be on *The Leftover.*"

Megan cleared her throat. Where was she supposed to look? "I don't know that I'm on the show yet."

The operator coughed. "Okay, what was it like when you heard it was a possibility?"

"I think I said something to the effect of 'not going to happen.'" Megan decided to focus on the dark background behind the camera.

"You were in shock, right?"

"I wouldn't call it shock, exactly. More extreme denial. As in no way, no how would I ever go on TV and compete against other locals like that."

Megan winced as she realized what she had said. She was telling the crew that she in no way, shape, or form wanted to be on the show. Her usual social awkwardness was coming across loud and clear. Megan tried to sit still, but she had to fidget. She scratched her nose and re-crossed her legs. She was going down in flames.

But she had to try—for Molly. Megan sat up straighter. "My sister was supposed to be on the show," Megan filled the silent, oppressive air around her. "She's really athletic and she would have killed it. She asked me to replace her and now that I've had time to let it sink in, I'm honored that she considered me worthy to fill her shoes."

There. That was better. Awkward and rambling, but better.

"Are you and your sister a lot alike?"

"Well, we wear different-sized shoes. She's got these puny little feet and mine are more like boats." Megan held her foot up in front of the camera and giggled. "See?" As she brought her shoe back to the concrete floor beneath her, only one thought crossed her mind—if Molly ever saw this footage, she'd think Megan was intentionally trying to get out of the show. But she had to keep talking—it was better than her usual silence, no matter how silly she felt. "We also look completely different and are good at opposite things, but we couldn't be any closer."

"What are you most excited about experiencing on *The Leftover?*"

"Meeting new people?" Megan raised her voice at the end, making it sound more like a question than a statement. "I work out of my house so I don't get out much." She smiled awkwardly. She was coming off like such a geek! And meeting new people was probably the last thing she was excited about . . . other than the competitions.

"And what do you do?"

"Mostly read." Megan shook her head. That wasn't a good description. "I'm a freelance voice actor. I do a lot of audio books, commercials, some radio theater, that sort of thing."

Megan's job was unique and she felt lucky to make a living doing something she loved out of her home. No one ever had to see her in person and she seldom spoke to clients on the phone. Everything ran remotely through email. When she started in the radio production business, she worked behind the scenes at a studio. Her sister saw how painful going to work was for her and encouraged her to branch out on her own. Megan was good at what she did, but she was too shy to sit in a studio and record things with people looking at her. Working at the studio limited her to producing and editing. The more her sister prodded her, the more thought Megan gave to creating her own business. Eventually, she took the plunge. She credited her sister for her current success.

"We should be good here." The blinking red light on the camera went black and the operator stepped into view. Megan immediately looked down. "Nice to meet you, Megan. Hope to see you in a few days on set."

"Thanks." Megan stood and gathered her wits. One foot got tangled in the cords that ran across the floor as she tried to get out from under the hot studio lights. She quickly recovered and scurried out.

Whose idea had this been anyway? Oh right, Molly's. And they were meeting for dinner in less than an hour.

Megan rushed for the studio exit. She'd been around people long enough. She hoped she had enough energy to do her dinner date justice, but she wasn't sure. Tucking her chin to her neck, she threw her shoulder into the exit door.

"Whoa there, steam roller!" Cane jumped back on the other side.

"Sorry! Did I get you?" Megan groaned inwardly. She wasn't sure she could have another conversation, especially after her embarrassing interactions with Cane earlier. But his soft eyes beckoned and her car was close.

"No, but it was a close call. I was just leaving."

Megan fell into step beside him. "I didn't know my own strength. I couldn't wait to get out of there."

"Did it go that well?"

Megan frowned as she watched her feet move closer to her car. "Great." She knew the sarcasm in her voice told him there was more to the story.

"I gotta get these samples to the lab." Cane patted the black medical bag slung over his shoulder.

"Oh, so my . . . it's in there?"

Cane grinned. "It is."

Megan's cheeks flamed once again. After a few steps, she realized he wasn't next to her anymore. She turned to find him standing there, looking at her.

"I really hope everything goes well for you, Megan. I think you'll be a great addition to the show."

"You do?" Megan searched his gaze, realizing he was being genuine.

Cane shrugged. "I know TV can be intimidating. It's hard to be yourself with so many eyes on you and plenty of expectations. But if you relax and let your true self come out, everything will fall into place."

Her eyes flicked from his eyes to his shirt and back to his eyes. "Well, thanks. I appreciate that." And she meant it. If Cane were an average medic, he wouldn't know so much about TV. But Cane was a TV star in his own right.

Cane smiled and Megan felt herself melt into the cement. Oh, the things his smile did to his eyes. They somehow got softer and deeper and she was certain if she didn't blink a few times or look away, she would be lost forever. She remembered that smile on the show, but it was much more attractive in person. She would have chosen him any day of the week. Of course, she had felt that way about Steve and Mitch on the show too . . .

"Tell Molly hi and I'll give you a call soon."

Megan shook herself from her reverie and hoped her lack of speech hadn't showcased her awe. He was going to call her!

"The lab results shouldn't take more than a day."

With lab results. Of course. He was going to call her about her tests.

"Have a good evening." Cane waved and ducked into a sensible Chevy four-door.

Megan watched him place the black medical bag carefully on the floor of the passenger seat before she fumbled her keys out of her pocket and got into her own car.

Chapter Four

Cane tapped the steering wheel and squinted into the rain. His delivery was complete and he had the evening to himself. Of course, he had every evening to himself if he wasn't working, but that was his own fault. His friends sometimes offered to meet him for dinner or a movie, but since Eva, he'd tried to fill his schedule with work, and when he was free, he pushed people away.

Cane had been a paramedic for the past seven years. He'd planned on being a doctor, but he wanted to help people faster than medical school would allow, and paramedic training was more immediate. He loved his job, though it was certainly trying at times. Cane hadn't grown up in the city, but after he completed his training and found an opening in his field, he grabbed the opportunity, moved, and made the area his home.

He'd made good friends from work that almost felt like family to him, but they didn't understand what it was like to get rejected on TV in front of the entire city. They all told him to get over Eva and move on with his life, as if it were as easy as wiping a slate clean. That's exactly what he wanted to do, but a little compassion along the way never hurt. He just needed time, that was all.

And he needed to realize, once and for all, that Eva wasn't coming back to him. No matter how convinced he had been that she was the one, she had chosen someone else. At first he believed she'd change her mind, but it had been a year and she hadn't called.

When he took the temporary job at KETO, part of him wondered if they might run into one another. She was the promotions director for the Furry Friends Rescue League and he'd seen her on TV as she was interviewed about the animal charity. But the chance to see her wasn't why he accepted the position, and in fact, he hoped he didn't see her—it would be too painful. He simply needed to occupy his time and work gave him a positive focus.

Cane turned his wipers off as the rain started to clear. What was left of the sun shone through the clouds and a brilliant rainbow formed just outside the passenger window.

"Wow." Cane whistled.

After finding himself attracted to Megan earlier that day, Cane began to believe he really was getting over Eva. The side gig with KETO would require a nine-day, twenty-four seven commitment, allowing him to take a break from his normal paramedic work and forget about the social world completely for a while. He would shake his love failures off and move on with his life . . . finally. He had family, friends, and a job he loved. What more did he need? After a little time away from his regular schedule, he would pick up where he left off with his friends and maybe even start looking for Ms. Right again.

He chuckled, remembering Megan's embarrassment over the urine sample. Despite her very shy nature, he was rooting for her. She was a real person with obvious limitations. He hoped she would do well on the show—and that her clumsiness didn't cause her to need his help.

Ringing took over the interior of his car and Cane pushed a button on the steering wheel to activate the hands-free phone. "Hello?" He recognized the hospital's number that popped up on the dashboard's screen.

"Hey, man, it's me. I know you're off today, but the rain really did a number on the streets. We've got accidents all over the metro and some are serious. Do you have a few hours to spare?"

Cane knew his colleague wouldn't have called if they weren't in dire need of extra hands. "Be there in five." He turned at the next corner and sped up. Cane was good at his job and he would give it all he had. For now, it would have to be enough.

Megan wrung her ponytail with one hand while closing the restaurant door behind her. It was just like her to leave her umbrella at home and get caught in the downpour. It hadn't been raining when she left the TV studio, but the clouds had had their fun and now that she was inside, the rain had stopped.

Molly burst through the door thirty seconds later, completely dry. She gave Megan the once over. "Shower in the rain?"

"Very funny."

The girls waved at Pete, the owner of their favorite haunt, Peter's Diner. It was just around the corner from the house they had grown up in. As children, they had stopped by daily in the summer to beg ice cream from the kind staff. Now that they were adults, they ordered meals—a payback of sorts. They met at least weekly, sometimes more.

Molly slid into their booth in the back. It was almost always empty when they arrived, like it had their name engraved on the side and no one else dared use it. As Megan started to take a seat across from her sister, her wet jeans stuck on the vinyl seat, making it impossible to scoot without completely lifting herself up and moving over with short hops. *Graceful, as always.*

"So, how did it go?" Molly leaned over and placed her palms down onto the table.

"Forget the show, how are you?" Megan squinted at her sister. She didn't look pregnant. She looked as long and lean as ever.

Molly waved her hand. "Fine, fine. Forget about me, tell me about the show!"

Megan shrugged, face solemn. "I'm a little ticked at you, to be honest."

Molly sat back in her seat as the waiter brought waters and quickly disappeared. "You don't want to go on TV, do you?"

Megan tried to hold back a grin. "I'm mad because you didn't warn me about Cane!"

Molly tilted her head with an impish grin on her face. "You recognized him immediately, right?"

Megan nodded. "How could you keep that a secret from me? He was my biggest crush!"

"I couldn't help myself. I only wish I could have seen the look on your face when you saw him."

"It was probably something like this." Megan widened her eyes to look like a deer in headlights and dropped her jaw.

Molly laughed. "Wow, I bet that made quite the first impression."

"He was adorable on *Accept this Dandelion*, but the cameras didn't do him justice."

"Cute, right?" Molly agreed. "He kind of looks like Mark Feuerstein with that curly hair."

"Mark who?"

"Feuerstein. You know, the guy on *Royal Pains*? Oh come on, we *have* to get you Netflix."

"Well, whoever he looks like, he's cute and he knows it." Megan stared at the table.

"He didn't come across as arrogant to me. How did he act with you?" Molly stirred her glass of water with a straw.

"It wasn't how he acted, it's the fact that I told him."

"Told him? That he was cute?" Molly's eyes bulged.

"Yup. Just blurted it right out. Honestly, I thought I said it in my head and not out loud, but based on the look on his face, I'm pretty certain it was audible."

"Oh, Megan!" Molly reached across the table and grasped her sister's wrist. "What did he say?"

Megan shrugged. "Something medical. I don't know."

Molly waggled her eyebrows. "Did you get his number?"

"What? Of course not. Are you kidding me? I was too busy doing the screen test." Megan bit her lip at the memory. "Another thing you *forgot* to tell me about."

"That part was fun. Did they ask anything unusual?"

"I don't think so. Just what I'd like about the show, if I was excited, things like that."

"And are you?" Molly took a sip of water, an expectant look in her eyes.

"I'm ready to do this. For you."

"That's not what I asked."

"I was hoping you wouldn't notice." Megan sighed. "You know me too well."

"Tell me what you're thinking." Molly moved the menus aside. No one came to take their order anymore—Pete knew what they wanted.

Megan leaned her head back against the booth so she was looking at the ceiling. "It's just so out of my element, you know? I'm used to sitting in my house, all alone, talking to myself. How am I going to go from that to actually talking to other people . . . on TV, no less?" She looked at Molly, hoping she'd have some encouragement.

"I don't have an answer for you." Molly leaned back in her seat.

"What? I was expecting some kind of pep talk."

"I don't know how you'll do it or how things will turn out. But I know you'll be great. Megan, you're so lovable. I want this just as much for you as I wanted it for me. You get a chance to show this city who you are. And the city deserves to meet Megan Malone. They'll love you just as much as I do."

"Now that's more what I was expecting." Megan smiled. "We don't even know if I'm on the show yet. They have to wait for the tests to come back and once the producer sees my screen test . . . well, let's just say it could be a deal breaker."

"You charmed their pants off and you know it." Molly swatted at her sister.

"I'm fairly certain everyone was still wearing pants when I left."

Their food arrived and interrupted the conversation. They thanked Pete with a wave across the diner. He would come talk to them before they left, like he always did. He was like an adopted favorite uncle.

"Well, we can't wait for the test results. We need to start training right away." Molly took a bite of her grilled chicken sandwich.

"Training?" Megan's mouth was full of her burger, but she managed to get the word out while chewing.

"Mmhm. We only have a few days and you have a lot to learn. Have I shown you the list of things to bring?"

Megan shook her head.

"That's okay, it's pretty small. This is a *Survivor*-like show, after all. We'll get to that. I need to see what you're made of first."

"Sugar and spice and everything nice, of course, just like any girl."

Molly kicked her under the table. "See? You're charming. Just bring that to the show and you'll be the last one left over."

"Ah." Megan stroked her chin. "I get it now. *The Leftover!*"

Molly rolled her eyes. "What, did you think they were talking about food from last night?"

Megan shrugged. "Instead of being the sole survivor like on the national show, the winner will be crowned *The Leftover*. That's kind of silly." She surveyed her sister's serious face. "I mean cool. That's very cool."

"You bet it's cool. You could find yourself on *Survivor* next if you're not careful."

"Don't worry, I'll be very careful."

"This is so exciting. I can't believe you're doing this!"

Megan looked at her sister with incredulity. "And I can't believe you're pregnant. I want details, girl!"

"That's rather personal," Molly joked.

"Come on, spill. Do you want a boy or a girl? Got any names? Megan has a nice ring to it, don't you think?"

"You win *The Leftover* and you can name the kid anything you want."

"Promise?" Megan stuck her pinky finger across the table.

"Pinky swear." Molly wrapped her finger around her sister's and shook.

Done deal.

Chapter Five

The phone rang once, twice, three times. Cane prepared himself to leave a message when the fourth ring was interrupted, followed by some muffled sounds and a loud clunk. After a moment, her smooth voice came over the line.

"I'm so sorry! I dropped you. Are you okay?"

Cane smiled. Her tone was a breath of fresh air. No wonder she did well in the voice-over world—he had picked up on her engaging voice while watching her screen test. "I'm fine. Everything okay there?"

"Yes, yes, of course. Just wrapping up a project."

"I didn't mean to interrupt."

"Not a problem. Who is this anyway?"

Cane chuckled. "I suppose that would be a good thing to reveal. This is Cane Trevino, the medic from KETO."

There was a loud inhale. "You have news?"

"I do." Cane paused, enjoying the element of power he had.

"I already know I'm not pregnant so if there's something else of concern, spit it out."

Cane smiled and pictured her haphazard ponytail and wire-rimmed glasses. Since she worked at home, she didn't have to get fixed up for anything unless she wanted to. And he guessed she usually didn't want to.

"You're the epitome of health. You get the all clear for the show.

I informed the producer and he's sending you detailed information this afternoon. Since time is short, I wanted to let you know as soon as possible."

"So there's no reason at all I shouldn't go on the show?"

"Nothing physical." Cane hesitated. He was the medical professional on *The Leftover* staff and he didn't want to cross any boundaries. But his contract didn't say anything about making new friends. "Are you having doubts about the opportunity?"

A shuffling sound echoed over the line. Cane wondered if she was pacing.

"Yes. I mean no. I'll do the show. I have to. For Molly."

Cane cleared his throat. "Megan, in my opinion, you're just what the show needs."

The shuffling stopped. "How so?"

"I've met the other contenders and I can't give anything away, but . . . I don't know, you're different." Cane scratched his cheek. Different was one way of putting it. She was shy, soft spoken and, well, awkward. But he had seen glimpses of the real Megan under the timid exterior, and she had spunk. He didn't think he'd be alone in rooting for her.

"Like I haven't heard that before."

"I mean it in a good way. You'll add a deeper layer to the cast and I think you'll do well." Cane understood TV shows often added as much eye candy as possible to keep viewers interested. If Megan could get over her shyness fast enough, he hoped her quick wit would come through and endear her to the audience and the other contestants.

"You do?"

"You've got a spark. I think the viewers will take to you. Remember Renee Lockhart from the first season of *Accept this Dandelion*?"

"You think I'm like her?" Megan sounded offended.

Cane made a face. Renee might not be a good comparison. She

was a disaster around every corner. She lit herself on fire, jumped into pools fully clothed, had embarrassing allergic reactions on camera, and bucked every rule the station put into place. But she was also a regular, everyday girl, and the audience loved her. She was still quite popular around town. "Not in so many ways. I just think you're relatable and that will draw people to you."

"I prefer to be alone." Megan's quiet statement was hard to hear over the phone.

"I got that when we met." Cane remembered how she avoided his eyes. Social situations made her uncomfortable, that much was clear. He didn't have that problem himself—he wouldn't make a very good paramedic if he did—but he was sympathetic toward her plight. She needed all the reassurance she could get. "Look, I'm in no position to tell you what to do. But if I were you, I'd give it a chance. Worst-case scenario, you lose a few days of your life and you make your sister happy."

"That's the worst case?" Megan's tone brightened.

"Well, maybe not, but it's the most likely worst case."

"And being a paramedic, you're good at figuring odds, right?"

"The best."

"Okay, Mr. Trevino. If you run into the producer, tell him I'm in."

"Will do, Miss Malone. Will do." Cane ran his hand through his curly hair. He felt unreasonably glad that Megan would be on the show. What would she bring to the table?

Megan hung up the phone and dropped over the edge of the couch into her favorite position. She had been nearing full freak-out mode about being a contestant on a *Survivor*-type TV show. She had allowed herself to delve into notorious "what ifs" and none of them had done her any good. What if she had to swim? What if no one liked her? What if she couldn't bring herself to talk to anyone? What if she was the first one kicked out? Or what if she embarrassed herself—or her sister—in front of the whole city?

Cane's call had pulled her back from the edge in just a few moments. She was still nervous about the show, but after talking to Cane, her demeanor was calm, cool, and collected. Megan knew her sister believed in her, but Molly was biased. Cane seemed to think she was taking the right path as well. Hearing reassurance from a near stranger sent relief coursing through her.

She hugged the phone to her chest. She was due to meet Molly for their first shopping/training session, but she wanted to savor the moment. She didn't interact with many people by choice, but her conversation with Cane was different. She felt good about herself . . . about the prospect of the show . . . about life in general. Maybe this opportunity wouldn't be so bad.

Megan peeled herself from the couch and adjusted the messy bun on the back of her head. At least she wouldn't have to wear a glittery dress like on the dating shows the station taped. For a show like *The Leftover*, she would fit right in with messy hair and a come-as-you-are appearance.

Ten minutes and a layer of ChapStick later, Megan found her sister outside their favorite mall so they could go through her list of needed items.

Molly waved the bright yellow sheet in front of Megan's face. "I have what the show gave me so you'll be ahead of the game when they call."

"Actually, they already called." She bowed her head in feigned disappointment.

"They did? And you're in, aren't you! Come on, Megan, you can't play this game."

Megan looked up, smiling. "You're right. I'm no good at faking it. I'm in."

Molly squealed and jumped up and down.

"Be careful, you'll jostle the baby too much," Megan scolded.

"She likes it, don't worry."

"She?"

Molly shrugged. "Better than calling her 'it.' If it's a boy, I'll switch gears. Until then, she'll have to deal with it."

Megan grinned as her sister looped her arm through Megan's elbow, chattering with excitement about the show. After a short walk, Molly dragged Megan into the large sporting goods store at the end of the mall. "Here's our first stop."

Megan shrugged. At least it wasn't ball gowns. If Molly were to find her some comfortable sweatshirts to take for the cold evenings, she'd be happy.

"Okay, I want you to have a seat here and I'll grab some things." Molly left Megan near a stool in the center of the women's athletic section. She disappeared behind a rack, leaving Megan alone with her thoughts.

Megan sat as directed and glanced around at the tight shorts and tops and too bright colors. She preferred jeans and t-shirts, but it could be worse. Megan picked at the seam of her jeans and inspected her cuticles. She should offer to help Molly, but she knew her take-charge sister preferred to choose things on her own.

"Your dressing room awaits," Molly's voice sang out. "You get started and I'll take another swing around the section and hand other things to you."

Megan stood and sidestepped the racks until she found Molly. "This one?" She pointed to the open curtain closest to Molly, who was already buried in another rack.

"That's the one."

Megan closed the curtain behind her and surveyed the hangers jammed on the hooks in the wall. She let out a low whistle. Her sister worked fast. She grabbed the closest hanger and her eyes widened.

"Um, Molly?"

"Yeah?"

Megan flung the hanger over the door to show the item to her sister.

"What does this go under?"

Molly's voice grew louder as she moved closer. "Nothing. It's hot in the summer. You'd die of sun stroke if you wore too much."

"But what about sun*burn*?"

"Sunscreen is on the list of approved items." Her voice grew softer and Megan knew she was walking away.

She sighed. She would let Molly have her way for now. She'd try it on and show her, but that was as far as this little number would go.

Megan threw her t-shirt to the floor and squeezed into the tight sports bra. She removed her jeans and paired the top with an item that looked like a swimsuit bottom. The tag read "running shorts," but they fit much more like underwear than shorts. Once Megan was situated inside the so-called clothing, she pulled back the dressing room curtain.

"There is no way in—" Megan stopped dead in her tracks.

"Megan, you remember Cane, the paramedic from the show, right?" Molly placed a hand on Cane's shoulder. The two stood ten feet away, and Megan was in full view.

Megan crossed her arms over her chest and studied the floor. Her mind was telling her to bolt in no uncertain terms, but she couldn't seem to get her feet to obey.

"I just stopped in to grab some more Ace bandages for the show and I spotted Molly over here and came by to say hello," Cane explained.

Megan slid her feet on the floor, one behind the other as she edged her way back into the dressing room behind her. No one was supposed to see her in this getup, much less the cute medic.

"Um, hi," she said as she jerked the dressing room curtain closed behind her. Too little too late. He'd already gotten an eyeful.

"Well, I better get going. Nice to run into you, Molly." Cane's voice raised a decibel. "Looking forward to spending time with you on the show, Megan."

Megan peeked out from behind the curtain and caught Molly watching Cane walk away.

"Well, that was embarrassing," she hissed.

"What are you talking about?" Molly frowned and walked over to her, looking her over with a critical eye. "You look great. Did you see Cane? He was definitely checking you out."

"Shut up, Molly."

"He was! He even said he was looking forward to spending time with you." Molly dug her elbow into Megan's exposed side. "If I didn't know any better, I'd say something was a-brewin' there."

"Whatever. He was just being polite." Megan blushed and rolled her eyes.

Molly winked. "We'll see about that. Anyway, that looks good on you. Does it fit okay?"

Megan looked down at the limited amount of fabric covering her chest. She let go of the curtain and, in the privacy of her booth, craned her head around to see her backside. There were definitely pieces of her cheeks hanging out in the rear. "That depends on your definition of 'fit.'"

"You have a nice figure," Molly called. "Whether you believe it or not."

Megan pictured her sister on the other side of the curtain. Molly was tall, thin, and muscular. Megan was short and squat, in her opinion.

"Just try on the rest." Molly's voice faded away.

It took Megan multiple attempts and several unladylike grunts to get the sports bra off, but once she did, she felt free. Cane had already seen her in it, but that didn't mean she had to show so much of the goods to the rest of the city. She was going on the show to please her sister, but she had to draw the line somewhere. It was time to take a stand.

"I don't think these are going to work for me, Mol." She tossed a few of the skimpier clothes over the top of the dressing room's curtain rail.

"I'm just trying to help."

Megan pulled her clothes back on and her body sighed in relief at their comfortable, well-covered surroundings. Megan pulled back the curtain and stepped out of the dressing room to face her downcast sister. "I know and I appreciate it. You're the only one in the world I would go on this show for. But you told me the other contestants would love me once they got to know me so I have to go onto the show as, well, me."

Molly held her hands up as if to show defeat. "You're absolutely right and I'm sorry. You wear whatever makes you comfortable. I'm in your corner whether you're wearing a sports bra and running shorts or," she gestured at Megan's wrinkled t-shirt and old jeans, "that."

Megan looked down at herself and smiled. Molly understood her better than anyone. She tried to push Megan outside her comfort zone more often than not, but she was okay backing off when Megan pushed back. Megan had committed to doing the show. Now that she was up to her ears in this challenge, the least she could do was wear comfortable clothing.

Chapter Six

Cane spotted the news anchors chatting over coffee before the next live program. It was surreal seeing people he knew from TV in person, but then again, he was one of those people as well. People still remembered his stint on local reality TV. He rounded the corner that led to the back offices and picked up speed. He had a lot to organize. He needed to pack his makeshift exam room and double check his supplies. Living on location would be complicated and he should be prepared. He was carrying a stack of newly purchased Ace bandages and wished he hadn't rejected the offer of a plastic bag. He pushed the packages under his chin and tried to watch his step.

When his shoulder rammed into another moving body, the precariously balanced bandages flew in all directions. But nothing startled Cane like the sight that met his eyes when he raised his chin.

"Eva." He breathed her name.

"C-Cane, what are you—"

"I took a job as the medic for the new show KETO is taping next week."

Eva nodded. "You'll be great."

"And what are you doing here?"

Eva blushed. "I just stopped by to see . . ."

Brian. Of course. She didn't have to say it. Brian was the

morning news anchor at the station and had been the host of *Accept this Dandelion*, the dating show where Eva and Cane had met. When Cane heard that Brian had not been asked to host *The Leftover*, he was relieved. He was on his way to getting over Eva, but he still did not want to work with the man she chose over him.

"I'm sorry," Eva continued. "This is very awkward. I didn't mean to put you in this position."

Cane shrugged and stuffed his hands into his pockets. "You didn't know I'd be here." He allowed himself a moment to study her. Her shiny hair glistened, even under the dull hall lights. Her nervous smile made his heart beat faster.

"No, I didn't."

Cane remembered how his heart had ached the day she turned him away. There she'd stood at the end of the long aisle, the studio decorated with dandelions and landscape rocks. She'd looked glamorous, as usual, in an off-the-shoulder black dress with a diamond necklace, her hair loose and wavy, framing her face and catching every ounce of the bright studio lights. He'd been certain she would choose him all the way up until the moment she told him he was everything she was looking for, but . . . Inserting "but" into any conversation like that meant it was going downhill. She'd told him that as much as she wanted him to be "the one," her heart led her elsewhere.

In shock, he'd walked off-screen and learned she also turned down Steve, the other contestant among the final two. Moments later, she ran into the arms of the show's host, Brian, who was also the KETO news anchor. After that fateful day, she had let a full month go by before calling him. When she finally had, she told him she was worried that if she had called sooner, he would have jumped to the wrong conclusion. There was no hope of a relationship.

"I just wanted to tell you how sorry I was and that I never intended for any of this to happen," she'd said on the phone.

"Honestly, I planned to pick you, but when it came down to it, I just couldn't."

"That's supposed to help?" Cane had asked in reply, bitterness coloring his tone.

"I suppose not." He had heard the hurt in her voice over the phone. She hadn't come out of the situation without anguish either, even if she did have a happy ending. "You need to know it's nothing you said or did. You know more about how the heart operates than I'll ever know. I hope you understand that as much as I expected things to work out between us, my heart chose Brian."

Hearing the words didn't feel good, even a month after they'd split on TV. But Cane had appreciated her concern. "I'm glad you're happy, Eva." And he'd meant it, though a part of him still hoped it was her calling every time his phone rang in the past year.

But that didn't make seeing her in person any easier now. Cane shifted his feet. He had no idea what to say. Their relationship on *Accept this Dandelion* had been easy, but this was downright hard.

She opened her arms and took a small step forward. Cane took his hands from his pockets and allowed her to initiate a brief hug.

"Good to see you, Cane," she murmured as she pulled away. Then she walked down the hall.

He turned and watched her go. He thought she was the woman for him, but Eva was right. If she didn't feel for him what he felt for her, their relationship never would have worked. Perhaps it was better that it ended sooner rather than later. Any additional time spent with her would have caused him to fall harder.

Cane knelt to gather the bandages. Seeing Eva wasn't easy, but his heart hurt slightly less now that he realized how awkward things were between them. She'd found someone to love. Perhaps it was time he started looking again himself.

"Those stairs?" Megan shielded her eyes and craned her neck, trying to see the top of the metal stadium steps.

"Yeah, remember when I used to come here to train for track?" Molly positioned herself on the bottom bleacher.

"Of course. Remember how I brought my magazine to kill time while you ran?"

"I didn't forget." Molly pulled a magazine from her oversized bag and leaned back on the second step. She hitched her thumb over her shoulder. "Get to it."

Megan shook her head. She was already exhausted. The stair workout was last on a long list of items Megan had already checked off that day, none of which she had enjoyed. Molly had started her out easy with a walk through the forest. Then she had ramped up the intensity with an obstacle course Megan was fairly certain was meant for dogs. Then, laps at the pool—where Megan again felt like a dog, given that her stroke of choice was the doggy paddle— followed by weight lifting. And now this stair climb torture.

Molly made the physical stuff look so easy. Megan realized she was probably lucky her sister was pregnant so she wouldn't run beside her and egg her on. *May as well get it over with.* She jogged up two stairs, three, four. Her breath came faster and she could feel the sweat forming on her upper lip.

She counted the stairs all the way up. Forty. Now, the easy part—time to go down. When she reached her sister, she put her hands on her knees and gasped for breath. "There," she said when she could. "Happy?"

"Ecstatic." Molly glanced at her over the magazine. "Again."

Megan glared at her sister as she turned and took the stairs again, this time slower. What good would this do? There weren't going to be any stairs on the show. How much could she improve her level of fitness in two days?

By the time Megan got to the bottom of the flight again, her glasses were steamed over and sliding down her nose.

"You can't do it a third time, can you?" Her sister's challenging tone bounced off the magazine and hit Megan's ears like fingernails on a chalkboard.

Megan scowled but didn't answer. She threw herself up the stairs again, this time taking her aggravation out on the metal beneath her. When she returned, her sister was standing and clapping.

"That's what I like to see," Molly yelled.

"Me drenched in sweat? Again?"

"The determination in your eyes. It's not that you can't do things, Megan, it's that you need someone to challenge you. You *can* and you know it. I know you don't like lying, but you're going to have to get used to it if you want to make it anywhere on the show. Now tell me, how do you feel?"

Megan felt like a wet dog. "Great?"

Molly narrowed her eyes.

"Great!" Megan raised her arms above her head and waved them around. *Ouch. That hurt.*

"Better. I almost believe you." Molly slapped her magazine shut. "Now go get cleaned up. Your meeting is in an hour."

Megan wanted to respond, but she didn't have control of her breathing yet. Her sister had put her through the wringer, but instead of feeling stronger, Megan felt sore, weak, and ready to collapse. She climbed into her waiting car without so much as a wave to Molly and blasted the air conditioning, turning the vents to point at her overheating body. Perhaps Molly's goal was to run her so hard that a week and a half on *The Leftover* would feel like a piece of cake.

Mmm, cake. Megan's mouth watered, but she shook the delicious thought from her mind. No time for food. She needed to get home, jump in an ice cold shower, cool down, and head over to KETO. Mike had called an organizational meeting to explain everything to the contestants. Megan was anxious to check out the competition, especially because that was literally all she would be allowed to do. Mike had stressed that there would be no talking—the number one rule until the show began the next day.

Megan pulled to a stop in front of her home and opened the car door. She was unsure as to how she would make it all the way to the bathroom, but swinging her legs out of the vehicle was a good start. One step at a time, up the walk, Megan cheered herself on. When she opened the door, she lost all resolve. Her comfortable couch beckoned and she fell over its side, splaying out. *Just for a minute*, she promised herself. She'd rest and then get ready for the meeting.

Chapter Seven

Megan stretched and rolled to her side. She didn't need anything more than her couch. And maybe a burger . . . She opened her eyes halfway. What day was it? She thrust herself up into a seated position. The meeting! She sat up and squinted at the clock across the room. She had ten minutes until she was supposed to be among the other contestants at the mandated silent meeting. She grabbed her glasses from the nearby coffee table and slammed them onto her face.

There was good and bad news. The good news was she could still make the meeting if she hurried. The bad news was she had to leave immediately. Forget the cool shower or even a comb.

Megan grabbed her keys from the counter and stuck them in her mouth as she pulled the hair tie from the depths of her disheveled ponytail. The humidity combined with her dried sweat had turned her hair into a frizzy mess—even by her standards. Without a shower, there wasn't much she could do. She pulled her front door shut behind her with a foot and wrangled her hair back into a messy bun. It was in no way smooth, but it was better than leaving it down.

Cane shuffled some papers and reviewed the safety guidelines. Preparing the contestants on the show for what could happen was part of his job. He would much rather respond to an emergency situation than speak to a room full of people about one. When he was on *Accept This Dandelion*, he had been able to forget the cameras around him and interact with people as he normally would. Dating Eva came naturally, and he never had to make big speeches with everyone looking at him. His confidence had risen a bit after his encounter with Eva the other day, but now that he was standing at the front of the conference room and the contestants and other station staff were starting to gather, his blood pressure was rising.

Cane tore his eyes from the papers and studied the people entering the room. It was weird that everyone was so quiet, and the silence only heightened his nerves. He recognized the men and women from when he had performed their medical exams, and he already had formed opinions about a few. He searched the room. Someone was missing. Where was Megan?

Mike, the show's producer, took his position beside Cane and cleared his throat. The quiet guests sat at attention as Mike snapped his clipboard on the podium in the front.

"Welcome, everyone," Mike's confident voice greeted them. "And thank you for agreeing to be a part of *The Leftover.* We have a lot to cover today so listen closely. And keep in mind if anyone breaks rule number one, he or she will be replaced. Get used to the silent rule. We're a small operation and we will maintain only a skeleton camera crew overnight. While we will film all day long, at night, silence will reign. One camera operator will stay on set at all times just in case, but between the daylight hours, no talking." He narrowed his eyes and swept them across the room, making his point loud and clear. "Now, I'd like to introduce you to the show's medic, Cane Trevino. You've already met him during your exams and now he will go over some important safety information for you to keep in mind as the taping progresses. Cane?"

Cane nodded and stepped behind the podium as Mike edged into a seat in the front row. He began writing something on his clipboard and Cane was certain he wasn't listening, but everyone else in the room was. Cane opened his mouth to speak. *What was it you were supposed to do when you were nervous in front of a group? Imagine people in their underwear?*

The conference room door opened and Cane's attention, along with everyone else's, swiveled to the back of the room. Megan appeared, biting her lip. She gave the others a small wave and pushed her glasses up on her face before lowering her head and making a beeline for the nearest chair. Cane frowned. *What had she been doing? Walking in a wind tunnel?* She wore a ratty old t-shirt, boy's basketball shorts and sneakers, and her hair had definitely seen better days. He smiled and his shoulders relaxed. She was more of a mess than he could ever be. He'd focus on her and try to get through this session.

Cane took a deep breath and settled his gaze on Megan's wire-rimmed glasses, which had tilted up in his direction as soon as she sat down. "Congratulations on being chosen for the show. While this is a local production and not nearly as strenuous as *Survivor*, there are still some dangers that we need to address."

Cane went on to detail the signs of sun and heat stroke and encouraged contestants to come to him if they had so much as a headache. He talked about muscle strains, fire safety, and the other elements Mike wanted him to cover. Every time he looked up from his notes, he made eye contact with Megan. Sometimes she was studying the contestants around her, but mostly, she stared at him.

"Good luck to all of you. I look forward to being a part of *The Leftover.* I hope you understand I'm here to help in any way I can. I have no office hours. I'm available to you twenty-four hours a day for the duration of the show. I'll be checking in with each of you periodically to get base information on your health so I am able to spot sudden changes, but I hope you will feel comfortable coming to me at any time." Cane smiled as he spoke the last sentence. He stepped back from the podium and let Mike take over.

"Thanks, Mr. Trevino. Everyone is doing well with the silence rule so far. I trust that the trend will continue, especially during the taping overnights. I'll be escorting the entire group to the parking lot myself to make sure no one violates the agreement."

Cane understood why they wanted to capture as much as they could on camera, but the complete silence in the room was a little unnerving.

Cane, a *Survivor* fan himself, only half-listened as Mike described what would be the contestants' regular routine, which included a daily group or individual competition, with the winner or winners getting protection from elimination that night and sometimes other rewards. The group would have to find their own food, build a shelter to protect themselves from the elements, and boil water they found to drink. Cane smiled when Mike got to the part about the Protection Piece—that would add a unique twist. But what really caught Cane's attention was with regards to any ties in the elimination votes. In the event of a tie, both contestants would be sent home. This was the biggest difference between the national *Survivor* and KETO's version.

"I know you're all dying to hear where the show is being taped." Mike paused and tapped a pen against his clipboard. "But I am not going to divulge that information. We do not get access to the location until a few hours before we begin taping, and I don't want anyone vetting the area beforehand to grab an advantage."

Mike didn't seem to trust the contestants any farther than he could throw them. And judging by the size of the guy in the front row, he couldn't throw them very far.

"Grab a sheet on your way out. It has the current approved list of items you can bring with you for the taping. Don't try to sneak anything else onto the set. We will find it. Return here the day after tomorrow at six in the morning. We will shuttle you to the location." Mike turned and glanced at the other staff members in the room. "Anyone have anything else?"

No one violated the rule of silence. Not even the crew.

"Okay, then. I advise you to rest up tomorrow and come prepared for a week and a half unlike any you've ever had."

Megan wrung her hands in her lap. She knew she looked like something the cat dragged in and the glances she got from the other contestants confirmed as much. Her nerves were going full force when she walked into the room, but after she caught Cane's eye, she felt more at ease. His speech should have been scary with all of the precautions, but instead she simply sat back and enjoyed his easy smile and the way his curly hair bounced when he moved.

But once Mike started talking, it all came back to her. She was really doing this. She was going to be on TV, competing against the people sitting around her. She took stock of the contestants. There was an enormous building of a man—like a skyscraper—sitting in the front row. His shoulders were so wide she was pretty sure two of her could fit behind him side by side. At least he would make her feel petite—which not many men could do—but he would also crush her in any type of physical competition. She frowned.

Next to Skyscraper sat a well-dressed woman who Megan thought might be a remainder from the dating show. Her makeup was perfect and not one strand of hair was out of place. It also looked heavily hair sprayed. Her nails were long and, based on the tiny stars they sported, professionally manicured. Megan shivered. Those kind of nails always made her think of bird talons. Megan tried to envision what Talons would look like after a day or two on *The Leftover*. Probably still better than Megan looked right now.

There were other athletic-looking men, and one man she was certain she'd seen in her bank. He would henceforth be known as "the Banker." Some of the women reminded her of Molly—long, lean, and up for anything. A girl on the other side of the room caught her eye. She was sitting, but her head was a good six inches lower than the woman next to her. She had beautiful light brown skin and Megan wondered if she might be Polynesian. Her short black hair curled around her ears and her eyes glowed with excitement—and spunk.

Megan needed all the spunk she could get on her side. She hoped petite Spunky Brewster was as friendly as she looked.

Megan's eye moved to the next woman. Her diamond nose stud glinted under the light of the conference room. When she scratched her arm, Megan noticed a barbed wire tattoo encircling her right bicep. Her auburn hair was chin length in the back and gradually lengthened in the front, so Megan decided to call her "the Wedge."

As Mike ended the meeting, Megan silently rose, clutching her information sheet. She tried to stay away from the others as much as possible. They'd get used to her smell soon enough, but she wanted to spare them as long as she could. Over a week of body odor . . . with complete strangers!

Megan glanced over her shoulder and caught Cane watching her as she left. She gritted her teeth and made a face at him. He winked and Megan's pulse quickened. A week and a half . . . with Cane Trevino.

Chapter Eight

Megan pulled the rubber band out of her hair and ran her fingers through it. Her sister had finally gone home after forcing her to watch a *Survivor* marathon to get in "the right mental mode" for the game. Megan wasn't sure how prepared she was, but she knew one thing . . . she was in way over her head.

The competitors on the national TV show were fierce, not only physically, but also mentally. Did Megan have the right intuition to know who was lying, who was forming alliances, who could be played, and how? She was fairly certain she couldn't pull off any of those maneuvers herself. Many players flat-out lied just to get an advantage. Megan didn't like the idea of lying to get ahead, even in a game. She wasn't prepared to stoop that low. But she promised Molly she would do her best—her sister couldn't expect anything more from her.

Megan flopped onto her bed and tried to calm her breathing, but her racing mind prevented peace. The producer prescribed rest. Watching TV was better than running stairs, but she didn't feel relaxed. She had too many questions coursing through her brain. Where would they hold the taping? Would she be able to sleep? What would the other contestants be like? Would she even survive the first vote?

She rolled over and Cane's face appeared in her mind. Her heart skipped a beat, but her breathing slowed. She went over their few embarrassing encounters. He had to think she was a total freak, but that didn't mean she couldn't dream about him. He probably had plenty of fans throughout the city who acted foolishly in front of him, and she had become one of them. Megan closed her eyes and tried to hold onto the image of Cane's curly hair bouncing on his forehead as he spoke to the group. The way his eyes had held hers made her feel like the only person in the room. And the fact that she had been banned from speaking entirely took a lot of pressure off. Now if she could just avoid tripping . . .

She sighed and fell into a restless sleep.

From his work as a paramedic, Cane understood odd hours and his body had grown accustomed to waking in the middle of the night. He wasn't the first one to arrive at the beach, but he had a lot of work to do before the contestants appeared.

The crew had set up a tent for him just off the main taping site. The lightweight fabric would give him shelter from the sun and the wrap-around sides would keep any blowing sand and bugs at bay. It wasn't the Ritz, but it was better than what the contestants would have.

Cane unpacked the cartons he carried in and stashed various first aid items on plastic shelves the crew had carted in for him. He needed to be organized so if an emergency arose, he would know where everything was. They were only fifteen miles from the nearest hospital, so if anything serious happened, they could get the contestant to the facility quickly. But Cane hoped he could handle anything that occurred.

If nothing else, the next two weeks were going to be an experience. He had enjoyed camping as a child, but he hadn't had much time for it as an adult. The show allowed him to stay within his profession while enjoying some time away from his day job as an EMT. If life had taught him one thing, it was to follow the paths before him and see where they might go. If he stood still too long, he'd miss whatever was ahead.

For too long, Cane had stood still, waiting for Eva. Now that he had decided to move forward, he knew each step he took was one more away from Eva—and that was okay. He still felt a twinge whenever she came to mind, but she wasn't the girl for him, as much as he wanted her to be. Eva was in his past and though he still had a soft spot for her in his heart, he had a much larger space reserved for the woman he was actually meant to be with.

It took hours to organize all the supplies and inventory everything he had on hand, but as the sun rose over the horizon, Cane was ready. He glanced at his watch. The contestants would be arriving at the studio soon. It wouldn't be long before they filled the beach near his tent. *The Leftover* was about to begin.

Megan bumped along in the back of the van with her small bag on her lap. It contained every item on the allowed list including two changes of clothing, a swimsuit, sunscreen, lip balm, and hair ties. They were also allowed one personal item, and she had chosen to bring something her sister made for her when they were children. She often carried it in her pocket when she was trying something new—it was a kind of good luck charm. It helped remind her that Molly was always there for her.

The van was too quiet, the contestants still not permitted to speak. Megan was annoyed that Skyscraper was next to her, blocking most of her view. She didn't know where they were going and it was hard to see out the window.

The Banker sat in front of her and she was surprised to see he was still wearing a suit. At the first stop light, he'd turned and raised his eyebrows at Megan. Megan didn't know if he was flirting or if he had some kind of facial twitch. She stifled laughter when he turned back around. Were giggles allowed? She couldn't take any chances. She didn't expect to make it far on the show, but there was no way she could justify getting kicked out before she was even allowed to speak.

When the vehicle halted, the energy within shifted. Spunky Brewster bounced up and down in her seat with excitement. Megan admired the woman's enthusiasm—Megan herself felt as though she might throw up. Her tight nerves wound tighter as she leaned to her right and tried to catch a glimpse of their destination. Her eyes widened. She knew where they were!

Cove Bay Beach was a small residential neighborhood situated around a man-made lake. The shore of the lake offered ample space for the development of new beach properties. However, there were plenty of sandy stretches that didn't yet have houses. Not everyone wanted beachfront property in Nebraska—it wasn't exactly usable year round.

Molly had dragged her to a party a couple years ago, and the host had lived a few blocks over from where the van was now parked. She was certain the taping was going to be stationed on an empty portion of the beach. They may be able to see houses across the bay, but they would be isolated. It was probably as close as they could get to the national TV show in terms of location.

At the front of the van, Talons folded her long, beautiful nails around a designer bag and stepped delicately out of the vehicle. Spunky Brewster threw herself from her seat. Megan followed as soon as it was her turn. She held her bag behind her so Skyscraper wouldn't get too much of her rear in his face. Her feet landed on cement, but the wind blew sand from the nearby beach around her legs. She noticed the Wedge jumping from the other van, her auburn hair half pulled back so it didn't look asymmetrical anymore. She joined the others, who were gathering in a semi-circle around Mike, a pretty woman, and a row of cameras.

The vans drove away and Mike cleared his throat. "Welcome to *The Leftover* beach. We've already started taping, but I want to introduce you to your host. She will be present at competitions and eliminations. Wendy?" Mike took a step away from center stage as all eyes turned to Wendy.

Wendy Weathersby. Megan always wondered if she changed her name to suit her profession. She was the weekend weather girl on KETO and while she was gorgeous, she didn't come off as all that intelligent.

"Hey, everyone!" Wendy waved her hand at the contestants. "You might recognize me as Wendy Weathersby, an important part of the KETO weather team. But for the next week and a half, I'm Wendy Weathersby, host of *The Leftover.* And let me tell you, Wendy Weathersby is excited about this journey."

Could you say your name another time, please?

"As Wendy Weathersby . . ."

There you go.

" . . . I will be here through thick and thin, helping you through this experience. I'll watch every challenge, help you talk about elimination decisions, and trek through the sand with you."

Megan glanced at Wendy's shoes. Trekking through the sand in those high heels was not likely.

"I want to personally welcome each and every one of you to the show. We'll have time to get to know one another later, but first, your beach." Wendy waved her hand behind her and the contestants directed their gaze at the sandy area.

The beach featured two tents. A large tent toward the parking lot held crew members and equipment. The smaller tent in the distance was closed off. Between those two tents, it was all sand. A block behind the beach, the trees started and the small wooded area stretched over to the road.

"Take the morning to figure out shelter and do a little strategizing. We'll have our first challenge this afternoon and we'll say good-bye to one contestant later tonight. Good luck, everyone. And remember, Wendy Weathersby will be watching!"

For some reason, that thought scared Megan.

Mike stepped back into view and cast an annoyed glance at Wendy. "If anyone has any injuries throughout the taping, that's the medic tent on the other end of the beach. The no-talking ban is officially lifted." He extended his hand toward the beach, inviting the contestants to start the game.

Megan took a step forward and was suddenly hit from behind. It felt like a Mack truck and she went down hard on both knees. Without so much as a sorry, Skyscraper rushed by, anxious to see what the sand looked like a few feet ahead of them.

Megan stood, brushed off her knees, and adjusted the bag on her shoulder. The blinking camera light nearby told her the fall had indeed been recorded.

"Let the fun begin," she muttered as she focused on placing one foot in front of the other.

Chapter Nine

Megan caught up to the other contestants who had formed a circle in the sand. The Banker was talking animatedly as Megan took a spot next to Spunky Brewster.

"Why don't we just go around and share our names and professions. Then we can get to work on the shelter and chat more later. Everyone good with that?"

Megan wondered how long it would be until he got too hot and took off his jacket. The sun wasn't scorching yet, but she could feel the humidity rising. Several heads around the circle nodded at the Banker's idea, but all she could do was focus on his horrendously ugly tie. *Why was he wearing a suit?*

"Okay, I'll go first," he said. "My name is Andrew and I work in insurance sales."

Insurance, not banking. Megan had already spent enough time thinking of him as the Banker that it was going to be hard to make the adjustment.

"I'm Kat and I'm a beauty consultant."

So Talons was actually Kat. Her face wasn't as heavily made up now as it had been at the first meeting, but it certainly wasn't make-up free either. And her form-fitting sundress looked more like something you would wear to an afternoon tea party than a roughing-it adventure on the beach.

"Hey, everyone. I'm Grace and I'm in the Army."

Megan stared at the small woman beside her. She had pegged Spunky Brewster wrong too. She had thought perhaps she was a hairdresser because of her stylish short hair. She was adorable and petite and Megan couldn't picture her in fatigues next to a bunch of much larger men.

Grace smiled at Megan.

"I guess it's my turn." Megan's eyes darted around the circle. The camera over her shoulder was invading her personal space. Her eyes dropped to her feet. "I'm, um, Megan, and I, uh, I talk for a living."

Skyscraper chuckled and Megan scowled at him.

He held up his hands. "Sorry. Hey, my name is Hunter, but my friends call me Tank and I'm a personal trainer." He flexed his arm and nearly knocked Megan over.

"And I'm Danae," said the Wedge. Megan was glad to know Danae's name since her nickname didn't suit her with half her hair pulled back. "I'm a high school counselor." *Interesting.* Megan would never have guessed her profession. She almost looked young enough to be a high school student herself. Or perhaps a college attendee.

Megan listened as Leo, Carson, Nathan, and Juan introduced themselves. Carson was roughly her age and Leo was much older. Nathan and Juan were both tall, lanky, tanned, and dark-haired. Juan wore a ragged Cardinals baseball hat and Nathan flaunted a large, shiny belt buckle. The other women were Lucy and Sabrina. Lucy was young and fresh-faced and Sabrina reminded Megan of a grown-up Melissa Joan Hart. Twelve people on the beach, including Megan. The names, faces, and professions would take a little time to learn, but Megan already knew there were a few people she wanted to work with and some she might want to avoid.

Megan figured Tank would be hard to beat in any challenge that took strength, but she didn't like his obvious love affair with his muscles. Andrew the Banker—or insurance salesman, as it turned out—had a take-charge attitude, but Megan wondered if he could be a team player.

Leo, on the other hand, was very intriguing. He was older than the rest of the group, but his wiry muscles told her he wasn't afraid of hard work. He'd worked in construction for thirty years, so he had both determination and skill. She knew she liked Grace's attitude; her enthusiasm was almost contagious. And Carson had the boy-next-door look going. The fact that he was a PE teacher and Little League coach told her he was good with kids, which added to his charm. It was hard to make snap judgments, but the other contestants were likely doing the same about her. She hoped the ones she was eyeing would approach her. She didn't know if she had the courage to go to them just yet.

"Okay!" Andrew, the insurance salesman, clapped his hands together. "Let's get started on the shelter." He turned to Skyscraper. "Is it okay if I call you Tank?"

"Sure." Tank shrugged.

"Great. Tank and I will walk around and find a good spot for the shelter. The rest of you guys, start finding wood that might be useful for building something. Ladies, grab as many big leaves as you can. Everyone good?"

Megan nodded slowly, suppressing the urge to roll her eyes as people began splitting off. *Who made him queen of the beach?*

Grace spoke up beside her. "Wow, he's bold. But hey, let him think he's the leader. Then, when things go wrong, he's to blame, not us."

Megan smiled. Molly had told her to try to blend in on the first day. If she came on too strong, she might stand out as an early target. Coming on strong was not in Megan's repertoire, so she figured following her sister's advice would be easy enough.

As Megan fell into step beside Grace, she remembered her surprise at hearing Grace's profession. Since Grace had already initiated talking to her, Megan thought that she could continue the conversation.

"I can't believe you're in the Army."

"I get that a lot," Grace answered.

"When did you know you wanted to do that?"

"It's all I've ever known. My dad was an Army man and he always wanted his son to follow in his place."

"Did your brother go into the Army too?"

"I don't have one."

"Wait, so . . ."

Grace giggled. "Since I'm the only child in our family, I had to be the son my father always wanted, you know? I didn't want to let him down."

"By being a girl?"

"I can't help that, but I can make him proud of what I do."

"I bet he's very proud." They reached the wooded area and Megan bent over and gathered a pile of large leaves. "I'm impressed. I, for one, could never do it."

Grace shrugged. "When it comes to the daily tasks in the service, you do what you have to do."

Megan stopped her leaf gathering. "Just put one foot in front of the other."

"Exactly."

Megan turned her head as Lucy and Sabrina joined them. So far, so good. Molly told her to make good connections on the first day and keep her head down. She was obeying her orders and blending in with the group. She pushed the glasses up on her nose. If only the first challenge would be something easy. Maybe they would have to read a script or do a puzzle.

Megan followed the group of women back to the beach where the men were dragging tree limbs and sticks and Andrew was waving his arms and giving directions. She couldn't pretend to be someone she wasn't, but maybe she could fit in for once. Grace didn't seem to mind her company. With any luck, she could hold back her awkwardness. Time would tell.

Cane had the best view on the beach. From one side of his tent, he was able to observe the contestants. On the other side, the studio crew members were busily setting up the first competition. He wasn't sure what to watch so he moved back and forth, trying to take it all in.

The contestants on the beach seemed to be trying to fashion a shelter for the night. It looked like there was already a rift. The well-dressed man, Andrew, wanted to build something in the middle of the open beach. A few dissenters were setting up a different shelter back in the trees. Cane was surprised that most of the group went along with Andrew's idea. The open beach didn't provide any natural shelter from the sun, wind, or other elements that might arise. He smiled when he spotted Megan among those in the trees. She may be shy, but at least she wasn't a pushover.

Cane walked to the other side of his tent. The beach was getting a makeover. There were logs being fashioned into balance beams all over the sand. Whatever the crew was doing, he was glad he didn't have to participate as a contestant. The contestants were most likely to get hurt during the competitions. The studio wanted him close by and on hand at all times, but especially during the injury-inducing portions of the game.

"Everything set in here?" Mike approached from the contestant side of the beach.

"I think I have all the supplies to tend to emergencies." Cane opened the side of his tent and glanced in at his stocked shelves. "What's going on over there?" He tilted his chin at the contestants on the beach.

"It's great stuff," Mike answered. "Andrew took charge and gave everyone a task to set up the shelter, but apparently not everyone agreed with his location. Grace suggested a different area under the trees and a few others went with her. It seems we have alliances forming already."

Cane squinted into the mid-morning sun as he counted silently. The group on the beach was in the majority with eight people. Those under the trees numbered only four. "It will be interesting to see how that works out."

"Just wait till they get hungry." Mike's eyes lit up at the possibility of contestants suffering, which would heighten emotions and drama. "We'll do the competition at one, okay? Until then, keep an eye on them."

Cane nodded as Mike shuffled back across the beach to remain behind the cameras, observing the activity.

The two shelters were coming along nicely. They both appeared to be well-formed. He shook his head. "You're on the wrong side of the numbers, Megan," he whispered. He was rooting for her and though he thought a shelter along the tree line was much smarter than one on the beach, he didn't want to see her go home early because of a numbers game. But whatever happened, happened. The only aspect he had any control over was how well any injured parties were treated.

Chapter Ten

Megan heaved a large branch onto her shoulder. Since Grace suggested the second shelter location, her job had changed from leaf-gatherer to wood-dragger. When Grace came up with her idea, Megan had immediately recognized that a shelter under the trees made much more sense. When Leo jumped ship to go with Grace, that sealed the deal. He would know exactly what to do to build something that would work well as a shelter. Carson was the last to join their shelter group.

Megan had hoped more contestants would sway away from the beach, but the fact of the matter was that she had landed on the wrong side of the numbers. That concerned her, but she was excited to work with Grace and Leo, two people she was interested in right away. The shelter was their first order of business, the competition their second. She would worry about the votes later.

The morning sun was starting to beat down and Megan wondered what the temperature was out on the sand. Andrew had to be feeling it by now. She glanced at the second group on the beach. They had collected enough to get started on their shelter and it was coming along quickly. Andrew's horrendous tie was no longer around his neck, but tied about his head like a bandana instead.

Megan giggled as she approached the others in the tree-line

shelter area. "I wonder what his insurance buddies will think of that look."

Grace stopped leveling the ground and shaded her eyes from the sun. "It's a good look for him." She shrugged. "Maybe they'll all start doing it."

"How's it coming, Leo?" Megan asked. Leo had offered an overall plan for the shelter and then volunteered to tie branches together with the long reed grasses they found on the lake's edge.

"Good," Leo answered without looking up. His tongue stuck out between his lips and there was a look of great concentration on his face. "These Boy Scout knots are a lot harder than I remember."

"That's because you haven't been in a troop in, what, twenty years?" Carson ribbed as he dumped his latest pile of large branches on top of what Megan had brought back.

"Hey," Leo answered. "I resent that remark."

All four contestants laughed as Megan sat in the dirt under a nearby tree to catch her breath. They were a motley crew, but she liked them already. Grace was by far the smallest person on the beach, but she had already proven her quick, sensible thinking, and she was obviously physically capable by the way she picked up large branches and heaved them around like they were a fraction of the size. Leo was tall and wiry with a good skill set with his construction resume and survival background from the Boy Scouts, even if he had graduated high school decades ago. His age might seem like a disadvantage to some, but Megan thought it gave him more experience and determination to succeed. She felt unexpectedly comfortable around Grace and Leo.

Carson was the one who surprised Megan the most. He was handsome, athletic, and looked much more like he fit in with the beach crew than their bunch. Since Megan found him attractive, she had a hard time making eye contact with him. She mostly just lowered her head and blushed when he was around. She hoped she'd feel more comfortable around him with time. Not likely, given her nonexistent history with good-looking men.

Megan's stomach rumbled. "What do we have to do to get room service around here?"

Grace laughed. "We have to catch some fish and bring it to our room . . . after we make our room, that is."

Megan took a deep breath. She'd have to get used to the hunger pangs. "Do we have enough sticks?"

"Yeah, I think so. Want to start on the roof?" Grace asked.

"Yeah, it looks ready," Leo agreed. He showed Megan, Grace and Carson how to take the leaves they had gathered and "sew" them together with the long grasses and small sticks. It was an ingenious idea.

Megan gathered some leaves and sat back beneath the tree to start sewing. The cameras whirred around her and she wondered if she would ever adjust to their constant stare. When she looked up from her work, she caught a glimpse of the blue medic tent. The side flapped in the slight breeze and a figure appeared.

Megan stared as Cane shaded his eyes and inspected their handiwork from afar. He raised his hand and waved and she smiled. There was no way to tell if he was greeting her or anyone else on the beach, but she liked to think the wave was just for her. And what harm would that cause? Molly wasn't there for her to confide in and no one had to know about her little crush on the show's medic. She had a crush on Carson too. *Crushes were harmless!*

Both groups worked the morning hours away and by early afternoon, two shelters had formed. The beach group had a sturdy-looking makeshift box in the middle of the sand. It resembled something a family would have lived in during settler days. The organized branches coming out of the sand acted as walls and the stick roof was covered in leaves woven through the crisscrossed branches. Megan wished she had a camera to document the ingenuity of the shelter, but then she remembered *everything* would be on camera.

The shelter in the woods was more of a lean-to. The four outcast contestants used the V of a large tree to hold fallen branches they found in the woods. They created an angled wall that would hide them from the elements at night. The sewn leaves draped over the top and down the sides to keep out at least a few bugs.

"It's a masterpiece." Megan clapped a hand onto Grace's shoulder. "And we have Leo to thank."

Leo shrugged. "I didn't work any harder than the rest of you. If there's one thing I learned from my years in construction, it's that nothing is built by one man alone."

The group took a moment to enjoy their triumph in the shelter they had built together before Grace spoke up. "Hey guys, if we're going to be bunking together, is it safe to assume we'll vote together too?"

"'Bunking together' is giving this shelter a bit more credit than it's due," Carson replied. "Unless there's a second level I don't know about."

Leo laughed. "I'm in, but I think we have a problem already."

Megan turned and stared across the beach. The numbers. They weren't even. By a long shot.

"Let's get through the competition first," Grace said. "Maybe one of us will win protection and we can sway the votes before the elimination. I like this group and I want it to stay put."

Everyone agreed, but their conversation was interrupted by a buzzing sound. The group turned and watched as Wendy Weathersby rode onto the beach in a bright orange dune buggy.

So that's how she's going to get around the sand wearing those heels, Megan thought.

Wendy gestured for the group to gather around her and put on her brightest smile for the cameras. "It looks like you've all been busy. Wendy Weathersby has been too."

Megan shook her head. *Busy refreshing your makeup.*

"Your first competition will start shortly on the other side of the medic tent. Meet me over there in a few minutes." Wendy gingerly stepped back into the dune buggy, which spit sand at them from the back tires as it zipped away.

The group started to walk over to the medic tent to see what was in store for them. Megan pulled at her t-shirt, glad for the third time that she wasn't wearing just the tight, low-cut sports bra and teeny shorts Molly wanted her to bring.

Andrew sidled up next to Megan, his voice startling her from her thoughts. "Let me know if you get cold tonight." He wiggled his eyebrows. "I might just be able to make a little room for you in our shelter."

Megan narrowed her eyes. "I'm not sure the moonlight will keep your shelter any warmer than ours."

"Maybe not, but we have body heat." He leaned his arm against hers.

She made a face. *Gross.* She was hot and sweaty and so was Andrew. She didn't want to be pressed against him. Megan wanted to duck away from the conversation and Andrew as quickly as possible, but she remembered Molly's advice. *Don't ruffle feathers and stay under the radar.* Megan gave him a tight-lipped smile and trudged around the blue tent.

Cane stood on the other side, watching the contestants entering the competition area for the first time. Instead of checking out the strategically placed logs, Megan took a bit too long watching Cane and stumbled over her own feet. She saw his eyes dart to her as she righted herself, and she gave him a sheepish grin as she fell back into step with the others.

Wendy stood on a small board that Megan bet they had set on the sand just for her shoes' sake. "Wendy Weathersby welcomes you to the first competition on *The Leftover.* These competitions will be your lifeblood out here on Cove Bay Beach. Not only will the winner receive protection from elimination, but there are also prizes that go along with winning. Sometimes, I will tell you what the prizes are. Other times, they will be a surprise. I know you're all hungry so suffice it to say the winner and two chosen friends will not have empty stomachs at the end of the day."

Megan's heart beat harder in her chest. She was trying to listen to Wendy, but her mind was preoccupied with the logs laying on the beach . . . and the fact that Cane's piercing eyes were watching.

"This afternoon, you will be working on your balance. The logs around you are your paths to protection. Pretend the sand is fire—something you don't want to touch."

Balance-beam logs. To a normal person, that would be simple enough. Megan, a classic klutz to the highest degree, wanted to bow out before it began to save a little face. Her nerves started winding tight. This challenge would be, well, a challenge.

"The first time you walk the path might seem easy. If you put even one foot in the sand, you have to start over. Since there are only three courses available, we will run the competition in heats. The first person down the logs in each heat wins and will move on to the second part of the race. I'll explain the next element of the competition when we get there. For now, Wendy Weathersby will choose those racing in the first heat."

Megan was having trouble breathing. Why did the first competition target one of her biggest weaknesses?

"Tank, Leo, and Lucy, you're up first."

Leo's name pierced through the growing haze of Megan's panic, and she refocused on her surroundings. She wasn't doing this for herself. Molly had been her initial inspiration, but now she had team members—friends, even—that she needed to support, and who would support her. She could get through this for them.

Megan joined Grace at the edge of the contestant area closest to the starting line for the competition. Grace was calling out encouraging words to Leo. Megan was nervous for her newfound friend. If their group had any shot at sticking together, they needed one of them to win. Megan watched the three contestants in the first heat line up at the logs. She crossed the fingers on one hand for Leo.

"Leftovers, ready? Go!" Wendy threw her hand down to start the race.

The logs were not nearly as sturdy as they looked. Tank went down hard as his log rolled beneath him. He got up quickly and raced back to the end of the log. Leo was making fast work down his log, but Lucy looked well-balanced and highly focused, arms out to either side. Leo hopped from one log to another until he reached the last one and it rolled, sending him flying to the sand. Megan gasped as Lucy passed Leo's position and landed safely on the other side of the logs. She threw her arms into the air.

"Lucy wins!" Wendy shouted. "Lucy, you'll move on to the second round. Leo, Tank, you're out."

Megan was sorry Leo lost, but at least he took Tank down with him. Tank hadn't made it farther than a few steps. Maybe his size wasn't an advantage after all.

Kat, Carson, and Nathan ran in the next heat and Carson beat them soundly. Megan was elated that someone from her group made it to the second round.

The third heat included Andrew, Grace, and Juan. Megan cupped her hands over her mouth. "Come on, Grace!" Her enthusiasm took hold as Grace got into position. When Wendy shouted for them to start, Grace nimbly took off and grabbed an early lead. The first time Juan fell off, he left his Cardinals baseball cap in the sand. He started over several times as the others made progress. He didn't look like he was going to be a very big threat, but Andrew was right on Grace's heels.

When the two leaders jumped onto their last log, Andrew suddenly shouted, "Watch out!"

Grace glanced over just long enough to lose her footing and

slip from her beam. She shook her head and rushed back to the start. Andrew jumped to the finish as Megan stared at him, aghast. *What a dirty trick!*

"Andrew moves on!" Wendy cheered. "The final heat . . . Sabrina, Megan, and Danae. Ladies, take your positions."

Megan wiped her sweaty palms on her shorts. She wanted nothing more than to get into the second round, just to beat the pants off Andrew. Even if he was the only one still wearing pants.

Megan squatted at the start line, determined to do right by Molly, Grace, and her team.

"And . . . go!" Wendy shouted.

Megan tentatively stepped onto the log and pulsed her arms through the air to get her balance. It didn't work and the log rolled, sending her to the sand on her backside.

"Ouch!" she heard someone shout from the sidelines.

"It's okay, Megan, get up and go again!" Grace encouraged.

Megan glanced down the course. Sabrina and Danae were on their way, but the logs could roll at any time. She wasn't going to give up. She got up and brushed herself off as she tackled the log a second time . . . and got thrown to the ground again.

Megan shook her head and rubbed her hipbone. *What am I doing wrong?* The logs beside her shook as Danae hit the sand. Megan saw her chance. She got up a third time and stuck the tip of her shoe out onto the log. She steadied the wood and tried not to flinch when she noticed Sabrina step into the sand before her. Her competitors were starting over!

She stepped out onto the wood beam and straightened her arms beside her. One step at a time. One foot in front of the other. That was all she could do. She looked down at the log as it wiggled. She was better off staring straight ahead and letting her body find its center. Megan focused her eyes on someone who was standing at the far end of the course behind the cameras. She was transitioning to the second log when she realized her focal point was Cane Trevino himself, standing at the end of the course behind the cameras.

Megan would analyze this to death later, but for now, she needed him to stay put. She could hear the other women gaining on her. She quickened her pace and narrowed her focus. It was just her and the log . . . and Cane. *You are the log. Become one with the log.* She felt silly, but the mantra and her focal point seemed to be working.

Before she realized it, she set her foot in the sand on the other side of the course, just seconds before Danae hit the end of her log.

"In our closest finish yet, Megan wins!" Wendy hollered. "Since four contestants remain, we'll run heats of two people each. Lucy and Megan will go first, then Andrew and Carson."

Megan's moment of elation turned back to focus as she nodded at Lucy. The young girl looked like she was still in high school, though she claimed to be a senior in college. She could probably stand on the back of a chair for an hour without so much as bobbling. But Megan was mature and had life experience behind her. Perhaps she could take her.

"This time, you will carry a bucket of water in each hand." Wendy announced. "If you spill the water, you have to run to the bay and refill it. Ladies, grab your buckets."

Megan and Lucy picked up buckets near Wendy's board and filled them in the bay side by side.

"Good luck," Lucy said as they approached the starting log.

"You too," Megan returned. At least it seemed like she didn't have to worry about Lucy being a bad sport like Andrew.

"Ready? And go!" Wendy shouted.

Megan put her toe on the first log and wobbled. She could see Lucy a few steps ahead of her already. She raised the buckets on either side to get balanced. She swayed first one direction, then the other. Her eyes searched the horizon. Where was Cane? She needed to find her center. As soon as he stepped into view and clapped and cheered with the rest of them, Megan stopped weaving on her log and started stepping forward.

"Water hazard!" Wendy shrieked. "Lucy, you spilled—return to the bay!"

Megan's pulse quickened. If she could keep it together, she could get through this heat. She kept her eyes fixed on Cane and her breathing steady, even as her legs wobbled beneath her.

When she got to the other side of the log course, she couldn't believe it. Not a drop of water had spilled from her bucket and Lucy was an entire log back.

"Slow and steady wins the race," Wendy announced. "Andrew and Carson, you're up next."

Megan fell into Grace's embrace and celebrated the fact that she was moving on in the competition, against all odds. If the other contestants knew what a klutz she was in regular life, they'd be astounded with what she'd accomplished. Megan searched for Cane around the group, and when their eyes met, she gave him a slight nod. He nodded in return. She didn't know if he understood she was thanking him for his help, but she planned to do so in person later.

She returned her attention to the competition and watched Andrew crush Carson soundly. She had high hopes that the PE teacher would triumph over the insurance salesman in a suit, but to no avail. It was down to two . . . her and Andrew.

"The buckets were easy enough, but what if you had to carry something bigger . . . something heavier across those logs?" Wendy asked. "Choose another contestant. You will be carrying *them* across the logs."

Megan's eyes widened. She had to carry a *person?* She immediately turned to Grace, the smallest in the bunch. "Do you mind?" She hated to ask.

"I'd love to be in the winning race!" Grace gave her a high five and moved to the log course to get into position.

Andrew chose Kat and picked her up like they were a honeymooning couple. Megan had Grace jump onto her piggyback-style. Grace didn't weigh much, but she was still way more than Megan was used to having on her back. She took a deep breath and hunched over.

"The final race of the first competition. Ready, Leftovers? Go!" Wendy stomped on her board.

Megan stuck her toe out onto the log for a third time, realizing what was different this time around. She couldn't lift her head up far enough to see Cane.

Her ankle rolled off the log and Grace's leg hit the sand. "It's okay," Grace said. "Let's go again. They could fall."

Megan rushed to the start and Grace jumped onto her back again. Megan got a few more steps this time, but she still couldn't spot Cane and the result was the same. The duo ended up back at the start three times before Andrew and Kat crossed the finish line.

"Andrew! You have protection from tonight's elimination!" Wendy screeched.

"You made it to the last race," Grace encouraged. "Way to go!"

"Better luck next time," Andrew called from the other side of the logs.

Megan sighed, her emotions in conflict. She was proud she had made it through more heats than she expected but disappointed she couldn't follow through one more time when it really mattered. Was it really Cane that got her that far? Staring into those remarkable eyes and watching his curly hair wave in the breeze seemed to have an effect on her center of balance. If that was the case, she was in a whole heap of trouble—trouble of an entirely different kind.

Chapter Eleven

It was hard for Cane to watch Andrew choose two fellow contestants and sequester themselves down the beach with sandwiches. He knew what hunger pangs were like, but he could always grab a sandwich. He didn't envy that the remaining contestants could not. They were going to have to figure out a way to feed themselves fast or it would be a long nine days.

Cane went back to his tent and closed the flap. His own sandwich awaited and he certainly wasn't going to eat it out in the open where the hungry contestants might see him. When he was done, he inventoried his supplies. Again. If no one got hurt, there wasn't much for him to do other than watch the game progress.

Mike stuck his head through the tent's door. "I put an order of silence on the contestants again. We only have so many crew members and it's easier to give them all a break at once. No one can talk for the next hour. If anyone needs medical attention, they can talk to you, of course. But they are not to speak to each other. If you see anyone out of order, let me know."

Cane saluted the producer. "10-4, good buddy. Over and out."

Mike frowned and his head disappeared outside the tent.

Those on the show had gotten through their first competition and reward. They were probably dying to strategize and talk about the elimination that night. On the other hand, they were likely exhausted as well. The hour break might give them a chance to rest and return to the game with a new perspective.

Cane didn't want to observe the contestants for fear he might catch someone cheating. He didn't want to tattle on anyone and get them kicked from the game. He'd stay in his tent and do a little light reading. He picked up a textbook on updated medical procedures and opened the cover. He had to take tests every two years to retain his certification and it was necessary to stay up on the latest.

He had just turned to the first page when a fist came through the tent flap.

"Oops," a voice on the other side called. "Sorry, I was trying to knock."

Cane chuckled and closed his book. "Come on in, Megan." He stood to greet her.

Megan parted the flaps and ducked her head unnecessarily as she stepped into the tent. "Nice digs," she said as she looked around.

Cane shot a look at the cot in the corner of the tent and the small tray where he ate. "Thanks. It sure beats what you guys have out there."

Megan shrugged, eyes going over the organized medical supplies. "We'll see after tonight. The lean-to seems pretty sturdy, all things considered."

"Everything okay?" Cane asked. "Do you need anything?" He frowned and looked for external injuries.

Megan blushed and looked down. "Oh no, sorry. Mike said we could talk to you but not each other. Everyone seems to be meditating or sleeping and I'm not into either."

"You're not into sleeping?" Cane raised one eyebrow.

She looked up at him earnestly, the bright lights in the tent making her eyes sparkle. "I am. I mean, I love nothing more than a good nap. I just can't relax right now."

Cane smiled. She still didn't meet his eyes half the time, but she already seemed different than their first encounter at KETO. More confident, perhaps? He wondered how she'd come across to the other contestants thus far. "What's up?" He gestured to his cot and Megan sat down.

"I just wanted to thank you." She was looking right into his eyes.

"For?" Cane sat in the lawn chair next to his supplies.

"Helping me in the competition."

"I'm sorry." Cane stroked his chin. "I'm not sure what I did."

Megan examined her feet. "Oh, yes, I suppose that would be confusing. I guess I was using you as my focal point. It might have seemed as if I was staring at you . . . and I was. I was just looking for something to center my focus and you happened to be in the way."

Cane grinned. He'd noticed her stare and while he'd found it strange at first, he couldn't look away from the concentration her features held during the competition. It was both inspiring and, well, attractive. "You're welcome. Glad to help. What happened in that last round? I was rooting for you."

"I couldn't see you anymore. With Grace on my back I couldn't raise my head enough."

Cane nodded. "I see." He scooted his chair closer to the cot and leaned toward her, his elbows on his knees. "Can I be honest with you?"

"Of course." Megan folded and unfolded her fingers in her lap while staring at her knees.

"I was going to apologize when I got the chance."

Her confused eyes met his momentarily. "Apologize. Why?"

"You might have felt like I was staring at you in the informational meeting. And now, I realize you were the exact same thing for me that I was for you in the competition. A focal point."

"I . . . I didn't mind."

"Neither did I." Cane tried to catch a glimpse of her eyes as the wind played with the tent flap.

Megan couldn't believe what she was doing. She'd spent a good twenty-five minutes talking herself into walking over to his tent and another five minutes convincing herself to knock. She never initiated social situations! And now, here she was sitting on Cane's cot inside his tent while the rest of the beach slept. She usually ran from situations like this, but she felt drawn to him. Perhaps it was because he wasn't a contestant on the show. Maybe she was more relaxed because the cameras weren't whirring around her. She could be awkward in front of him without setting off a domino effect and ruining her chances of advancing on *The Leftover*.

Silence settled around them. Megan had said what she came to say and she didn't know where to go from there. The idea that Cane used her as a focal point in the same manner she had used him thrilled her. A man—and a cute one at that—had actually noticed her!

Just as it became too much for her to stand, Cane broke the silence.

"Want to make a deal?"

Megan leaned back on his cot and inspected his ears so she wouldn't have to look directly at him. "What kind of deal?"

"People have already started forming alliances out there." Cane tilted his head in the direction of the beach. "What if you and I have one of our own on the side?"

"That sounds interesting. What would it entail?"

"Oh, nothing much really. Let's just promise to help each other through these next few days. You know, if I have to stand in front of the group, I'll look at you. If you need help in a competition, you can stare at me."

Megan chuckled. "I think I can agree to that." She rocked forward on the cot and stood to leave.

"What if we take it one step further?"

Megan shifted her eyes back and forth on the tent wall behind Cane. "How so?"

"Friends. I'd like for us to be friends. I can be your sounding board when you need an ear."

"And I can give you advice on, well, medical stuff." Megan glanced at the nearby textbook.

Cane laughed. "Yeah, you can choose the color on the band aids . . . if anyone ever gets hurt."

"Oh, they will if I have anything to say about it." Megan's eyes widened as she blushed. "I mean, I'm not wishing any ill will on anyone, I just . . ."

Cane stood and put his hand on her shoulder. "I know. So, what do you say?"

The warmth of his fingers radiated through her shirt. His touch was so different from Andrew's. "You've got yourself a deal." She stuck her hand out and bumped her fingers against his midsection. "Sorry." She stared at her feet. She had talked more with Cane than most people on the beach, but touching anyone's abs was still out of her comfort zone.

Before she could withdraw her hand, Cane's hand enveloped it and firmly pumped it up and down.

"Why do I have the feeling this is a match made in heaven?"

Megan tore her eyes from her feet and forced herself to look at Cane. What did he mean by that? Her eyes drifted to the curls just above his eyes. She wanted to touch them and see if they were as soft as they looked. But that would be creepy.

She shook her head. The lack of food must be getting to her. "I . . . I better get back. I have a lot of people to, well, not talk to."

Cane's fingers slid from her hand. "Good luck tonight, Megan. I'll be around if you need anything. Medically or otherwise."

"Right. And you know where I'll be too."

"That I do."

Megan pointed two fingers at her eyes and then over to Cane to indicate she was keeping her eyes on him as she backed out of his tent. When she turned back to the beach, she shook her head. "You're such a geek," she scolded herself.

But at least she'd talked to him. It had taken her half an hour to do so, but she'd done it. It was a good first step. Approaching a man like that was a big deal. And now they were officially friends. At *his* suggestion. She almost didn't care if she went home that night. Except that would mean no more Cane.

Chapter Twelve

The group worked together during the afternoon to build a fire pit between the two shelters. They needed to get a fire going so they could boil water from the bay and stay hydrated. The hot Nebraska sun was draining their energy and every drop of sweat they produced pooled on their skin like glue that never dried. They needed water . . . and fast. Then they would worry about food.

Megan knew the bay was filled with all kinds of fish. If they could fashion a rod out of sticks, maybe they could catch something to cook over the fire. But that all depended on whether or not they had a fire.

Juan, Nathan, Andrew, and Leo had been rubbing sticks together over dried out leaves for two hours. Sometimes they managed to get smoke, and once even a spark, but nothing that had staying power.

Megan had an idea, but she hated to insert herself into the macho man hour, and she didn't want to come across as pushy. However, her need for water overruled everything else.

"I don't know if this would work . . ." She approached tentatively.

Leo gave her a tired smile, but the other men gathered around the pit scowled at Megan as she interrupted their stick rubbing.

"But maybe if we use my glasses . . ."

"You think we can start a fire with your glasses?" Andrew scoffed.

Megan shrugged. "Might be worth a try. I know what you're doing can work, but it hasn't yet and it will be elimination time soon. We'd probably all be better off with a little water before voting."

The normal Megan would have slunk off to the lean-to after the look Andrew gave her, but the thirsty Megan wasn't backing down. Her primal side was overpowering her meek nature.

"Just keep doing what you're doing and I'll try my idea on this side of the pit, okay?" Megan grabbed a few dry leaves and twigs and made a pile away from the stick-rubbers.

The men went back to their method and Megan removed her glasses. She poked a hole in a large leaf with a sharp stick and held the leaf against her glasses. She looked up at the sun and angled the glasses just so. The hours she and her sister watched *Survivor* just might pay off. She never would have known how to do this without the recent binge.

Megan tried to hold her hand steady as the hot sun did its work. She had no idea if her severe astigmatism would help. She knew its hindrance in everyday life, that was for sure.

She squinted at the leaves below her lenses. *Was that smoke?* Without her glasses on, it was hard to tell. She bent over the pile and blew softly. Yes, it was definitely smoke. Her eyes widened as a small spark lit the edge of a leaf. She blew again and the leaf burst into flames.

"Guys! Guys!" she called.

Tank appeared at her side. "She's got fire!"

"Way to go, Megan!" Grace called from the outskirts of the pit. "She did it, everyone."

Megan stepped back and placed her frames on her nose as Andrew and the other men added sticks and leaves to enlarge the flame she had started. First she had made it into the final two of the competition, then she had started the fire. Maybe she wasn't so out of place on the beach. She smiled.

Once the fire burned hot, Grace and Megan took the buckets from the challenge down to the bay to fill up with water.

"Have you heard the talk around camp?" Grace asked.

Megan shook her head. "Is it about any of us?" The elimination was looming. Andrew was safe and since eight people were together under the beach shelter, the four lean-to people assumed they'd be picked off one by one.

"Apparently Tank didn't take kindly to losing the log-walking competition to Lucy. It seems as if everyone on the beach is in agreement that she'll be the first to go."

"Not any of us?" Megan was incredulous.

Grace shrugged. "Not unless they're trying to pull a fast one."

"Does Lucy know?"

"I think they told her they were voting for Leo because he's the oldest."

"But they see Lucy as a bigger threat and they still have the numbers so they figure why not keep Leo and get rid of someone they might not be able to beat." Megan worked the plan through out loud.

"Exactly." Grace bent over and filled her bucket.

"I'm not sure I'll be able to keep up with the mind games."

"You'll do fine. Besides, you're not alone." Grace smiled as Megan thought about her conversation with Cane. "You've got the lean-to crew."

Megan giggled. "Is that what we're calling ourselves?"

"Could be worse."

Megan scooped water out of the bay and balanced a bucket in each hand. "It *has* been worse."

"Let's get this water boiled and have a drink. I prefer drinks with lots of ice in this weather, but right now, I'd lick the sweat off Tank if it weren't so salty."

Megan winced. "That's a visual I'm not going to get over anytime soon."

Grace laughed. "Sorry, didn't mean to traumatize you. I'm just thirsty. Getting a drink will help us forget how hungry we are."

Megan's stomach rumbled. "Really?"

"It can't hurt."

The two women of the lean-to crew delivered the water and partook of their share once it was boiled and safe to drink. The group sat far enough away from the fire to avoid its heat, but close enough so they could keep an eye on it so it wouldn't die down.

The dune buggy's motor startled all of them as the sun began to hide behind the horizon. Half of them stood as Wendy Weathersby appeared in a bright yellow pantsuit and high-heeled sandals.

"How's everyone doing out here?" she called without exiting her vehicle.

Contestants shrugged, waved, and grunted in response.

"Great!" Wendy answered. "The elimination area is set up on the other side of the medic tent. Take a few minutes to gather yourselves and meet me over there for our first elimination. Is anyone else as excited as Wendy Weathersby?"

Grace and Nathan shouted enthusiastically while the others shifted their feet in the sand with nervous energy. Even though everyone thought they knew who was getting eliminated tonight, it would be hard to relax until after the votes were counted.

"Okay, then. It's a date! See you in a few." Wendy took off in the cart and left the contestants to fend for themselves.

"Let's do this thing!" Tank beat his fists against his chest.

"Ouch," Megan muttered as she fell in with the group. When they neared the medic tent, she flitted her gaze to the door, hoping to catch a glimpse of Cane. His curly hair bobbed through the entrance as the contestants reached the far side of the beach. Megan raised her hand in a wave and Cane winked.

Ahead of her, Carson said, "Wow, this is really something."

She leaned around him to take in the transformed area, her eyes widening.

A large rock for each contestant was set in a semi-circle in front of a small platform. A fire burned in the center and Wendy stood on a board at the opening of the circle. "Welcome to the first elimination of the season. Take a seat on a rock, and we'll get started."

Megan sat on a medium-sized boulder, and Andrew and Tank took their seats on either side of her.

"How has the first day been?" Wendy asked.

Andrew didn't wait a beat before voicing his opinions. "This is a phenomenal group," he said as he adjusted his tie around his neck. Megan didn't remember when he had removed it from his head. "We've worked together well and we've really come together as a team."

Megan held back a snort. A team working well together would have only one shelter.

"I noticed two shelters over there." *Way to go, Wendy.* "What's that all about, Grace?"

"Well, Andrew insisted we build a shelter on the beach, but I thought it might be better to use the natural shelter of the trees as protection for whatever we built. A few people in the group agreed with that idea, but since Andrew wasn't willing to bend, some of us built a shelter of our own."

"Ooh, I sense a rift in the group. Is there a separation forming, Tank?"

Tank ran his hand over his bicep, which looked flexed even when he was relaxed. "I don't know, but I'm definitely on the right side. I mean, there's more of us than them."

"Us . . . them . . . sounds like a separation to me. Leo, you're with those along the tree line. How does it feel to have fewer numbers?"

"I have more numbers than anyone here, age wise," he replied, smiling. "But really, I'm okay with the numbers. The game is just beginning. Anything can happen."

"I heard that you were essential to getting the fire started, is that right, Megan?" Wendy leaned in her direction.

Megan's pulse raced. Her sister told her to float through the first day and try to blend in and what had she done? Started a fire for the group. That might be enough to put a target on her.

"I wouldn't say that, Wendy." Megan shuffled her feet and studied the small flames in the center of the circle. "Everyone in the group worked very hard so we could have a drink."

"But you had the idea to use your glasses."

"I . . . I guess."

Wendy moved on. "Does anyone think there will be any surprises with the vote tonight?"

"I think we all know what we're doing," Kat said, lounging back on her rock. "We don't know each other very well yet and it's more about making us strong as a group."

Megan squinted through the smoke in the air. Kat was making it sound like Leo was the obvious choice since he was the oldest.

"No one's thought about those who might be a threat in other ways? Megan started the fire, after all, and almost won protection."

Thanks, Wendy.

Grace cleared her throat. "Megan is a huge asset to the group. I think we just want to get through this first vote without causing too many waves. It'll get interesting soon enough."

Megan made a mental note to thank Grace later.

"Okay, well, if everyone knows what they want to do, let's vote." Wendy rubbed her hands together in excitement. "There's a wooden box on the podium. Take a few minutes to cast your vote one at a time and reveal your vote only to the camera near the podium. When all the votes are in, we'll see who the first person to leave the show will be. Carson, when you're ready, you can go first."

Megan watched as the group voted one by one. At first, she tried to guess what each person wrote by the way they moved their hand. It wasn't like reading lips, though, and it was dark enough that she couldn't see well enough to tell anything at all. When it was her turn, her hand shook as she held the pen above the paper. She wrote the name down and held it up for the camera.

"Sorry, Lucy." Megan spoke softly. "I didn't get a chance to know very much about you and you seem like a very sweet girl. But I heard most of the group was going with you and I don't want to do anything out of line at this point. I wish you the best of luck." Megan folded her paper, placed it in the box and sat back down on her rock. Once the rest of the group voted, Wendy gestured for a crew member to bring her the box. She couldn't step off her board into the sand, after all.

"I'll read the votes one by one," Wendy said as she pulled the first piece of paper out and opened it. "Leo."

The second paper read Lucy and the third Leo. The vote went back and forth. After eleven votes were read, Lucy was ahead by one vote. The last vote would either bring it to a tie or eliminate Lucy. Megan held her breath.

"And the last vote," Wendy paused to heighten the tension. "Lucy. I'm sorry, Lucy, you are not *The Leftover*. Please take a few moments to gather your belongings and leave the show."

Lucy stood with tears in her eyes and walked away from the fire. She didn't speak to anyone or say goodbye. Megan could tell she was hurt, but she was young and had a bright future ahead of her. She'd get over it and move on to the next adventure.

"I hope you all sleep well on your first night. Wendy Weathersby will see you in the morning for tomorrow's competition." Wendy stepped into her waiting orange dune buggy which spit sand as it took off.

The rest of the group sat in stunned silence. No one was surprised that Lucy had left except Lucy. But watching her walk away made the process more real.

Megan's mind whirred. The vote told her several things. First, she didn't want to come off too strong or they'd see her a threat and take her out. Second, the group on the beach wasn't united. Assuming all of the lean-to crew voted for Lucy, that meant a majority of the beach group had voted for Leo.

Megan smiled as the contestants stood and began to shuffle to the shelters on the other side of the beach. Perhaps her crew had more power than she thought.

"Danae, Sabrina, you're on fire watch," Andrew ordered. Danae looked like she might protest, but Sabrina tugged her toward the fire.

Megan shook her head. "He hath spoken," she muttered. At least she'd dodged his command this time.

Chapter Thirteen

Cane rolled over on his cot. He could hear the laughter settling down the beach. The contestants were calling it a night and would soon be in their respective shelters. The cameras would turn off and the crew would break for the day.

Being close to the show was exciting. Cane wondered what kind of emergencies might pop up over the days to come. So far, he had only treated Kat for splinters after the log competition. He was certain no one else would have complained of that particular "injury," but Kat was in a league of her own.

Cane sat up when he heard a rustling noise. It wasn't going to be easy to sleep with so many different sounds.

"Are you awake?" The loud whisper rang through the tent.

"I am. Why are you?" Cane smiled and pushed his thin blanket aside. He parted the tent flap to reveal his visitor.

"The ground is pretty hard." Megan shrugged.

"Want to come in?"

She glanced over her shoulder. "I better not. I don't want to get caught cheating or even have it look like I was trying to cheat. The cameras aren't rolling, but still."

"Good point. Why don't you take a seat out there and we can talk for a while."

"Really?"

"My cot's not much softer than the ground."

Cane sank to the ground on his side of the tent and watched Megan do the same. "Turn around and lean against me," he suggested.

Cane felt the pressure of her back against his as he leaned in her direction. They could support one another.

"Tell me a bedtime story?" Megan asked.

Cane chuckled. "You like ghost stories?"

"On a dark beach near the woods? Um, no."

An owl hooted and Megan started with a small gasp.

"It's a lot to get used to." Cane chuckled.

"I'll say. I usually go to sleep to the hum of the air conditioner."

"Air conditioning . . . don't remind me." Cane wiped his brow.

"I know. The humidity today was killer. But it'll cool off tonight." As if on cue, Megan shivered. "So, no ghost stories. Just tell me about you. Did you always know you wanted to be a paramedic?"

Cane leaned the back of his head against hers. "As long as I can remember. I always wanted to help people at least. When I was little, my friends played G.I. Joe and when they'd get hurt in battle, I would fix them up. My parents were always running out of bandages in the medicine cabinet because I would steal them for the Joes."

Megan giggled. "I can picture that. You have a compassionate heart."

Cane shrugged. "The world is so messed up. I just want to do what I can to make it better, even in a small way."

"If I'm ever hurt, you'll be my first call."

"I better be." Cane glanced over his shoulder, wishing he could see her face through the tent wall.

They settled in against each other again. "What's it like to have a sister? Someone you can rely on like that?" Cane envied their sibling bond. They seemed closer than he was with his brothers.

"Molly's great. We're close in age so it was almost like growing up with a twin. Except we're rather different, in case you hadn't noticed."

"There are a few contrasts," Cane agreed. His few interactions with Molly had gone smoothly. She was charming and full of grace. Megan, on the other hand, was reserved and understated. He smiled, thinking about the way she pushed her glasses up her nose and looked through her eyelashes at him.

Megan let out a snort. "Like the fact that she'd choose to do a show like this and I never would."

"And yet here you are."

"Here I am." Megan sighed.

Cane was enjoying the conversation and her closeness. Since Eva, he had pulled away from his friends, and he realized he was lonely. He hadn't had a simple, easy conversation like this in a long time. Would they be talking like this if Megan could see him? He smiled. Perhaps the darkness gave her shy tendencies the cover she needed to step out in boldness.

"What brought you on the show?" Megan asked. "You know why I'm here."

Cane drew in a sharp breath as visions of Eva flashed across his mind. "I don't know. I guess I was trying to get away from everyday life."

"You aren't happy with your job?"

Megan was prodding him, but he didn't mind. "I love what I do. I think I just needed a change of pace."

Megan turned slightly. "What are you running from, Cane Trevino?"

He drew his knees up toward his chest and placed his elbows on them. "Okay, you got me. A broken heart."

"I couldn't believe my eyes when she turned you away," Megan said wistfully.

He smiled. She was sweet. "We weren't right for each other."

"Well, I guess that's true, but still. I can't imagine having a man like you and dumping him. It just doesn't make sense."

"Thanks."

The pair listened to the night sounds of the woods and the soft lap of the water for a few moments.

"Did you see how much sand blew up around Tank when he fell off that log today? It was like some kind of sand storm."

The abruptness of the comment and the image of Tank caught up in a sandstorm was too much. Cane threw his head back and laughed. It felt good to let loose. "Thanks, Megan. That was just what I needed."

"I wasn't joking." Her voice was serious.

Cane laughed again. "I know. I saw it with my own eyes." He appreciated the change in topic and the fact that Megan didn't delve too deeply into his past. She knew what had happened. Everyone did. They'd all seen it on TV.

For the next hour, they talked about his college days and how she got into voice-overs. The time went fast and the night noises faded away until all he could hear was the sound of her deep, melodic voice.

※※※※

Megan smacked her lips. Her mouth was dry. She brushed her fingers across her cheek. Sand stuck to her face and her arms were freezing, but her back was very warm. She opened her eyes to get her bearings. Ah yes, *The Leftover*. She was on the beach . . . but wait. She wasn't in the lean-to with the others. Her eyes darted around. The blue tent at her side told the story.

"Cane," she whispered as their conversation came flooding back. They'd spent well over an hour talking about their lives. She'd enjoyed every second—which was very unusual for her. The fact that she had sought him out the night before was unprecedented. She smiled. He had a way of making her feel comfortable.

She pressed her hand against the blue tent and felt his back on the other side. He must have laid down when she did and eventually, they had both fallen asleep.

"Hey! Watch it!"

Megan drew back her hand in surprise as the tent flap flew open and Cane's head appeared, confused and sleepy.

"I'm so sorry, did I goose you?" Megan's face was on fire despite the chill in the morning air.

"Goose? No, but you grabbed my rear."

Megan stood. *Oh my gosh, oh my gosh.* She stumbled backward. "Again, so sorry."

"Wait," Cane called, reaching out to her.

But Megan was picking up speed across the beach. They'd had a lovely conversation. Their friendship had grown by leaps and bounds. And then she ruined it by waking him up with a hand on his butt cheek. Thankfully, with no cameras around, the moment would be between the two of them. But that was bad enough.

Megan crawled into the lean-to, lay in the space next to Grace she had vacated the night before, and tried to calm her breathing. With any luck, no one would know she had been gone. Especially all night. She didn't need rumors to start, and she certainly didn't want anyone to think she was trying to cheat.

She gave herself a few moments to revel in the late night conversation, trying to forget the embarrassing morning event. Cane made her feel like a real person, not someone easily overlooked as she was by most people. He cared about her opinion and laughed at her jokes. She closed her eyes. It was a good thing they had sat back-to-back. She never could have said half as much had she been looking into his dreamy eyes.

Grace rolled over with a moan and the rest of the contestants in the lean-to began to stir. Megan pretended to be waking up too, which wasn't hard. She was sleepy from the previous day's exertions and late night conversation.

Too soon, she was following Leo to the fire pit to help boil water. Danae and Sabrina looked the most haggard since they had taken turns keeping the fire going throughout the night. Stomachs rumbled all around. Megan couldn't remember the last time she'd been this hungry.

Everyone drank their fill of water to try to calm their complaining tummies.

"How was the lean-to?" Andrew asked with a cocky smile. His tie was in place around his neck, but his suit was wrinkled.

Megan ducked her head and let the others in her group answer. "Lovely," Leo said. "No wind, no bugs, just enough moonlight. How about your shelter?"

Andrew cracked his knuckles. "Never better."

Megan noticed Kat rolling her eyes as she rubbed the small of her back. Life on the beach wasn't paradise after all.

The contestants began to ponder what the day's competition would be as the station's crew members were making plenty of noise on the other side of the medic tent. Before long, Wendy appeared in a bright flower-print sundress and strappy high-heels.

"Morning, everyone." Wendy's voice was bright and cheery, like that of someone who had slept in a cozy bed.

"Morning," the contestants muttered in sleepy voices.

"I hope you don't mind getting started bright and early. Our competition for protection will begin in a few moments on the other side of the beach. You'll have the rest of the day to figure out who you will eliminate tonight. And," she paused for dramatic effect, "the reward that goes along with protection is one all of you will want. Wendy Weathersby will see you over there in a few minutes and we'll get started."

Megan watched Wendy take off in her dune buggy. Maybe the

reward was getting to ride around the beach in that thing. Megan was tired of the sand in her shoes. But a little sand was the least of her problems. She was starving and she had to compete on little reserve energy.

She fell into line with the group as they trudged up the beach and around the blue tent. Cane appeared as the contestants neared and Megan averted her eyes. She'd hold on to the conversation they enjoyed. It would have to be enough. Now that she had touched his buns, she'd never be able face him again. Her cheeks flamed with embarrassment.

"Welcome to Day Two of *The Leftover!*" Wendy greeted the contestants from her board. "Today's challenge has several parts. It will be a timed event and you will each have a turn. First, you'll do a little beach bowling." Wendy gestured dramatically at the long aisle of boards lined up in a makeshift bowling lane. There were ten pins at one edge and a plastic ball sitting at the other end. "You have to get all ten pins down before you can move on to the second stage. You'll throw the ball and then retrieve it yourself. Remember, time is of the essence." Wendy tapped her wrist. "Then, once all ten pins are down, you are allowed to start digging in the sand behind the pins. There, you'll find a box that holds a key. Use the key to unlock the puzzle pieces at this station." Wendy tapped the wooden treasure chest next to her. "Once the puzzle is free, put it together and hold up both hands to indicate you are finished. Wendy Weathersby will stop the timer at that point."

Megan smiled. She stank at bowling, but she was decent at puzzles.

"You can watch one another from over there." Wendy pointed to a flagged area twenty feet away. "That way, no one else can see what the puzzle is and gain an advantage. Who's ready to play?"

Megan took a deep breath. She didn't know if she wanted to win or not. Her sister told her to keep a low profile, and she already came close to winning last time. Then again, if she won, she could relax for the rest of the day knowing she was safe from elimination. Plus, maybe the reward was a cheeseburger.

"I'll draw names for order." Wendy reached into a bucket and picked out a slip of paper. "Nathan, you're up first."

Megan watched Nathan take his spot at the end of the bowling aisle as the rest of them moved to the designated viewing area. She hardly knew Nathan. If her social game was going to go anywhere, she'd have to start talking to the contestants in the other shelter. That would be even more painful than getting to know the lean-to crew since the others were on the opposite side of the game from her.

"And go!" Wendy shouted.

Nathan tossed the ball down the aisle, and Kat sidled up to Megan's side.

"What do you say we make a deal?" Kat said out of the corner of her mouth.

Megan looked behind her. Could she be talking to anyone else? "Me?" she asked softly.

Kat nodded. "If I win today, I'll take you with me on the reward. If you win, you take me."

Megan shrugged. "Sure, deal."

Kat smiled and moved away. Megan wondered if she was making the same deal with everyone in the group. It didn't matter. Megan wasn't likely to win, given her aversion to bowling.

Nathan threw his hands up to show he was done, then stood up and adjusted his large belt buckle to tighten his pants at the waist as Wendy recorded his time. Juan took his turn next, knocking the pins down quickly but struggling with the puzzle. Megan cheered as Carson and then Grace took their turns. Carson did well, but Grace beat him by ten seconds and took the lead. Sabrina and Danae fell short by a few seconds and then it was Megan's turn.

Megan grabbed the plastic ball and prepared to toss it on Wendy's cue.

"And . . . go!" Wendy yelled.

Megan launched the ball down the aisle. It zoomed off to the side and into the sand. She jogged over, picked it up, and raced back to the other end. She heaved it a second time with similar results. Her face started to burn. This was not going to be pretty.

"Gutter ball!" Andrew called from the sidelines.

Not helping. Megan threw the ball again and managed to knock one pin off the side at the end. After a few more throws, there were still four pins standing securely in the sand. She was growing increasingly frustrated. It didn't matter how fast she did the puzzle if she couldn't knock down the pins.

She took a deep breath and glanced at the blue tent. Cane stood at its corner and gave her a slight salute. She smiled and returned her attention to the pins. She held the ball in front of her face, squinted, and lightly tossed it down the aisle. It veered to the side, then returned and hit the remaining pins in the center. When they all fell over, she jumped into the air.

Megan knelt in the sand and dug furiously. She needed that key fast if she was going to make up any time. Once the key was in her hand, she got the puzzle out of the box. She laid the pieces out right side up and surveyed the scene. It was some sort of beach picture with a lot of sand. It wasn't an easy puzzle. She found the corners and began to connect pieces. Once she saw the picture in store for her, the pieces fit together faster.

The last piece snapped into the puzzle and Megan threw her arms in the air.

"And time!" Wendy leaned over to look at the puzzle, which was a picture of the beach with *The Leftover* spelled out with rocks. "Puzzle correct," Wendy announced. "Megan, your time was . . ." She paused as Megan tried to slow her racing heart. The puzzle had taken more out of her than the rest since she was in such a hurry. "I'm sorry, you're four minutes off pace. Megan takes a spot at the bottom of the leader board."

Megan grunted and returned to the viewing area, disappointed but not too upset—at least now the other contestants wouldn't feel threatened by her. She crossed her arms over her chest and watched as Andrew got a strike on the first try and then put the puzzle together with ease. He took the lead from Grace like it was another day at the office.

Kat was last and Megan found herself cheering the woman on. Why not? She might be the key to the reward, even if protection was out of the question. When Kat threw a split with the first ball, Megan groaned, but the woman was fast on her feet and was throwing the ball again in no time. On her third throw, all the pins were gone.

She dug with precision and Megan wondered if she was worried about breaking a nail. Once she got to the puzzle table, perhaps the nails helped her slide the pieces into place—it went together in no time at all.

"Done!" Kat held her hands above her head.

"Wow, great job, Kat." Wendy studied her stopwatch. "We have a new leader . . . and a winner! Kat, you have protection from tonight's elimination."

Kat brushed her hands against one another and pumped her fist. "Yes!"

Wendy turned to the competitors as Kat took her place among them, receiving congratulations from all around. "No one can vote for Kat tonight and this afternoon, she will also get a reward. Kat, you can choose two people to enjoy the reward with you."

"I'll take Andrew and Megan," Kat replied.

Wendy nodded. "Everyone else can return to the beach. Andrew, Megan, Kat, you'll come with me."

Megan, pleasantly surprised that Kat had followed through on their deal, watched as the rest of the group commiserated their losses and walked around the blue tent to the other area. She also caught Cane's bug-eyed look as Kat swung her arm around Megan's shoulders as if they were long lost sisters.

"Now," Wendy said once the other contestants were gone. "I know it's only been a day, but I'm sure you're already feeling rather dirty from sleeping on the beach."

"You bet," Kat agreed.

"Near the parking lot, we have a staff shower set up. This morning, you will each be allowed twenty minutes to get cleaned up. The shower is equipped with shampoo, soaps, and even new toothbrushes and toothpaste. It's an outdoor shower, so it's not like having a long bubble bath, but it's certainly better than what the others get."

Megan leaned away slightly as Kat squealed and pressed against her side.

"When it's not your turn, you can get to know one another better." Wendy winked dramatically. "You never know what time away from the group can do for your game."

Megan felt Andrew's eyes run down her body and her skin crawled.

"Who's up for a ride?" Wendy hopped in her dune buggy and Andrew swiftly jumped into the front seat. Megan and Kat sat on the bench seat behind them and folded their legs into the small space available. They gripped the cross bars so they wouldn't fly off. "Let's do it! Wendy Weathersby over and out." Wendy floored the pedal, showering Megan's sandals and legs with sand. Megan hastily pulled her knees up and shook her feet as they rocketed toward the parking lot . . . and the warm, fresh water that waited.

Chapter Fourteen

When they arrived at the shower, Kat insisted Andrew take the first turn. "He's the best dressed man on the beach, after all," she said with a wink at Megan.

Megan could see his legs under the makeshift shower and averted her eyes when he flung his tie over the side. She didn't want to see any more than she already had.

"I wasn't sure you were going to pick me," Megan admitted as Kat tapped her nails against her leg.

"Were you going to pick me if you won?"

"Of course," Megan reassured her. *No need to make enemies.* "But I knew there wasn't much chance of that."

Kat smiled knowingly. "Yeah, I suppose not."

Megan frowned. *What did that mean?*

"What can you tell me about Carson?" Kat scratched her cheek with a manicured nail.

"Carson?"

Kat gave her an are-you-serious look. "You know, one of the guys you're sleeping with in the lean-to."

"Carson, of course. Carson." Megan was beginning to understand there was an ulterior motive to Kat picking her for the reward. Carson was a good looking guy—blond, strong jawed, and well built. Of course he would catch Kat's eye. "Carson's great. He's a PE teacher and coaches a local Little League team too."

Kat rolled her eyes. "I know all that. Is he single?"

Megan squinted into the sun. "I . . . well, he's not wearing a wedding ring." She didn't want to admit that she had yet to speak directly to him.

Kat cackled and bumped her shoulder against Megan's. "I like the way you think, girl. If he's not married, he's free for the taking."

"I didn't say–"

"And you're right. Girlfriends come and go. Even some wives too, I suppose."

"I really don't know if he's seeing anyone or not."

"Thanks for the info, Megan. I'm going for it." Kat sat back and started examining her nails, which had held up surprisingly well after digging in the sand for the puzzle.

Megan made a face, wondering what poor Carson was in for. Andrew stepped out of the shower with a towel around his waist.

"Now that," he said with a grin, "was refreshing."

His exposed hairy chest was too much for Megan, who blushed and stared at her feet. She hadn't enjoyed his business suit, but it was better than near-nakedness.

"Sorry. Am I offending you, Megan?" he asked with sarcasm in his voice.

"No offense taken," she mumbled. "Just trying to protect myself."

"Protect yourself?" Andrew scoffed, and his feet came into view as he stepped closer to Megan. "Now that you've seen the goods, you don't think you'll be able to keep your hands off me, is that it?"

Megan blinked. "Not exactly."

"Get a grip, Andrew. She has a crush on Cane." Kat shoved him away playfully.

"What? I do not." Megan's eyes shot up to glance at Kat as her cheeks turned a dark red. *How did Kat know?*

"Come on, I saw the way you stared at him during the first competition. What girl like you wouldn't want a guy like him?"

"Trevino, huh? That's how you like it?" Andrew backed away. "I understand now. I'm too much man for you." He stepped into the makeshift changing room and dropped the towel. Megan stared daggers at him as his tie flew from the side. She wanted to grab it and pull until it was too tight around his neck.

"Your secret's out now, girl. Sorry." Kat shot the glib comment over her shoulder as she took her turn in the shower.

When Andrew came around the corner, back in his suit, Megan refused to meet his eyes.

"Aw, I'm sorry, Megan," he said, almost sounding genuine. "I didn't mean to embarrass you." He sat down next to her and placed his hand on her knee, and when she looked at him, he feigned sheepishness. "Tell you what, I promise not to tell another soul about your little crush if you do a favor for me."

"What?" Megan spoke between her teeth. She felt like she was making a deal with the devil and she wasn't sure she even wanted to hear the terms.

"You came pretty close to winning that first competition for protection. Of course, I beat you out in the end. But if you were ever to win, I want you to hand protection over to me, no questions asked."

"And if I don't?" Megan seethed.

Andrew removed his hand from her knee. "I might fall ill just long enough to have a long discussion with our resident medic."

Megan stared at the sand below her. She didn't want Cane to hear she had feelings for him . . . especially from someone like Andrew. He would probably twist it in such a way that Cane would be repulsed and she would be humiliated. It was just a little crush, but still. And Kat had already spilled the beans without having any real proof. There was no telling who else she might tell.

"Fine. But you have to keep Kat quiet." She spoke with force.

"That's easy."

"Then you have a deal," Megan muttered between gritted teeth.

"What's that?" Andrew asked as he adjusted the tie at his throat.

"I said you have a deal. I win, you win."

"Ah." Andrew patted her knee again. "That's what I like to hear."

Megan stood and summoned every ounce of courage she had. "One more condition."

Andrew's eyebrows rose with interest.

"Don't ever touch me again." Megan turned and stormed into the shower as Kat pranced out and around to the changing area.

Megan ripped her clothes off and stood under the warm stream of water. She brushed her teeth so hard she was sure one of them would fall out, her thoughts a torrent of emotions and memories.

She was sick and tired of people like Andrew pushing her around. He was no different than the bullies who had teased her when she got glasses, the jocks who prodded her about her hair, the jerks who shoved her in her gym locker, and the former co-workers who whispered about her behind her back. All her life, she'd bowed to jerks like him just to get through the day, and here she was doing it again. She'd had enough. Her sister had stood up for her enough times that Megan understood how it was done. But Molly wasn't on the beach with her. It was time for her to take back her power, her life. *No more being pushed around!*

Megan reached for the small towel the crew had provided and wrapped it around her body. It barely covered her chest and backside at the same time. She felt renewed after the shower and she was ready to give a piece of her mind to Andrew.

She pulled back the shower curtain, prepared to lay into both Kat and Andrew. She was grateful to Kat for bringing her on the reward, but that didn't excuse the way she'd acted either.

Megan opened her mouth, ready to let them have it, but she

was met with a few empty logs. The cameras were gone too. Megan glanced about in confusion and reached for her clothes. Missing.

Panic welled up in her throat. *Think, Megan, think.* What would her sister do in this situation? She shook her head. That didn't help. Her sister would never be in this situation. She was too lovable and popular for anyone to pull a prank like this on her. Even if they did, she'd probably strut confidently back into camp in her little towel and find the perpetrator. But not Megan. The towel barely covered enough to keep out the breeze, much less allow her comfort in front of a camera. She would have to come up with another solution.

She had stepped into the changing area to think when she heard the telltale sound of footsteps on the beach.

"Megan!" the voice shouted. "Megan?"

Megan buried her face in her palms. Kat and Andrew were evil geniuses. It wasn't enough to steal her clothes and leave her with nothing but a hand towel. They also had to send Cane running.

"Are you hurt?" he called as he neared the shower. "What happened?"

"I'm fine," Megan called. "Physically," she muttered under her breath, then spoke at a normal level. "It seems as though my clothes may be in trouble."

Cane's voice came from just outside the curtain. "What?"

Megan sighed. "Nothing's wrong with me other than the fact that I don't have any clothes." She covered her face with her hands in embarrassment. At least the changing room gave her a bit more shelter to hide from his piercing eyes.

"They . . . took your clothes?" He paused. "But you're okay, right?"

"I'm okay," she reassured him. The worry in his voice made her smile. He still cared even though she'd grabbed his rear, however inadvertently.

"I'm gonna kill them," Cane mumbled.

"What? No, wait!" Megan peered out the dressing room flap and watched Cane storm away. "Cane, don't!" That was the worst thing he could do in this situation.

Megan rushed out of the dressing room and flew to his side. She grabbed his shoulder and turned him to face her.

His eyes met hers and Megan wrapped her fingers around his arms.

"Please don't poke the bear," she insisted.

"Poke the bear?"

"It's very nice that you want to stand up for me, but if you go after them, it'll only make things worse. Trust me. I know."

"This has happened to you before?"

Megan glanced down at her towel. "Not this exactly, but things like it."

Cane gently clasped one hand around her elbow. "You don't deserve this, Megan."

"I know. No one does."

"I didn't say that," Cane answered. "I said *you* don't."

Megan's eyebrows knit together as Cane's arm snaked around her waist. He hugged her gently and when he pulled back, he looked into her eyes.

"You're a special girl, Megan. Don't let anyone make you believe anything different."

Megan was speechless. Who was this man? He befriended her, promised to be her sounding board, and now wanted to defend her against bullying competitors? She never wanted the swelling emotion in her chest to disappear.

"I won't poke any bears," Cane promised. "But I am going to get your clothes back."

Megan's eyes widened as she backed away from him, acutely aware of the size of the towel. "Oh." She placed her hands across the small piece of fabric, holding it in place. "Oh yes. Please do." She slipped back into the changing area and peeked out the flap as

Cane shook his head, put his hands in his pockets, and turned back to the beach.

Megan put the back of one hand against her forehead. Was she swooning? She'd stood half naked before that man twice now and he still managed to make her feel better than anyone else in her life ever had. She didn't care what happened in the game. He made her feel worth the trouble.

Could he be right?

Chapter Fifteen

Cane pulled the folding chair outside his tent and sat angled toward the bay with his book in his lap. The air was stifling and the tiny bit of breeze was lifesaving. He eyed Kat and Andrew and watched as Megan returned with her clothes in place. He shook his head. Andrew denied it all, but Kat sheepishly returned the clothes when he'd asked. Ridiculous. They were adults, not teenage pranksters.

It looked like the others were trying to create a boat from branches and some of them were attempting to create a fishing pole. They were all hungry. And with good reason. The crew delivered food to Cane on a regular basis, but so far, nothing to the contestants. At least they had water. Dehydration was more dangerous at this point.

Cane read the same sentence three times. He couldn't keep his eyes off the beach scene. More than that, he couldn't stop thinking about the way he felt when Megan was wrapped in his embrace. She was an entirely different creature than Eva. When he held her, he felt needed, and he'd never experienced that in a relationship before. When he was with Eva, he hadn't realized that she had never needed him—they would have been good together, but he wouldn't have completed her. Cane wanted to fulfill something missing in a woman and for that woman to fill something missing in him. He wanted to be someone's other half.

He wished he were a camera operator so he could be part of

what was going on by the water. Eliminations were looming and he wanted to know who they were talking about voting out. He wished he had a say in the decision.

Cane returned to his book and was finally engrossed in reading about a new procedure when commotion on the beach caught his attention. Leo was running and waving his hands in Cane's direction. Cane slammed the book shut and jogged to meet Leo.

"What's going on?" Cane asked.

Leo struggled to catch his breath. "It's . . . Andrew . . ." Leo made his finger into a hook and stuck his finger in the side of his mouth, acting out the injury. It looked like Andrew had been hooked. Leo pointed toward the edge of the water.

"Got it, thanks." Cane picked up speed and broke through the ring of people standing around Andrew near the water. "Coming through. Andrew, are you okay?" He knelt by the man whose suit, though wrinkled, still looked rather decent.

"Not exactly." Andrew spoke in a muffled tone.

The hook was protruding through Andrew's upper lip and while there was a little blood on his shirt and chin, Cane was fairly certain the damage was superficial.

"Where did this come from?" Cane asked, examining the hook.

"It's mine." Kat played with the remaining earring in her right ear. The piece of jewelry was fashioned to look just like a fishhook. The only indication that it was indeed jewelry were the small stones on the edge. "It's pure silver, in case you were wondering. I wore this pair specifically in case we'd need something with a sharp hook."

"It's definitely sharp," Andrew muttered.

"How did you hook yourself?" Cane helped him to his feet to move him to the medic tent. He needed to sterilize the wound and remove the hook—er, earring.

"I didn't." Andrew's menacing stare fell on Megan.

"They were just plunking the line in the water," Megan explained. "I thought if we cast it out more like fly fishing, it might attract the fish."

"It worked too," Grace chimed in. "We could see the fish in the water. We didn't get a bite yet and then Andrew got in the way . . ."

Andrew's eyes widened. "This is my fault?" His words were garbled through his swollen upper lip.

"Come on, let's get you fixed up." Cane led the man away by his elbow, glancing behind him to see Megan trailing along.

"I'm really sorry, Andrew," Megan said. "I didn't know you were standing that close."

Andrew glared at her. "I'll send you the dry cleaning bill."

Cane opened the tent flap and helped Andrew enter the makeshift emergency room. "It's okay, Megan," he reassured her before ducking in behind Andrew. "He'll be fine."

"And his shirt?" she asked. "Dry cleaning can be costly, you know."

The twinkle in her eye made Cane wonder if she'd hooked the man on purpose as revenge for stealing her clothes. "I'll let you know."

Andrew rocked back and forth on the cot, examining his lip with his fingertips.

"Sit still." Cane pulled gloves on his hands and grabbed the disinfectant. He swabbed the liquid on Andrew's lip and allowed the man a moment to wince. "Okay, I'm going to slide the earring back out. Do you want me to numb the area?"

"No, I can take it."

Cane nodded and grasped the sharp earring. He carefully slid it around Andrew's lip and popped it out the other side.

"Ow!" Andrew proclaimed.

Cane set the hook aside and pressed gauze to the wound. "Hold this," he instructed.

"That idiot. Of all the stupid things to do. She can't catch a man so she goes and hooks one on the beach. Can you believe the nerve?" Andrew's words were muffled around the gauze.

"You think she was trying to flirt with you?" Cane asked. A camera had followed them into the tent, and he was certain the producer was eating up this situation. Andrew was opening himself to drama.

"I have absolutely no interest in her kind." Andrew straightened his tie, which now had a few drops of blood on it to match the splotch on his shirt.

"Her kind?" Cane pushed Andrew's hand away to examine the wound. It would sting, but as long as he kept it clean, it would heal fine.

"I can have any woman I want. Why in the world would I go for some washed-up geek?"

Cane blinked. Megan may have been a stereotypical "geek" in appearance due to her wire-rimmed glasses and low-maintenance look, but Cane found her witty and kind. Besides, name-calling was never okay. "I think Megan is very nice."

Andrew scoffed. "Do nice girls throw dangerous weapons at people?"

Cane glanced at the nearby earring. A weapon? He held back the laughter building in the pit of his stomach. "No," he agreed. "I guess they don't." Andrew was acting like she'd run him down on the beach with nunchucks. If the man couldn't hold up against one tiny little earring, he had more problems than Cane could count. As much as he wanted to make fun of Andrew's overreaction, he had to remain professional. All he could hope was that the group would get rid of the whiny, tie-wearing Mr. Andrew sooner rather than later. Maybe even that night.

"I'm going to place a bandage where the earring pierced the outside of your lip. There's a small tear, but don't worry—lips are one of the fastest healing areas on the body. You should be as good as new in a day or two."

"Yeah? Can't say the same for my shirt."

Cane could no longer resist the humor in the situation. "If you've ever dreamed of having a lip ring, you can keep the earring. I can put it back in now if you'd like."

Andrew narrowed his eyes. "No thanks." He stalked out of the tent, wiping at his shirt with the gauze Cane had given him to stop the bleeding.

Cane shook his head. "Wow." He didn't envy Megan's position within the group. She was already a target. Now she was dangerous as well. The earring-armed attacker. He chuckled. He couldn't wait to recount the experience with her.

"You don't think there's anything we can do?" Megan leaned toward Grace.

"I'm not sure what. Any ideas?" she replied.

Megan sat back against the tree under the lean-to. Grace had just informed her Leo was the target that night. The group on the beach had decided and the four people united in the lean-to crew wouldn't have enough votes to save him.

"Why Leo?" Megan lamented. "He's not a threat. He's sweet as molasses and he's a hard worker. Why would they go after him?"

Grace shrugged. "You got me, but this is trouble. If they get him, it's only a matter of days before they pick the rest of us off, one by one."

Megan nodded in agreement. She was shocked that the other faction was choosing to vote for Leo rather than her, assuming the intel was correct. After she'd hooked Andrew's lip she was certain he had it in for her. Why would they keep her over Leo? It didn't make sense.

"Maybe I'll go for a walk," Megan announced. "See if I can find anything out."

"Okay, let me know. I want to keep our group together. I'll vote whatever way necessary."

Megan appreciated Grace's willingness to bend. But at that point, it didn't matter who they voted for. It would be four against seven. The numbers didn't look good.

Megan crawled out of the lean-to and hit the beach. She walked down to the water and stuck her feet in. Her sandals were going to be wet for the duration of the taping whether she liked it or not. She surveyed the area. Andrew, Nathan, and Juan were near the shelter and Kat and Sabrina were just down the way, splashing water on their arms. Megan sauntered over to the other women.

"How's Andrew doing?" she asked, testing the mood. She had no kind emotions toward Kat after the clothes-stealing incident, but talking to girls was always less intimidating than approaching men.

Kat looked up. "He's okay, no thanks to you."

"I really didn't mean . . ." Megan almost turned and walked away. Nothing she could say would make them believe her.

"If it weren't for the little deal he made with you, you'd be the goner tonight." Kat spat.

"Deal? What kind of deal?" Sabrina asked with interest.

"I really shouldn't say, but Andrew told me he and Megan have a deal. If she wins protection, she hands it over to him."

Kat hadn't mentioned Megan's crush on Cane. Megan hoped leaving that out was Kat's way of staying silent about it herself, even if Andrew was the one forcing the issue.

"But what's he doing for her in return?" Sabrina frowned.

"Letting her cook him dinner, I guess." Kat rolled her eyes. "Keeping some secret or something."

Kat's pointed stare told Megan that Kat knew exactly what secret Andrew held over Megan. She was on board with keeping it quiet . . . for now.

"Ooh, Megan has a secret," Sabrina chanted in a singsong voice.

Megan took a step back. This is why she avoided starting

conversations. Things were going from bad to worse. She knew why the group was picking Leo and she didn't think she'd be able to sway them against it. She turned around and walked away swiftly. She only had one recourse—go straight to the power source.

Megan approached the small shelter on the beach with care. Andrew was talking animatedly and Nathan and Juan were soaking in his story. She didn't hear much, but it seemed to be some kind of boardroom victory tale.

"Sorry to interrupt, but Andrew, can I talk to you?" she asked in the middle of the saga.

Andrew sighed. "I'll finish later." He waved the fingers on his left hand, and the other two men took the hint and left the shelter. Andrew turned to Megan. "What?"

"I just wanted to apologize again, you know, about before."

"You think we're even now, is that it?"

"Even?" She remembered the feeling that ran to the bottom of her toes when she realized her clothes were gone. "I didn't do it on purpose."

"Oh, so I still have it coming to me later, huh?"

Megan narrowed her eyes. "I don't hurt people intentionally. I just wanted to tell you I'm sorry." She was getting nowhere and she needed to get to the point. "Anyway, I wanted to let you know the other girls aren't happy . . . about our deal."

Andrew tilted his head.

"I think they know I'm not good at everything . . ."

"You can say that again." Andrew cackled.

Megan steadied her hands at her sides. "But I do have a certain skill set. I almost won the first protection competition. Anyway, they're afraid of their position within your group. I just want you to be careful."

"What are you saying?" Andrew leaned toward her until he was close enough for his suit jacket to brush against her shoulder. "They're planning a coup?"

"I . . . I don't know what anyone's planning. I just think they don't like that you made a deal with someone from the other side of the beach." Megan was trying to act like a faithful informant, playing up to Andrew's ego.

Andrew nodded and stroked his chin. "Thank you for coming to me with this, Megan."

Megan forced a smile as Andrew waved his hand, dismissing her. Who did he think he was? The don of the beach? She didn't like it, but she took her cue and excused herself from the shelter. She was certainly in no position to unseat him. She was lucky she made it through the visit in the first place. Only once she was back under the lean-to did she get her racing heart under control.

"Any news?" Grace asked. Leo and Carson were starting to stir from an afternoon nap.

"Nothing much. You were right about the vote, but I don't know if everything is as settled as you thought. I think we should all vote for the same person and keep our fingers and toes crossed."

"Hey guys, let's talk." Grace called the waking men over to the edge of the lean-to. "Okay, Megan, lay it on us. Who are we voting for tonight?"

"There's absolutely no guarantee. But if we stick together, we might be able to pull it off. Are you guys ready?"

Chapter Sixteen

Megan's stomach was in knots, not only because she hadn't had anything to eat in two days, but also because of the vote that was about to take place. Wendy Weathersby stood before them in a bright pantsuit, balancing on her board as always. She was going on and on about the beautiful sunset they'd experienced a few moments ago. But Megan couldn't care less. She thought she was safe that night, but she was afraid for Leo. She needed all the friends she could get in this game, and Leo was part of the lean-to crew. He'd become like an uncle to the group, always making sure everyone's water bottle was full and that the shelter had enough leaf covering to keep them protected. Despite the short amount of time they had known one another, he had endeared himself to the group.

"I heard about the drama on the beach today." Wendy wore a serious expression as she touched her lip. "Andrew, how are you doing?"

"I've been better, Wendy, but it's nothing I can't handle." His tie was wrapped around his head like a man in battle. "I'm more concerned that the game is starting to get into people's heads."

"How so?" Wendy rocked forward on her shoes.

"This is a game of alliances. Deals have to be made. What goes around comes around. Megan will get what's coming to her and so will the others who cross me."

Megan frowned and her hands began to shake. She quickly sat on them. Was that a threat? Someone had to take that man down a peg or he would run the game into the ground until the very end.

"Megan, what do you have to say to that?" Wendy asked.

Megan opened her mouth, but no words came out. Her head pounded—she needed food. She glanced around the fire, trying to focus. Off to the right of Wendy's head, a camera light blinked red. She thought she saw a flash beside it. The flashlight blinked on and off and then settled under someone's chin. It was Cane. One side of Megan's mouth curled up in a slight smile.

"Andrew and I talked about the incident. I think he understands I didn't mean to hook him with that earring. I was simply trying to get something for the group to eat. Obviously, that didn't work out as I'd hoped. But Andrew and I have an . . . understanding. I think it's safe to say everything is fine between the two of us." Megan turned and gave him an eager nod. It sickened her to have to play along with his inflated power-trip, but if it would further her allies in the game, so be it.

"Where do you see yourself in the game, Sabrina?" Wendy asked.

"I thought I had a solid group," Sabrina answered. "I'm starting to learn you never know what's going to happen. I think Megan surprised us all with her fishing move. It's only a matter of time before more surprises pop up."

Sabrina's nerves were evident. The news of Megan's deal with Andrew was getting under her skin. She wondered if Kat felt as affected.

Wendy changed subjects. "How is it sleeping out under the stars, Grace?"

"Nothing I haven't done before," Grace answered. "Actually, this is one of the more pleasant places I've lived."

Megan smiled at her friend. She admired her ability to stay positive despite the trying situation.

"We have a big day ahead of us tomorrow and Wendy Weathersby is anxious to see how tonight's vote turns out. Let's get to it, shall we?" Wendy shook with anticipation. "Andrew? Will you do the honors?" She gestured to the voting table.

Andrew stood and confidently stepped over to the box. He looked at Leo and grinned. Megan's heart sank.

When it was Megan's turn to choose a name, her pulse beat hard in her temples. She needed a meal. If she could have eaten the paper, she would have, but her group needed her vote. She wrote down the chosen name and folded the paper into the box.

Once everyone had voted, Wendy retrieved the box from the stand and shook the papers around inside. "Let's see who's going home to their own bed tonight." She stuck her hand inside and pulled out the first paper. "The first vote goes to . . . Sabrina."

Megan noted Sabrina's shock, but her features quickly settled. The lean-to group had to vote for someone. Sabrina probably figured—correctly—that was her.

Leo took the next four votes and then Sabrina caught up with three votes of her own. "Leo," Wendy read from another paper. "That makes five for Leo, four for Sabrina."

Sabrina sighed and her shoulders relaxed. Megan tensed as the next paper was drawn from the box. This slip would tell her everything she needed to know. "Next vote," Wendy read slowly, "goes to . . . Sabrina."

Megan let out a breath. The tide was turning. She could feel it.

"We have a tie. Five votes Leo, five votes Sabrina. Two votes left."

Sabrina shifted uncomfortably when her name appeared on the next piece of paper as well.

"One more vote," Wendy announced. "This could tie things up." She pulled the paper out of the box, unfolded it, and smiled. "Sabrina, I'm sorry, you're going home tonight."

Sabrina stood as confusion settled over her features. "I . . . I . . ."

Megan rolled her head around on her neck. It had worked. Somehow, it had worked! She knew Andrew was an egomaniac, and she hoped placing a seed of doubt in his mind about the women he worked with would help turn things against them. Apparently, it had. Her group voted for Sabrina with little to no hope. Andrew must have gotten Juan and Nathan to vote against her as well.

"Take a moment to gather your things, Sabrina. Your ride is waiting in the parking lot."

Megan watched as Sabrina hugged her friends from the beach shelter. She hadn't yet figured out what had happened, but Megan bet she'd be pretty upset when she did.

"I can tell the line is being drawn in the sand." Wendy spoke as Sabrina walked back to her shelter to get her few items. "Tomorrow is another day and we shall see what it will bring. Until then, Wendy Weathersby wishes you all a good night." She blew a kiss to the group and stepped off her board into the dune buggy.

Megan sighed in relief as Carson placed an arm around her on one side and Grace on the other. Leo linked arms with Grace. The entwined group would remain intact . . . for now. Wendy was right. Tomorrow was another day and Megan would take things one day at a time, one second at a time, one step at a time.

～《《《》

The remaining contestants sat around the dwindling fire between their two camps. Someone needed to stoke the flames or risk losing the fire. Starting over was not an attractive option. But all they managed to do was sit in stunned silence. Andrew's features were arranged in a smug manner. Megan figured he was pleased that the group bent to his will, or so he thought. Kat looked confused about what she'd just witnessed, while Danae's face was a picture of exhaustion and hunger.

Leo finally stood up and put another log on the fire, the sparks shooting up into the night sky. The action seemed to wake the group from their stupor.

"Let's get to know each other better," Kat suggested. "Truth or dare always works."

Megan grimaced as the others agreed with the idea.

"I'll go first," Kat offered. "I pick truth." She looked around the circle, waiting for someone to ask her a question.

"Real or fake?" Danae asked. "Your hair."

Kat shook her golden locks. "A little of both. The darker color is natural, the highlights are added. My hair is about shoulder length, but I have extensions to add layers."

Megan took a deep breath. It was more than she wanted to know about Kat's hair, but it was a relatively easy question.

"Andrew, you go now." Kat lobbed the game in his direction.

"Dare," he said. "Always dare."

"Go moon the camera crew over there." Nathan guffawed and Juan took off his cap and waved it over his head as he chanted Andrew's name.

Andrew shrugged and jogged over to the unsuspecting camera operators. Megan averted her gaze as he dropped his pants and stuck his rear into the air before them. He shook it around a bit and returned to the circle to cheers and laughter, the other two men still chanting his name. They would have made good fraternity brothers with those antics.

"Megan, your turn." Andrew gave her a lopsided grin.

"Um . . ." Megan weighed her options. She didn't want to pick truth and have Andrew ask her about her crush. Dare wasn't a safe option either, but she didn't have any other choices. "Dare."

Andrew rubbed his hands together. "I got this one," he said to the group. "Megan, I dare you to kiss *The Leftover* medic. On the lips."

Kat gasped and fanned herself. "Cane Trevino? He's a hunk. She'll never do it." She raised her eyebrows with an eager expression, toying with Megan.

Grace leaned over and whispered in Megan's ear, "You don't have to. It's just a stupid game. Ignore them."

"No." Megan shook her head. "I'll do it." She stood and started walking toward the blue tent.

"Oh, and Megan—no ducking into the tent and faking it. We want to see it. It doesn't count unless it's out in the open."

Megan's pulse quickened. Andrew had called her bluff. It would have been easy to slip into the tent, concoct a reason to see Cane for a moment, and then come back out and lie to the group. Now she was in a pickle. She slowly put one foot in front of the other, her mind racing. She didn't want to give Andrew the satisfaction of winning this little game. He wanted her to back away from the challenge and embarrass herself.

She stopped halfway to the tent. She couldn't do this. It was ridiculous.

"Second thoughts, Megan?" Andrew called. "Let me guess—you've never kissed a boy before, right?"

Megan fumed. How did he know the buttons to push? So what if she was nearly thirty and had never been kissed. Lots of people waited for the right person to give away that first kiss. Okay, so she wasn't really waiting. She'd just never had the opportunity. Unless you counted that one exchange student who planted a chaste kiss near the side of her mouth after school one day. But that was another story.

Megan forced herself to move forward. She was getting closer to the tent and she still had no idea what to do. She raised her hand to knock before remembering how well that had worked the first time she had visited Cane.

"Cane?" she called, her voice cracking with nerves. "Could you come out here for a second?"

"Megan," he said when his head appeared between the tent flaps. "I was hoping you'd stop by. I have been dying to hear more about that fishing incident." His smile froze and he stopped just outside the tent as he studied her worried face. "What's wrong?"

"Nothing. I don't have time to talk right now." She glanced over her shoulder. She couldn't see the others very well in the dark, but she felt their eyes on her. "I just . . . needed to give you something."

"Give me something?" Cane frowned.

"Please just take it and I'll explain later, okay?"

"Okaaay."

Megan took two steps forward and closed the gap between them. She rose up on her toes and widened her eyes. She knew she was supposed to close them, but she couldn't tear her gaze from his concerned face.

When she was inches from his mouth, she whispered, "Sorry about this," and then planted her lips on his. She heard hooting back on the beach and jammed her eyes shut. She didn't want to see Cane's reaction after all.

Megan felt very awkward with her lips pressed against Cane's mouth, but a moment later, he grabbed her wrist and pulled her into his tent.

"Those lunatics are watching," he said softly against her cheek.

Megan nodded. Their lips were still only inches apart. "I know."

"I don't know what's going on here, Megan, but you started it." Cane tipped his head to the left, wrapped his arm around her waist, and drew her to him.

Megan's heart beat harder as he placed his lips on hers. She was so shocked she couldn't move, but her arms had minds of their own. They wrapped themselves around his neck as she sank into his embrace. After a few moments of pure enjoyment, Megan realized what was happening. *Cane* was kissing *her*. She drew back and stared at his shoulder.

She heard the other contestants chanting her name instead of Andrew's. "I . . . I have to go."

Cane released his hold on her waist. He looked almost as shocked as she did. She rushed out of the tent and back to the fire. Everyone wanted a play-by-play of the action, but Megan refused to give any details. She pushed them off with a quick comment. "I never kiss and tell. Grace, it's your turn."

Grace chose truth and the game continued around the circle until everyone had a chance. Leo had to skinny dip in the lake and Carson was supposed to sleep in a tree, but no one faced a challenge like Megan's. She had had her first kiss and though it started out awkwardly enough, it became something real. She wasn't sure she'd ever sleep again.

Chapter Seventeen

"Psst. Megan. Hey."

Megan jerked awake and rolled to her side, squinting into the darkness. Her eyes flew open as the voice's owner came into focus. Cane's face was inches away and when he tilted his head to the side to invite her out of the lean-to, she slowly sat up and edged away from her sleeping tent-mates.

"Sorry to wake you." Cane spoke in a soft voice as they put distance between them and the lean-to.

"I was only a little asleep."

"Huh, that's a new one." Cane chuckled and the hair on Megan's arms rose.

"So, what's up?" she asked as they neared the medic tent.

Cane gave her a look. "You didn't come over tonight to talk like you have the past couple days . . . and I thought we should talk. About before."

"Oh, yeah, that."

Megan averted her eyes as Cane stopped in the sand and turned toward her. She had been waiting for her lean-to friends to fall asleep before venturing out, but she must've fallen asleep herself.

"I guess I owe you an explanation," she said. "I didn't mean to put you in an uncomfortable position. I just . . . they dared me and I couldn't back down." She shivered, and Cane placed his hands on her elbows and rubbed her arms.

"You did that on a dare?"

She nodded, semi-shocked that he was touching her like it was no big deal. His hands burned her skin.

"Well, this is awkward." He exhaled. "I should have guessed . . . with the chanting and all."

Megan searched his face. It was dark and easier for her to look at him. "You weren't egged on?" she teased.

"Do you see anyone in my tent?" He threw back the flap.

Megan giggled. "No."

"I'm sorry. I got carried away."

"It's okay," Megan said. "It's not like I minded."

"I just felt . . ." He broke off, then coughed. "Never mind."

"What?" Megan asked. He had come to her this time and she was curious.

"I don't know . . . something."

Something? He really felt something? Megan didn't know what that was, but something was definitely better than nothing.

"Me too," she whispered. Not stopping to think, she took a step forward and leaned against his chest.

Time stood still as she snaked her arms around his waist and wrapped them around his back. His hands moved from her arms to her shoulders and she thought she felt his fingers toying with the back of her ponytail. It was dark and she didn't have her glasses on, but when she tilted her head to look at his face, she thought she saw a slight smile.

"Cane!" A deep voice rang through the darkness from the beach.

Megan jerked away.

"It's Tank." Megan recognized Andrew's voice—it sounded genuinely worried. Cane was already making his way toward the beach shelter, and Megan jogged behind him, concerned about Tank.

"What's going on?" Cane asked.

Andrew stood beside the shelter and waved him inside. Megan waited outside and tried to hear what was happening.

"He's breathing erratically." Cane's voice rang through the stick walls. "You said he was talking?"

"He said something about food and he even stood up and tried to grab me like I was his favorite candy bar," Kat said from within, sounding both scared and disgusted.

A moment later, the rest of the beach group joined Megan outside the shelter.

"Is Tank okay?" Megan asked.

"What are you doing here?" Kat scowled.

"I heard the commotion and wanted to see what was going on."

"I don't know what his problem is." Kat shrugged. She looked more put out than concerned. "He was snoring really loud and moaning about food. We just wanted to sleep so we tried to wake him but couldn't."

"He wouldn't wake up?"

Kat shook her head. Andrew leaned against the shelter around the corner, half asleep on his feet.

Megan ducked her head into the shelter behind the camera operator who had also awakened from the activity. "Is there anything I can do?" she asked. Cane knelt on the ground next to Tank as the camera's red light began to blink nearby. His fingers were on the larger man's wrist and had a serious look on his face.

"Could you grab my supply bag?" Cane asked. "It's on the bottom shelf."

Megan nodded and set out in a dead run for the medic tent. When she returned, she knew her sister would be pleased with her fast time. "Here you go." She dropped the bag next to Cane and waited in case he had more instructions for her.

"Thanks." Cane dug through the bag and slapped a glove on each hand. He inserted a needle into Tank's arm and held a bag of fluid above his head.

"What's going on with him?" Megan asked, unsure if she should stick around.

"He's dehydrated. He's a big man and even though you guys are getting a lot of water, Tank requires more than average. Add a little delirium from hunger and he's in a what they call a sleep coma."

"A sleep coma?"

"He's really just asleep, but he's in such a deep sleep that he's hard to awaken. Once we get him hydrated, he should wake up and be fine. But he really needs to get some food tomorrow."

Megan took a step back. She was impressed by Cane's fast actions. She knew he was a medical professional, but seeing him at work gave her a whole new appreciation for his job.

"It might be best if the others give him space tonight. I'm going to stay here and monitor the situation. I have my cell phone. If I need help, I'll call Mike and the hospital."

"I'll tell them." Megan promised.

"So there's nothing more to see here?" The camera operator lowered the lens.

"Not unless you want footage of him sleeping." Cane shrugged.

The camera operator swung the device from his shoulder and ducked back out of the tent.

"Are you sure you won't need anything else?" Megan asked.

Despite the serious situation, Cane glanced up with a smile. "Do you want me to?"

Megan smiled back. The shelter was brightly lit with a lantern Cane had pulled out of the medical bag, but her features were safe in the shadows. "Just offering."

"It might be good to have another pair of hands. Just in case." Cane returned his attention to Tank.

Megan exited the shelter to pass the news along to the others.

"Tank is going to be okay, but Cane needs some space to help him. He asked that the rest of you find somewhere else to sleep tonight so Tank can recover. He should be okay by morning."

Andrew rolled his head on his neck. "Where are we supposed to go?" he whined.

"The lean-to is close and there's extra room. It might be tight with all of you, but it's better than the open beach."

Kat grinned. "Dibs on the space next to Carson."

"He's in the tree," Andrew spat. "Remember the dare?"

Kat's face fell and Megan watched the group disappear toward the lean-to without a care as to where Megan would end up. She let herself back into the shelter and knelt next to Cane.

"How's he doing?" she asked.

"Salisbury steak," Tank muttered.

"Did he just . . ."

"He did." Cane shook his head. "The sleep coma is peculiar. Some say you can even influence people's dreams when they're in this state."

Megan bent over close to Tank's ear. "You're in love with Kat. Megan is *The Leftover*," she whispered. "There, that oughta wake him up. Or give him a nightmare."

Cane chuckled. "You have a big day ahead of you, Megan. Why don't you get some sleep? I'll be okay. If I need anything, I'll let you know."

Megan gazed into his eyes for a few moments. The bright lantern and dark night air gave him a fuzzy look that was almost surreal. She surveyed the shelter. It wasn't any more luxurious or comfortable than the lean-to. She chose a spot within touching distance of Cane. If she fell asleep and he needed something, she'd be within reach.

Between Cane's embrace and the emergency with Tank, Megan's adrenaline was still pumping. She wanted to relax and take Cane's advice, but it would take a while to calm herself. Since he was going to be awake keeping watch over Tank, she grabbed the opportunity to find out more about him. "Tell me about your first day on the job," she said as she settled into the sand.

"It was a disaster. I couldn't even remember my own name, much less the proper medical procedures."

Cane's voice lulled her to sleep as her pulse slowed and she eventually drifted away with a contented smile on her face.

‿‿‿‿

Cane woke when a hand stroked his cheek. He allowed himself a few moments to enjoy the sensation without opening his eyes. He remembered the night before very well. Megan had fallen asleep next to him on the sand as he told tales of medical marvel . . . or something like that. Once Tank was fully hydrated halfway through the night, the large man had settled into a fitful but normal sleep. He was out of danger, but Cane had wanted to stay nearby. He must have drifted off himself at some point.

When he opened his eyes, he discovered his head was resting on someone's chest—someone's rock-hard chest. The hand against his cheek was large enough to cover his entire face. He jerked into the upright position. Somehow, he had fallen asleep half sitting, his head resting on Tank's torso.

Cane shuddered. Thank goodness no one had seen him sleeping there, or Tank's stroking–

He glanced at the spot Megan had occupied the night before. Empty.

He slowly swiveled until he saw her grinning from her seat by the shelter opening.

"Good morning, Cane."

"Morning." Cane ran his hand through his mussed hair.

"I was going to wake you, but I didn't want to interrupt . . ."

Cane made a face. "It would have been a welcome interruption."

Megan's smile grew and a burst of laughter escaped her lips. "Sorry. It's just . . . he was . . . oh my gosh!"

"I know, I know, I was there." Cane grimaced. He wasn't going to live this down anytime soon.

The laughter woke Tank, who rolled to his side and rubbed his eyes.

"Where's Mimi?" he asked in a confused voice.

Cane turned his attention back to the large man. "Mimi?"

"My poodle. She always sleeps right here." Tank patted his abs. "I swear I was just petting her."

Cane glanced at Megan, who was turning purple trying to hold in the laughter.

"Hey, what are you two doing here? Where's everyone else?" Tank sat up and noticed the IV running from his arm. "What's this?"

Cane calmly explained the situation. "You really need to make it a priority to find some food today, Tank. If you don't eat soon, I'm afraid they might have to pull you from the game."

"I'm not one to miss a meal." He patted his stomach. "Gotta keep the protein flowing to grow the guns, you know."

"Guns?" Megan murmured.

"Yeah, you know, it's all about keeping the ladies happy with the gun show." Tank flexed his arm and kissed his bicep.

"You know what the ladies like." Megan stood. "I'll go tell the others you're awake." She bent and spoke near Cane's ear. "And leave you two alone for a minute."

Cane swatted at her as she left.

"Can't they just deliver some food to us like they do the rest of the crew?" Tank asked. "I don't know if I have the energy to hunt today."

Cane squinted at the much larger man. He might still be a bit disoriented. He was on a beach in a residential neighborhood and the only weapons he had were the "guns" on his arms. There would be no hunting.

"The producer might think food delivery was cheating. Finding your own nourishment is part of the game, I guess. And you've got a whole team of contestants behind you. Let them do the work and hope for the best. If you're going to make it through the competition later, you'll need the extra energy."

"Thanks for the help, doc."

"Anytime." Cane wasn't used to being called doc, but he didn't bother correcting Tank. He pulled the IV from the man's arm and placed a Band-Aid over the small wound. "If you feel dizzy or disoriented today, please come see me."

"Will do."

Cane packed up his bag and headed back to his own tent. He slept for an hour or so, but he certainly didn't feel well rested. He kept thinking about the hard set of abs he had rested his head upon instead of a soft pillow the night before. He stretched his neck. Tank wasn't going to win any awards for best pillow, that was for sure. He wondered why Mimi the poodle chose to sleep there.

He was glad he had helped someone in the game. He hoped Tank's problem was a one shot deal, but he felt a thrill that he'd been able to rush to the scene and take care of the issue without involving the hospital. His job was important, even if it didn't seem like it every hour of the day. He was available when needed.

Cane placed his supply bag in its place on the shelf and sank onto his cot. Tank's emergency hadn't come at a very convenient time. He lamented that it interrupted his moment with Megan. He needed to figure out what was going on between them. He'd only known the woman a few days, but as usual, he was falling for her hard and fast. It was probably a good idea to back off.

But at the same time, he couldn't help but pay attention to what his heart told him. Megan was nothing like the other girls he had dated, who were meticulous in their appearance and very outgoing. Eva, who he had thought was his perfect fit, was Megan's polar opposite. Eva loved to wear the latest styles, which meant a lot of shopping, and she went to the gym religiously. Every weekend was filled with social events, and everyone seemed drawn to her. Megan, on the other hand, initially came across as a mess. She didn't seem to care a whit about her appearance and she was almost painfully reserved. Yet Cane had been attracted to her from the beginning, and as he had gotten to know her, he realized she had other priorities than how she looked—like her sister and her job. And he found that refreshing.

Deep down, Cane wondered if he was subconsciously using Megan to get over his broken heart. He wouldn't do that, would he? He had to admit, he didn't like being alone. Whenever things hadn't worked out with women in the past, he'd been fast to jump back into the dating pool—his current year-long single streak was a big exception. And rebound relationships never ended well for him.

As he lay back on his cot, he had plenty of questions on his mind and very few answers. He knew two things for sure. One, he liked the way Megan fit into his arms. And two, he needed to sleep and clear his head.

Chapter Eighteen

"Got one!" Grace's arm flashed out of the water, something splashing wildly in her grip.

"You . . . what?" Megan stared at her in shock. Her friend said she was trained in survival skills with her Army background. Megan hadn't realized that meant Grace had the ability to catch fish with her bare hands.

"I think it's a little upset." Grace held the fish over her head. "It's a crappie."

"It's a decent sized fish. Can you do it again?"

Grace smiled. "Take this one off my hands and watch me."

Megan blinked at the fish Grace held out in front of her. She wasn't opposed to slimy things, but a live fish? It might go a bit beyond her skill set.

"Here, I got it." Carson appeared at her side. "Ladies shouldn't have to do this kind of job." He winked at Megan as he took the fish from Grace. "I'll clean it in the woods and you can help at the fire."

Megan frowned at Grace, who was waist deep in the water, concentrating. "I clean. You cook." Grace grunted. "Me man. You woman." Grace raised her hands by her side and became still. Her eyes swiveled and her hands moved lightning fast through the water. "Ha!" She held up another slippery fish.

Megan glanced over her shoulder. Carson was long gone. Who

would take this one? She took a few steps off the beach into the water.

"Why didn't you tell us you could do this two days ago?" she asked as her stomach turned over. She was desperately hungry, but she wasn't sure she'd be able to eat a fish after staring it in the eye.

Grace slapped the fish into her hands. "I didn't want to come on too strong. You saw what happened to Lucy."

Megan nodded. "That's why I haven't jumped out of that big tree and caught a bird for us to eat."

Grace giggled. "Please promise me you'll do that for the next meal."

Megan stared at the crappie in her hands, unable to think about anything but the feel of its scales. "I better get this to Carson for . . . prep."

"Think we'll need more?" Grace asked.

Megan shrugged as she held her arms as far away from her body as possible. "Probably. Tank could eat these two alone. More wouldn't hurt." She gingerly walked toward the woods and found Carson pulling guts from the first fish to create a fillet. "She got another one." Megan held the jerking fish out to him.

Carson shook his head. "Amazing. Forget the hooks and lines, all we need is Grace. I'm glad she's on our side."

Megan smiled as he removed the fish from her grasp. She hadn't talked to Carson much, more because of her embarrassment around cute guys than anything. But she was starting to think of him as a brother-like figure. That helped her now when she found herself alone with him in the forest with only a slimy crappie between them.

"Can you get this one on the fire?" he asked. "The sooner we eat, the better."

Megan agreed. They were all hungry. Starving, really. And the first fish didn't look much like a real fish anymore. In fillet style, it looked much more like what she was used to seeing at the supermarket. "I'll see what I can do."

She took the bucket with the fresh fish from Carson and turned to hit the beach.

"Hey, Megan," he called. "Do me another favor?"

Megan turned back in his direction. "What's that?"

"Put in a good word for me? With Grace?"

Megan cocked her head, half teasing. "What about Kat?"

"Kat?" Carson asked, looking confused.

Megan thought back to the past few days. Kat had placed her manicured nails on Carson's shoulder at every possible moment, but Carson hadn't reciprocated, or even noticed. Perhaps Kat wasn't his type. Megan assumed any man would like a put-together woman like Kat. At least in appearance.

"Never mind," Megan said. "I think Grace enjoys your company and I won't have a hard time saying nice things about you." She admired Carson's work ethic and he never said a bad word about anyone, even when those sleeping on the beach annoyed the lean-to crew.

"Wow, thanks, Megan." He beamed at her.

Megan nodded and spun on her heel to deliver the fish to the fire. She was glad she was over her initial crush on Carson. He was a charming, attractive man and now that she could speak to him, she considered him a friend. In her years working at home, relating to her clients via email, she had trouble calling anyone "friend." But here on the beach, she'd made several in a matter of days.

By the time she reached the pit, the others from the beach group were starting to stumble out of their shelter. They'd spent a long night in the lean-to and no one got much sleep. While Grace, Megan, and Carson got to work finding food in the morning and Leo kept the fire going, the others returned to their original shelter and went back to sleep.

Megan watched Leo stoke the flame then spear the fish on a stick and string it across the top of the fire to roast. She watched as Kat emerged from the beach shelter, stretched and looked around, probably trying to locate Carson. Andrew followed, buttoning his suit jacket as if he were preparing to prosecute a trial, and Tank appeared when the first line of smoke peeled off the fish.

"I smell food!" he announced. Everyone quickly gathered around the fire.

"Did you get that with my earring?" Kat fingered her empty ear.

"No. Grace caught it. And there's more where this one came from." Megan turned as Carson joined them from the woods with the second fish.

"Welcome to our feast." Carson bowed as he placed the second fish on another stick.

The group eagerly took spaces around the fire, watching the fish sizzle. Grace sent Carson back into the woods two more times with several more fish before she joined the circle.

"I don't even want to know where these came from," Kat said as she took her share from the first fish. "Don't tell me anything." She bit into the fish and made a face. "It's the most disgusting and most delicious thing I've ever had in my life." They each got a small bite of the first fish, just enough to whet their appetites.

Tank devoured an entire fish on his own. Given his recent medical emergency, no one complained. The rest of the group shared two more fish as they came off the fire. By the time the fifth fish was ready, Tank was back in the mix and no one begrudged him his share. All eyes remained on whoever was taking a bite as the contestants waited their turn with each fish. There wasn't enough to completely satisfy everyone, but their stomachs were fuller than they had been in days.

Andrew sidled up to Grace while everyone let the protein settle into their systems. "We should chat later."

Megan leaned in their direction. She wanted to hear what he had to say, and she needed to remember to warn Grace against deals with Andrew.

"We're chatting now, Andrew. What do you want?"

Megan stifled a laugh. She loved Grace's direct approach.

"I think you and I could work well together."

"Is that so?" Grace gave him the once over. "Are you willing to part with that tie?"

Andrew blinked down at his tie. "My tie? You want my tie?"

Grace shrugged. "It would make a cozy pillow."

"You want to use my tie . . . as a pillow?" Andrew looked aghast at the idea of his precious tie lying in the sand, acting like nothing more than a piece of fabric cushioning someone's head.

"At least that way I'd have my eyes closed when I was near it."

Megan snorted and Andrew turned and glared at her. He got up and stormed away. Grace giggled softly and bumped her fist against Megan's.

Megan should have known. Grace had his number. She wouldn't work with him if he were the last man on the beach. And if the lean-to crew had anything to say about it, he wouldn't be the last one left anywhere.

The morning sun burned into the afternoon hours and the contestants split off into groups. Some wandered by the water while others took refuge in the shade. Megan took advantage of the empty lean-to and napped for a while. She'd had a more spacious place to sleep the night before, but she'd been up late listening to Cane's stories, and she needed to catch up to be fresh for the competition. Now that her stomach had a little food in it, sleep would do her good.

As soon as she dozed off, she found herself back inside Cane's tent, his arms wrapped around her. One of his hands rested at the small of her back while the other one stroked her spine. She looked unabashedly into his eyes and puckered her lips as she stood on her toes. His eyes sparkled as he stared back at her and leaned down to press his lips against hers.

She moaned softly as she tilted her head and threaded her fingers through his curly hair. The curls were even softer than she imagined. The kiss went on much longer than Megan dreamed any kiss could last and when it finally ended, they pressed their foreheads together and gazed into each other's eyes. Neither spoke, but no words were necessary. They were perfectly in sync and completely comfortable.

"Megan. Megan, wake up!"

Megan jolted awake and found her hand in her own hair, tangled in her ponytail.

She blinked a few times and prayed she hadn't been talking in her sleep like Tank the night before. "What? What is it?" she asked as Grace's face came into focus.

"Wendy's on her way over. The competition is going to start soon. The crew said to wear swimsuits."

Megan rolled to her side and sat up. She was stiff in places she didn't know she had, and her mind was obviously preoccupied with things outside of the game. She needed to get her head back in the game.

As she changed into her swimsuit, she hoped Cane would be nearby to guide her through whatever the challenge held that day. And she tried to imagine a competition that required a swimsuit but no swimming.

Chapter Nineteen

Megan stood on the beach. There was nothing in sight but Wendy Weathersby on her board. She exchanged a look with Grace. There was nothing set up for them to do. Megan's body ached from head to toe. The beach was not her friend. She needed to start dreaming of soft, cozy mattresses instead of Cane.

Thinking his name caused her to search for him. She found him standing amidst the crew, just to the right of Wendy.

"Welcome, Leftovers!" Wendy greeted. "You may be wondering about today's challenge."

The group looked at each other.

Wendy gleefully pointed to the water behind them. "Today, Wendy Weathersby has organized a water competition."

Megan slowly turned as the blood drained from her face. Surely, Wendy hadn't jumped in that water and organized anything at all, but that was beside the point. They were going to swim.

Wendy picked up where she left off. "You will all swim out to the middle of the bay where you'll find a colored buoy."

Megan squinted. She could see five buoys lined up in a row. This was worse than she could have imagined.

"Each buoy has a series of knots below the surface. Dive down, find the knots and untie them. Once all the knots are untied, bring the buoy back with you to shore. The first person back wins protection from tonight's elimination."

Megan let the instructions settle in. Could she even make it to the buoy in the first place?

"Here's the catch." Wendy paused. "There are five buoys and ten of you. We will run the competition twice and two people will receive protection."

Danae gasped and Nathan cheered. Two people safe from elimination. It was huge.

Megan sighed. She would be lucky to survive the competition, much less win protection.

"I'll draw names for teams." Wendy pulled out the first five names, and Megan was relieved not to be among them. At least she could watch the first round. Maybe she would gather some useful tips.

Megan cheered Grace on as she swam the distance with long, wide, confident strokes. Grace took a large lead, even ahead of Andrew who had swiftly shed his suit all the way down to what looked like a Speedo. Megan tried not to look at him, but it was like a car accident . . . hard not to stare. Everyone else had come to the beach in their swim attire—Megan in her black one piece; Kat in her itsy bitsy, teeny tiny, yellow polka dot bikini; Juan in bright blue swim trunks; Grace in her red tankini. But Andrew had to go for the dramatic striptease.

Megan removed her glasses and wiped them against her swimsuit. When she put them back on her nose, she shielded her eyes and tried to catch sight of Grace. Her head was gone. She was below the water working on the knots. After Grace popped back up for air, Andrew reached his buoy followed by Nathan, Leo, and Juan.

"Come on, Grace, you can do it!" Megan called every time Grace's head surfaced. She was underwater at least a minute each time, if not more. The fifth time she disappeared, the buoy jerked and then started moving toward the beach. Megan frowned and watched as Grace surfaced partway back to the shore. Not only had she untied the knots, but she had started swimming in the right direction. She was amazing.

Grace reached the shore to a line of cheers. Even those who lived in the other shelter knew what she had done was quite a feat.

Wendy screeched through a mega phone. "Grace wins! The rest of you can return to the beach."

Crew members in canoes visited each buoy and retied the knots for the next round. Megan listened to Grace's excited descriptions while wondering if any buoy was looser than another. She needed all the help she could get.

"Second group, take your spot on the shore," Wendy commanded.

Megan glanced down the beach. She was up against Carson, Danae, Kat, and Tank. She didn't think Tank would be competition. He would probably sink to the bottom, especially after his rough night. Kat might have to fight to keep her top in place so maybe Megan could best her as well. But Carson was strong and athletic, and Danae looked determined with her hair piled atop her head in a high ballerina bun. She wore a purple and pink swimsuit that looked like it came out of an Olympic swimwear catalog. If Megan had to guess, she'd say Danae was not new to the swimming scene.

"I'm out," Kat called as she stood from her readied position.

Wendy's face registered shock. "You're not going to participate?"

With no explanation, Kat shook her head and backed away from the water.

One down, three to go. Megan shook her head. At least the crew wouldn't have to worry about blurring out Kat's chest if she had a swimsuit malfunction in the water. Megan found herself slightly disgusted by the high-maintenance woman. Megan wasn't a strong swimmer and she knew it, but at least she was willing to try. With that kind of attitude, Kat didn't deserve a spot on this beach.

"Are the rest of you ready?" Wendy was way too close with the megaphone.

Megan nodded uncertainly, searching over her shoulder for a glimpse of Cane. He raised a hand to her, his lifeguard flotation device gleaming in the sun. He was their medic and their lifeguard too, apparently.

"Megan, you want to leave your glasses here?" Wendy asked loudly.

"No glasses, no vision," Megan replied.

Wendy shrugged and yelled again. "And go!"

Megan waded out into the water, lifting her legs up high to gain as much time as possible. She watched as Carson and Danae started swimming. Tank floated on his back and made slow progress.

What do you know, Tank can float. Megan's feet could still touch the bottom of the bay. There was no reason for her to start swimming yet. It would be slower than walking in her case. She stretched her toes so she stood on their tips and took a few more steps. The water crept up to her chin. She was halfway to the buoy. It was time.

Megan kicked her legs and lifted herself from the sand below. She paddled her hands in front of her. Yes, she was doing the doggy paddle on TV, but what else was she supposed to do? It was her most commanding stroke. The other competitor's heads started to disappear as they worked on their knots. Megan's only hope was that they would struggle to untie their buoys.

When she reached her destination, her body was exhausted and she was out of breath. She clung to the large buoy, thankful that it kept her afloat. She watched Carson resurface to grab a breath and go back under.

"Here goes nothing." Megan gulped in as much air as her lungs could hold and pushed herself under the water. She squeezed her eyes shut and worked her hand down the rope and found the first knot. It came undone easily. Megan went back to the surface and wiped some of the water from her glasses. She took a moment to survey her competition. No one else was swimming toward the beach yet. Maybe this wouldn't be so bad. She could do it.

Megan gulped in a big breath of air and plunged back underwater. Her fingers moved down the rope until she found the next knot. She didn't bother opening her eyes or cleaning her glasses. It didn't matter where the other contestants were. The second and fourth knots were just as easy as the first, but the third gave her trouble, and she had to surface, gasping, before throwing herself down to finish it.

After the fourth knot, she struggled to the top and attempted to get enough air into her lungs to satisfy her body. With a final deep breath, she threw herself back underwater. By the time she found the last knot, her lungs were begging for air. The knot was more complicated and her fingers grew numb around it as she struggled to untie the rope. Her body screamed for air, but she really wanted to free the buoy to prove she could complete the task.

Megan let air bubbles escape slowly as she worked the knot. No luck. She had no choice but to surface. With a gasp, her head popped above. There was some garbled yelling coming from the shore, but water filled her ears and she was unable to make sense of it. Probably just Wendy narrating the race as she had the first. Megan guessed someone was heading back to the beach. She wasn't going to win, but she couldn't pull a Kat and quit trying until it was over for sure.

She dove back into the water and found the final knot again. She unraveled a bit more of it, surfaced for one more breath, and then freed the buoy with a final tug.

Megan was gasping for air when she returned to the surface. She ignored the now-free buoy and began to dog paddle back to shore. She couldn't see much around the drops of water that clung to her glasses, but at least what she could make out was more clear than blurry.

Come on, arms, keep going! She only had to make it halfway before she could stand and walk the rest of the way, but she was so tired. She felt her head slip under water and strengthened her resolve. *Go, legs, go!* Her arms weren't working very well anymore so she kicked harder with her legs to resurface. She sucked air in before resting her legs for a moment. Megan tilted her head back to keep her chin above the water as she tried to get her arms going again. She was concentrating so hard on telling her limbs what to do and failing that she didn't hear the splashing figure coming toward her.

"I've got you." The voice rang through her haze. "Just relax."

Megan turned onto her back, her muscles screaming even though she had stopped moving, and let herself be dragged toward the beach.

"I got the buoy," she said softly.

"You sure did. Well done, Megan."

Once Megan was sitting on the sand, her senses returned. Her glasses were blurred with water. She took them off and shook them. Cane was kneeling beside her. His hair was wet but still just as curly. He had the flotation device strapped around his bare chest. Megan blinked as embarrassment rose onto her cheeks. Her glasses were still in her hand so she couldn't see very well, but what she could make out was impressive. He definitely had the body of a lifeguard.

"I . . . guess I got tired." She wanted to explain herself and push the embarrassment away as quickly as possible.

Cane patted her shoulder. "You did well. You might have even made it to shore, but I was concerned."

Megan nodded, ducking her head. "Thanks for saving me."

"Why don't you lie back for a little mouth to mouth?" Kat cackled.

Megan blushed as she noticed the rest of the contestants gathered around them in a semi-circle. Cane took her glasses and wiped them dry on a towel. "Here." He placed them on her face.

"Thanks." Megan wanted to put her hand on his arm and tell him how much she appreciated his help. She also wanted to dig a hole in the sand and disappear. She'd shown one of her many weaknesses not only to Cane, but also to everyone else on the beach.

Kat and Andrew whispered to each other nearby. Kat threw her head back and laughed as Andrew rolled his eyes then looked right at Megan with a smirk.

Grace knelt down next to her, her eyes worried. "You okay, girl? We were all confused when you went back under after Wendy announced Carson had won."

Megan nodded, not looking up. "I didn't hear her. And I really wanted to prove I could do it . . ." Her voice died away. She could still see the circle of feet from the other contestants around her. Megan was the center of attention and she did not like it one bit.

Megan was saved from any further humiliation as Wendy called the group to reassemble around her. "Carson and Grace, you have won protection tonight. No one can vote against you. I suggest the rest of you return to the beach and decide what you're going to do."

Everyone dispersed and Megan let out a relieved sigh. As she slowly stood, she wished she had a walker. Her legs felt like rubber and her arms were shaking from exhaustion. But she had swam more than she ever had in her life, two people in her alliance were safe from elimination—and Cane stood nearby with no shirt. Now that her glasses were clear, the vision of his muscles glittering in the sun was not helping her think straight. How did someone even get eight-pack abs? She had only heard of a six-pack.

She shook her head to clear the water from her ears and the sight of Cane from her view. She needed to focus on the elimination tonight. Grace and Carson were out of danger, but the odds were against her and Leo. Maybe she could trick Andrew's ego again or pull someone over from the beach shelter to the lean-to voting side.

Cane stood behind the camera crew and ran a towel down each arm, his chest still fully exposed to Megan's view. She tried to draw her gaze away from his bare pecs by turning her head, but her eyes stayed on him. When he blotted the towel on one side of his neck and then the other, the rest of the fabric covered his abs and allowed Megan to tear herself from the sight.

She made a beeline for the lean-to. She had a few hours to figure out what to do about the vote. She'd have to come up with something—assuming she could get the vision of shirtless Cane out of her head long enough to devise a plan.

Chapter Twenty

The Leftovers were showing their wear and tear after several days on the beach. Cane liked the color that returned to their cheeks after eating some fish, but he still needed to keep tabs on them. He approached them one at a time after the competition and invited each to his tent for a round of vital checks. He needed to keep things under control and get a read on how everyone was faring.

Cane first checked everyone from the beach shelter group first, then moved on to the lean-to group. They'd heard about his checks and started to come on their own. Grace appeared first with Carson waiting just outside the tent.

"Congratulations on the win." Cane grabbed his files and flipped to hers so he could make notes.

"Thanks."

"You don't look excited." Cane strapped a blood pressure cuff around her arm.

"I was at first, but now I realize how vulnerable this leaves the rest of my team."

"You mean Megan and Leo?"

Grace nodded. "I know only one person will be left at the end, but I really want all of us to make it further than this."

Cane listened to her heart with his stethoscope. "You never know what the evening will bring."

"True."

"Okay, you're in good condition. I'm ready for Carson."

Cane took Carson's readings and asked him to send Leo in. Leo was holding up well, and Cane asked him to watch for Megan and ask her to come by.

Half an hour later, Megan still hadn't appeared. Cane set her chart on top of the others and peeked out of the tent just as she raised her hand to knock.

"Oh, hi," she said.

"I was looking for you."

"I heard. Something about vitals?"

"Yeah, come in." Cane had her sit on his cot, just as he had the others. "Where have you been?"

Megan shrugged. "Back in the trees wandering around. I needed to think through my options."

Cane assumed she was talking about the game. It wasn't his place to talk strategy so he moved past the comment. "I do need to take your blood pressure, but I wanted to see you too."

"Oh?" Megan studied her knees as she pushed her glasses up her nose.

"Yeah. Are you okay after that swim?"

"The swim? That was no big deal." Megan waved her hand.

"It looked like you were struggling. Was there something physical going on?" he asked.

"I had a cramp. Plus, I'm not a strong swimmer in the first place. Nothing more."

Cane lowered his head to catch her eyes. "Promise me you'll tell me if anything *does* come up. That's why I'm here, you know."

Megan made eye contact and held his stare. "I know."

Cane took her blood pressure, which was slightly elevated but not in an alarming way. He made a note in her chart and then placed the stethoscope in his ears to listen to her heart. As he scooted closer, his thumb and forefinger made their way under her chin and raised her gaze to meet his again.

"Megan." He was hoping to speak with her about the events that had occurred between them. "I want you to know I meant what I said at the beginning of this game. I'm here for you and I want to be your friend."

Megan shifted in her seat and stared at his nose, her face emotionless. "Friends, yeah."

Cane didn't understand her lackluster reaction to him. He thought she'd come a long way in her level of comfort around him, but now she didn't seem able to look him in the eye for very long. Was she embarrassed about the swimming incident? Or worse yet, did she regret the kiss?

"I just want to make sure you know that. Whether you're here tomorrow or not." Cane winced as soon as the words were out of his mouth. He didn't mean to bring up the very real possibility that she could go home that night. The game was no business of his. He was there for health reasons only. "Sorry." He removed his hand from her chin and listened to her heart and lungs.

"All good?" she asked.

"Everything sounds great." Cane looked down at her chart to mark the rates and when he looked up, she was gone.

Embarrassed to the hilt, Megan couldn't get out of the medic tent fast enough. She and Cane had reached a good point in their friendship—if "friend" included someone you kissed. But as soon as she had gotten back to the lean-to and had a minute to process her near-drowning, she had burned with embarrassment. He'd had to save her like a drowning toddler, and only because she hadn't heard Wendy announce that Carson had won. Maybe it would be a blessing if she got voted out. She wanted nothing more than to maintain the comfort she felt with Cane, but that didn't seem to be in the cards. After dragging her out of the water and emphasizing that they were just "friends" during her check-up, she was back to square one. He was the handsome medic, she the chaotic shut-in.

Megan pushed Cane from her mind and thoughts of her sister took over. Molly would be proud of what Megan had accomplished in the game and while Megan would bask in that praise, going home now was too soon. Megan had to admit that her sister's desire drove her at first, but the determination was catching—the swimming contest was testament of that. Underneath her embarrassment of Cane having to save her, she was proud of how she'd pushed herself to nearly finish a challenge that a week ago would've seemed impossible. She wanted to prove to herself and the others from her past that she could stick it out. Megan would fight to her dying breath to stay in the game as long as possible.

When she got back to the lean-to, Grace was walking toward their shelter from the woods.

"Oh Megan, good. We need to talk." She pulled Megan into the lean-to. "I just came from a walk in the woods." She paused and then said in a rush, "Okay, so I was on a reconnaissance mission."

"What did you find out?" Megan asked, smiling.

"I followed Juan and Nathan, who said they were going for firewood. Do you know how many times they've gone for firewood today and come back with hardly anything?"

Megan hadn't noticed.

"Anyway, I followed them and they haven't been collecting firewood at all. They're looking for the Protection Piece."

"The Protection Piece," Megan murmured. She'd forgotten all about that.

"Yeah, and if they find it, one of them will be in the final four whether they get eliminated before then or not."

Megan nodded. She remembered the tool now and wished

she'd thought to look for it herself. She'd been too distracted by other elements of the game . . . and men outside of the game.

"Do you think they found it?" Megan was worried what that would mean for the lean-to crew.

"No, I know they haven't."

"How can you be sure?"

"I read lips. They were talking about it on their way back." Grace glanced over her shoulder to make sure no one was encroaching on their privacy.

Megan let the silence settle around them as she squinted through the logs that made up their wall. She spotted Carson across the beach, his arm around Kat. She drew back in surprise

"What's Carson doing?"

Grace peered through the wall, then turned back to Megan with a wave of her hand. "Oh yeah, that. He's trying to get in with the beach group. It's obvious Kat wants him so I told him to let her fawn. Who knows what she might say. He's safe, so it can't hurt."

"Doesn't it bother you?" Megan thought about watching another woman hang on Cane and her stomach turned over.

"Why should it?"

Megan blinked. *Oops.* She sighed. Hopefully Carson's feelings weren't a secret. He'd asked Megan to put in a good word with Grace and now was her chance. "Well, because he's crazy about you, that's why."

Grace shrugged. It didn't look like news to her. "There will be time for that after the game."

Megan tilted her head. Grace never ceased to amaze her. She served the country, was in top physical form, and was even able to keep her mind in the game despite the gorgeous PE teacher who had feelings for her. Megan wished she could shove her own crush aside until after the game. And now that she'd been labeled a "friend," perhaps she could.

Megan narrowed her focus and shut everything out—Cane,

the bay, even the sand beneath her feet. She took a deep breath and when she opened her eyes, she had an idea.

"Okay, here's what we do."

Grace listened with rapt attention and immediately agreed that Megan's idea was worth a try. She clambered out of the lean-to so she could put the plan in action. Megan needed to stay in the background this time and, with any luck, let things fall into place.

She watched as Grace put a bug in Andrew's ear. She worried he might turn Grace away, but the lines around his mouth and in the corners of his eyes softened and Megan had hope that he might just come around. She'd leave it to Grace to work magic where Andrew was concerned.

When Grace was done talking to Andrew, she waded out into the bay and grabbed a fish. That would give Grace the opportunity to lure Carson away from Kat and into the woods to clean the fish as Megan suggested. She'd let him in on the plan there. Leo was asleep on a log out on the beach. By the time he got up, they could tell him what needed to be done. He'd go along with it. He'd be like Megan, happy with anything that didn't include votes against him.

Megan smiled. It was a long shot, but it felt good to have a plan. And it all hinged on one thing that she felt pretty confident in . . . Andrew's ego.

Chapter Twenty-One

The elimination ceremony came all too soon. Megan's hands shook. She was nervous about the way things would go down, but she was also excited. If her plan worked, it would be quite an accomplishment. Best of all, she hadn't needed to lie to put it in place.

"Welcome, Leftovers!" Wendy Weathersby's chirpy voice called from her board in the center of the circle.

"She looks well-rested," Megan muttered to Grace. Grace nudged her with an elbow, stifling a laugh.

"You've made it through several days on the beach and it shows." Wendy grinned.

Thanks, Wendy.

"There was no reward to go along with today's competition, but we do have a surprise for the winners tonight. Grace, Carson, at the end of the elimination, you will share this clue." Wendy held an envelope straight up in the air. "The clue gives you an advantage in looking for the Protection Piece. Sound good?" Carson and Grace nodded.

"Now, as for the rest of you . . . I have nothing to give, but let's chat before we say good-bye to one of you, okay?"

Do we have a choice? Megan glanced at the cameras surrounding the fire pit. Cane stood off to one side, next to the producer, Mike. She averted her eyes as soon as she saw him. He'd given her strength on several occasions, but tonight she needed to get by on her own. She hoped she'd get over her embarrassment where he was concerned, but until then, she'd have to use what little courage she had and stand on her own two feet in the game. No Cane-focal-point crutch needed.

"Leo, did you enjoy today's challenge?" Wendy asked.

"I wouldn't say I enjoyed it, but it didn't hurt me any. Nothing a nice nap on the beach couldn't fix, at least." Leo chuckled.

"Grace, you seemed to thrive in the water. Did you know you would do well going into the competition?"

"I always hope I'll do well, Wendy," Grace answered. "I can't ever guess how I'll do against the others. There are a lot of fierce competitors here. Who knows if I'd be safe tonight if I had gone up against Carson? Andrew held his own too."

Megan squeezed Grace's elbow in solidarity. Grace's comments were part of the plan and so far, things were going well.

"And how did it feel to need assistance back to the beach, Megan?"

Megan glanced around the boulders. Andrew snickered while Juan and Nathan bumped fists. Megan was especially frustrated with Kat's eye roll since she hadn't even participated in the competition to begin with. She slapped her hands on her knees, took a deep breath, and bolstered her courage. "I'm glad you asked, Wendy." Megan's voice rang through the night air with a hint of sarcasm. "I've never been a big swimmer, but I think it's safe to say I gave it my best and didn't give up."

Wendy tilted her head. "Very admirable. And how's life on the beach, Kat?"

Megan leaned over to inspect Kat's face as she answered. Kat deftly laced her arm through the crook in Carson's and tapped her manicured fingers on his bicep. One of her nails was broken, but otherwise everything looked to be in place.

"Swimmingly, Wendy. Just swimmingly." Kat smiled at Carson

with adoration. His eyes swiveled to Grace with an expression that said something more like *help*.

"Well, I'm glad to hear everyone is getting along so well. Let's see what happens when you have to vote out one of your own. As soon as the votes are read, whoever has the most will hit the parking lot and head home. Megan, are you ready to go first?"

Megan took a deep breath. "Ready as I'll ever be." She stood to cast her vote. Once she was standing at the box, she tapped the pen on the tabletop. She knew what she had to do, but she wanted an extra minute to run through the options. If it didn't work, she could go home. Too late now. She had to play the cards she dealt earlier in the day. She wrote the name on the paper, revealed it to the camera, then folded it, and returned to her seat.

One by one, the others cast their votes. She couldn't be sure, but Megan thought Andrew had a cocky grin on his face when he returned to his seat. That was a good sign, but he would probably look like that no matter whose name he wrote down.

"Okay, time to read the votes. Wendy Weathersby asks for silence as I show each name."

Megan made a face and then hoped the camera hadn't caught her disgust. Wendy was a nice woman, but her dramatic flair and attachment to her own name was getting old.

"First vote goes to . . . Nathan."

Megan heard rustling across the fire as Nathan adjusted himself in discomfort. The light of the fire glinted off his belt buckle.

"Second vote . . . Juan."

Juan and Nathan exchanged a worried look, and Juan pulled his Cardinals cap up and down on his forehead in nervousness.

The votes included two for Leo and then went back and forth between Nathan and Juan until Nathan was up one vote and there was one vote remaining.

"The last vote is for . . . Juan. We have a tie." Wendy slammed the box shut. The glimmer in her eye told Megan this was big.

"*The Leftover* rules state in the event of a tie, both participants would be asked to leave immediately. I'm sorry Nathan, Juan—you'll both go home tonight."

Nathan and Juan sat on their rocks with their jaws practically in the sand. Neither had any idea what had happened or what to say. Megan certainly wasn't going to fill in the blanks, but things had worked perfectly. When Grace planted a bug in Andrew's ear that Nathan and Juan were looking for the Protection Piece, he automatically felt betrayed and wanted them gone. Then, it was just a matter of finding out which man the beach crew was voting for and the lean-to crew voted for the other. Carson had to pull ranks with Kat for details, but that had been simple enough.

"Good riddance to you both, traitors." Andrew spoke loudly enough for the entire group to hear. Nathan frowned and Juan scratched his head.

"You need to leave now." Wendy stated firmly.

The two men got up from their rocks and slowly walked back to their shelter. Megan imagined them gathering their items and stuffing them back into their bags. It would be interesting to see their reaction when they saw the show on TV next month and realized her crew had orchestrated their demise. But in reality, they'd done it to themselves when they'd aligned with the egomaniacal Andrew in the first place.

"That was interesting," Wendy mused. "I didn't see that coming." She smiled with satisfaction at the turn of tide. "Anyway, Grace, Carson, come get your clue. The rest of you can return to the beach."

Megan stood and hugged Grace, Carson, and then Leo. Their little crew was still intact. She couldn't believe her plan had unfolded just as she'd hoped. She gleefully leaped over the rock she'd occupied—and her toe caught, throwing her hard onto her hands and knees. She grimaced. She'd made a dumb move in the dark and now paid the consequence.

Pain lanced through her foot, and she winced.

"Holy mackerel, that hurts." Before she could utter another word, Cane was at her side. She looked up at him from the ground, his worried eyes searching her body.

"What is it? What's hurt?" he asked.

Megan's cheeks warmed. She looked like a fool in front of him again. But the concern on his face was genuine. Sure, it was his job to care for the contestants, but he looked truly worried about her. "I'm not sure. My foot." Her toes were still wedged between the rocks. Pain radiated up her leg.

"I need to get you under some light." He pulled out his bag and snagged a long needle from a case.

"What's that?" Megan asked warily.

"You won't feel much. I'm going to give you a shot in the ankle to numb the area and we're going to get you out of there. I'll be able to assess the damage better in the medic tent with more light."

Megan nodded and looked away as Cane administered the shot. Her body relaxed and her foot went numb.

"Oh, that's nice."

Cane smiled to give her a show of confidence, but he didn't like seeing her in pain and he was concerned about what the injury would do to her chances in the game. "I'm going to slide your foot up and away from the rock. If you feel any pain, just yell."

"Oh I will, don't worry." Megan's eyes took on a faraway look.

Cane knew her pain had vanished, and she might feel a bit strange if she wasn't used to this type of medication. He eased her foot out of the rocks, needing to tug for a moment, but she didn't complain. "Okay, you're free and clear." She nodded happily, gazing up at him. He looked around and saw the contestants gathered around. "I need a camera to light our path back to my tent. Then I want everyone to back off until I get a handle on this. If I need help, I'll let you know."

Before Megan could agree to anything, Cane swept her up into his arms. She wrapped her hands around his neck and pressed her forehead against his cheek.

"Oh!" she proclaimed as he began to walk. "This is nice." She smiled and brushed her cheek against his rough, unshaven chin. "Does your facial hair get curly like the hair on your head? Or has it never been long enough to know?" Megan giggled.

Cane raised his eyebrows. The medication was having a strange effect on her. The expression on her face made her look like a whole different person. "Let's just get you fixed up, okay?" He wasn't sure how to handle her forward remarks, especially with the camera crew lighting their path.

"Yes, sir, Mr. Medic, sir." Megan saluted him in a slow, sloppy manner and then placed her hand around his neck again as he hoisted her into a better position.

"Let's move." He followed the camera, which lit the path so he could avoid the same fate that had befallen Megan. He carried her quickly across the beach and into the medic tent. He set her gingerly on the cot and thanked the camera operator who accompanied them.

"I have all the light I need in here—you can go now. It's just an injured toe. You've already got plenty of the accident documented." He turned on several exam lights and pointed them in her direction.

The camera operator nodded and left the tent.

"I didn't do it, I swear." Megan snorted. "Please, don't let them arrest me, officer."

Cane's eyes widened as he raised her foot and removed her sandal. She was almost acting drunk with her bad humor and uncontrollable actions.

"You have really pretty eyes, you know that?" Megan leaned forward and brushed a curl from his forehead. "And your hair, I've always wanted to touch it." She ran her fingers through his hair just above his ears. "Ooh, it's just as soft as I imagined."

Cane swallowed and paused what he was doing. It would be so easy to pull the hair tie from the back of her hair and run his hand through the messy waves, but there was no way he could take advantage of a patient in this state. He felt like Megan had taken a big step away from him earlier that day, and now she was acting the complete opposite. He took her hand from his head and bent over her foot. "I think most of the bones in your foot are okay." He pressed down on a few ligaments and ran his hand down the center.

Megan burst into a fit of giggles as she jerked her foot. "That tickles!" she cried.

"Sorry. If you had been wearing shoes instead of sandals, you might have escaped injury." He was doing his best to remain professional despite the circumstances.

"Are you scolding me, doctor?" Megan asked in a coy voice.

Cane couldn't humor her, as much as he wanted to. Playing into her change of attitude would only make it worse. He didn't want to cause her any further embarrassment if he could help it. "As it is, I think your pinky toe is broken. There's not much to be done for that. I'll tape it to the next one and let it heal. You'll have a limp, but there's no reason you can't stay and finish the game."

He was relieved that her injury wasn't so bad she needed a hospital or to be pulled from the game. He needed to figure out why she had distanced herself, and it would be a lot harder if she wasn't in the game. Besides, he really enjoyed their nightly conversations. Not to mention she'd made the game very interesting. The plans she'd come up with and orchestrated within her small alliance were impressive and he couldn't wait to see what happened next. There was a smart, deep individual beneath the shy exterior. However, shy was the last way he would describe her at that moment.

"Does that mean you aren't going to take me away from it all?" Megan grinned in a sly manner.

Cane was the one avoiding eye contact now. He was afraid of even harmless flirtations with a woman under the influence. In all his years as a medic, he'd only seen the painkiller work like this on one other person. And that had been an old man in his eighties who refused to take anything stronger than aspirin on rare occasions.

"Actually, I do think you should stay in here tonight. I'm not sure you would want the cameras seeing you this way." Cane placed a hand on her shoulder and examined her injured toe again.

"I don't want anyone seeing me but you, handsome medic."

Cane blushed and looked up at Megan in surprise. She batted her eyes and he chuckled. He couldn't help it. This was so out of character for Megan he couldn't believe it. At the same time, he was flattered. If her truthful side was on display, she thought he was handsome. It was the second time she'd said as much in the short time they'd known each other.

He let the statement hang in the air and gripped her toe, holding it against the next one.

"Ow!"

"Sorry. I know it's tender." He fumbled around on the supply shelf nearby with his free hand and located the tape. He secured her toe and elevated her ankle on his pillow.

"Lie back. I'm going to have a word with Mike. I'll be back in a moment."

Cane watched as Megan did as she was ordered before he ducked out of the tent. Mike and some of the camera crew were waiting outside.

"What's the news?" Mike asked as he tapped his clipboard against his side.

"Megan's going to be fine," Cane replied. "Her pinky toe is broken, but I've secured it and she'll heal in time. I think she should stay in the medic tent tonight. The medication I gave her seems to have made her a little . . . woozy. If it isn't cheating, she's better off here."

Mike nodded. "Fine, but she sleeps on the ground, not the cot."

"Deal." Cane waved as Mike and the crew scurried off down the beach to check in on the others.

Cane slipped back into his tent and closed the tent flap behind him. Megan awaited with big eyes and an even bigger grin. "Mike said you can stay here tonight because of your injury. It won't be cheating if you sleep on the ground and not in the cot."

Megan gave the sand a despairing look.

"The sand'll actually be better because you can put your foot up on the cot and get better elevation." Cane held his hand out to her and helped her settle on the sand. "Okay?"

"Okay." Megan looked sleepy and Cane half-expected her to drift off immediately. Instead, she spoke again in a slurred voice. "I've always wanted to be more like my sister."

"Molly? Why's that?" Cane crossed his legs in front of him and leaned back on one elbow. He hadn't been out of the tent long, but apparently her focus had changed from him to her sister.

Megan propped herself up on her elbows in the sand. "She always knows what to do and what to say. She can make any situation feel normal and comfortable. I don't know how she does it. It's like everyone she meets is her best friend."

Cane thought that was a fair assessment of Molly. She seemed very comfortable in her own skin and with everyone around her. "I didn't get a chance to know Molly well, but I think you have a lot in common."

"You do?" Megan sat up straighter. Her eyes sparkled in the bright lights he'd turned on to examine her foot. For once, her glasses were doing nothing to disguise their depth.

Cane nodded. If she was going to new levels of honesty, so would he. "You're both striking, but in completely different ways. Molly seems to know what she wants and she goes for it. You have more of a quiet confidence that takes some time to come out. But when it does, your beauty really shines."

"You . . . you think I'm beautiful?" Megan adjusted the glasses on her face.

"Of course I do. I'd be crazy not to." Cane ran a hand through his hair. She was far enough away that he could see every inch of her. Her body language told him she was astounded by the compliment as if she'd never heard one before in her life.

Megan parted her lips but remained silent. Cane noticed it was taking her longer to open her eyes between blinks. She scooted down into the sand and gave into the heaviness of sleep. As he watched her drift away, he settled himself onto the cot to rest. He turned off the exam lights and waited for his eyes to adjust to the darkness. When he couldn't make out her features, he sat up and dropped down onto the sand next to her, laying on his side with his head propped up on his hand. He removed her glasses and laid them next to her.

Cane allowed himself a few moments to study her face. It was hard to tear himself away from the deep sense of peace that rested across her features. But eventually, he laid his head on his arm and succumbed to his own need for sleep.

Chapter Twenty-Two

Megan's eyelids were heavy, but she managed to open them after a brief struggle. She felt like she had sand ingrained into her skin, but she was warm. She smiled as she ran her hand over the arm that was slung over her midsection. As she realized the arm was real and not a dream, she pushed it away and sat straight up.

Cane rubbed his eyes and looked nearly as disoriented as Megan felt. "How's the toe?" he asked.

Megan glanced down at her foot. "Still there." It was throbbing, now that he mentioned it. "Where are my glasses?"

"Right next to you." Cane pointed to a spot on the sand on her other side.

Megan grabbed her glasses and slid them onto her nose. Flashes of the previous evening flooded back to her as the tousled curls on Cane's head came into focus. "Um, did I say anything . . . " she began.

Cane waved his hand, still groggy. "Don't worry about it. Everyone reacts to medication differently."

So she *had* said something. *But what?*

"I didn't mean to invade your space." Cane rose to his feet and stretched.

You can invade my space any time. Megan turned crimson at the thought. She covered her mouth with both hands as the bold notion brought back memories from the previous night. "I totally hit on you."

Cane grimaced. "I wouldn't call it that . . . exactly."

"What would you call it?" Megan tried to stand and pain shot through her foot. The toe was very tender. It looked like she would be walking on her heel for a while.

He shrugged. "You called me handsome and asked me to take you away from it all."

Megan slapped her forehead and covered her eyes. She wanted to limp from the tent immediately and hide in the woods, but Cane's hands wrapped around her wrists and pulled her fingers from her face.

"Do you think you would have woken up the way you did had I minded?" he asked softly.

Megan stared at the sand and visualized his arm around her waist the way it had been when she'd awakened. Had they slept like that all night? His fingers cupped her chin and she raised her eyes.

"Megan, I've enjoyed getting to know you. I think we both know there's more to our story than friendship."

We do? Megan's heart skipped a beat. Her bold statements the night before hadn't turned him away. Nor had her lack of confidence in social situations. Or even her messy appearance and less than stellar physique.

Cane leaned forward and Megan panicked. Was he going to kiss her? She could taste her own breath, and it was less than minty. She allowed herself to enjoy his hand on her face for another second before she snaked her fingers between them to cover her mouth. His lips were inches away.

"Sorry," she muttered through her hand. "I haven't seen a toothbrush since I won that reward."

Cane's eyes gleamed with amusement—and a hint of disappointment—as he backed away. "You're right. There's time for that later. You don't need me distracting you from the game. Let's take a look at your toe and you can get back out there. Concentrate on being *The Leftover* for now and we'll figure this out later."

Megan sat on his cot as directed, thoughts in a whirlwind. *Time for that later? We'll figure this out? What exactly was he referring to?* His gentle examination of her toe brought her back to the moment. It felt so nice to have him close, even if he was just handling her foot.

"Your toe has good support from the next one over. It'll sting to walk, but as long as you don't injure it again, the area should heal properly. You'll need to be careful in competitions. And please, come to me if you have any shooting pain, okay?"

Megan took Cane's hand and allowed him to help her stand. "What, so you can give me another shot and let me make a fool of myself again?"

Cane pulled her closer. "You're no fool. I really am very handsome."

Megan giggled, then outright laughed.

"You said so yourself!" he protested.

She pushed his chest playfully. "And I'm never going to live it down, am I?"

"Not if I have anything to say about it." He pulled her into his embrace and toyed with the hair falling from her ponytail.

Megan took a deep breath and inhaled his scent. He had access to the staff showers, but he didn't smell soapy. He smelled like wind and woods and she never wanted to forget the moment. She'd never had a real boyfriend and never dreamed she would come across a man like Cane who would actually be interested in her. He had given her a first kiss that she'd remember for the rest of her life. She feared their flirtation would end in heartbreak, but she could enjoy the sweet sensation in the present and worry about the rest later. It was about time she got a little male attention!

Cane stepped back and held her at arms' length. "Now get out there and show them how it's done."

"Like in the swimming contest?" Megan made a face.

"How about like the log contest?"

"I didn't win that one either."

"No, but you were close and I was with you the whole way."

Megan looked into his eyes and held his gaze. It was hard for her to allow him to search her features this close, but he gave her something she'd never had before—an element of self-confidence.

"You were," she agreed. "You really were."

Megan promised to check in with him later to make sure her toe wasn't giving her any problems. As she exited the tent, she saw a telltale suit jacket disappear into the woods. "Andrew," she whispered. Either he'd been spying or he needed medical attention and didn't want Megan to know. She smiled. Either way, it was a glorious day on the beach. The sun was shining, the water was blue, and Cane was interested in her.

❧❧❧❧

Cane wasn't sure what had come over him. He felt like a schoolboy with a crush. He couldn't wipe the grin from his face or erase the thoughts of Megan from his mind. She was completely different from any other girl he knew. She was beautiful, especially when she allowed herself to smile—or better yet, laugh. He loved the way she scrunched up her nose when she was uncomfortable and the cute little freckle just under her right eye. Her glasses would look out of style on anyone else's face, but somehow suited her perfectly.

Cane ran his hand through his hair. He was a mess, inside and out. He hadn't felt like this since . . . since Eva.

He took a deep breath and sank onto his cot. What was he doing? He was letting himself fall for someone at lightning speed again. He had fallen in love with Eva in a matter of weeks—and on TV, no less. And then, just like that, she'd chosen another man over him and dropped out of his life.

Cane rubbed his forehead. Was he setting himself up to get hurt again? This wasn't a dating show, but things with Megan were still happening fast and circumstances were throwing them together. What would things be like between them in the real world? Would she climb back into her shyness, never to let him in again? Once she was off the set, she might drop him faster than Eva had.

Cane didn't want to involve his heart any further than he already had. He wasn't sure his heart could mend itself if it was broken a second time. He was right when he told Megan there would be time for a relationship later. Now, he needed to back off. Megan was a contestant on the show and he was the medic. It wasn't professional.

Megan was having trouble letting anything get to her. The group had let the fire burn out overnight—apparently Andrew had forgotten to assign anyone to the duty—and they were struggling to get a new one started. Andrew was barking orders at everyone. "Danae, get water! Leo, get more wood! Carson, work on the fire!"

Megan wondered what Andrew himself was actually doing to help. Perhaps he thought his role was to simply tell everyone else what to do. She spotted Grace out in the water, fishing. They were all hungry and thirsty and the whole contest was getting old, but Megan grinned through it all. Nothing and no one could touch her happiness with a ten-foot pole.

When the day's competition rolled around, Megan was still on cloud nine. She even found it charming when Wendy Weathersby repeatedly said her own name.

"Today's competition is going to be a challenge for each of you." Wendy pointed to the wooden boards sitting at seventy-five degree angles all around the beach. "You will have to climb each wall and slide down the other side. This is a group event. Since there are eight of you left, there will be two teams of four. Every person on the team has to make it over all of the walls to complete the competition. The first group to get everyone over wins the reward. The reward today is juicy, let Wendy Weathersby tell you. It will satisfy a different taste bud than the fish."

Megan's mouth watered as several stomachs nearby growled. Food. The reward was food. The fish kept them going, but anything different would be heaven. Even if it was pizza, something she normally avoided.

"The twist to today's game is that the winning team will also receive protection, but only one person can have it. The team will have to decide unanimously who gets protection from this evening's elimination. If the decision cannot be unanimous, the entire losing team will be protected from elimination. Understand?"

Megan nodded along with the others. It was a unique twist. She was anxious to get started—she felt ready for anything. Her stomach joined in with the symphony of other stomachs growling around her. She wanted that reward.

"I'll draw for teams." Wendy reached into the bucket she carried and pulled out a slip of paper. "Grace," she read. She pulled another piece. "Kat." Megan's heart sank. If she was going to be with Grace, she'd have to deal with Kat too. "Andrew." *Ugh*. As much as Megan wanted to be with Grace, she detested the idea of sitting on Andrew's team. "And the final person on this team is . . . " Wendy drew another slip. "Megan."

Grace gave her a big smile and a hug while Andrew and Kat walked over to them. Wendy continued her monologue. "Leo, Carson, Danae, and Tank, that leaves you for the other team." Megan sized up the competition. Carson was physically fit and he would easily be able to scale the walls. She wasn't sure how they would get Tank over, but perhaps his muscles would end up being an advantage. And Danae had proved to be more fit than Megan had first thought. Time would tell.

"I'll give you two minutes to strategize before we begin." Wendy brushed the sand from her hands after she set the bucket of names aside.

Megan huddled with her group and assessed the walls behind them. Each group had its own walls to climb. They started out small but grew in size as they moved down the beach. She was fairly certain she couldn't scale even the shortest on her own, much less the tallest—especially with her wounded toe. It throbbed dully.

"What do you guys think is the best approach?" Grace asked.

"Can't we just all climb the walls and get to the end? I'm hungry." Andrew straightened his tie. It was bloodstained and dirty—almost an improvement.

"This is a team event," Megan reminded him. "I think we're supposed to work together."

"If we're all over the wall, who cares how we do it?"

Megan narrowed her eyes.

"Oh, I get it. You don't think you can get over." Andrew stroked his chin. "It's okay to admit your weaknesses."

Megan scowled.

"Teams, time is up," Wendy called. "Take your positions."

What a waste. They'd made no decisions and formed no strategies. Megan took position at the starting line, pausing to search the crew for Cane. She spotted him behind the cameras by the second pair of walls and smiled. Who cared about Andrew? She had Cane on her side. Their connection could make her scale any wall in record time even with two toes taped together. Or so she hoped.

She bent her knees, crooked her arm and set a determined expression on her face. She was ready.

"And, go!" Wendy shouted.

The sand kicked up around the two groups as they scurried to the first set of walls. Megan reached the wall last and watched as Grace catapulted herself over like it was a vault. Andrew took a split second longer but used the same move. Kat grabbed the top of the wall and climbed with her legs until she disappeared behind it as well. The wall was only shoulder-high. Megan shouldn't have a problem.

"Come on, Megan!" Grace encouraged from the other side.

Megan threw herself at the wall and grabbed the top. She wasn't able to clear it like Grace and Andrew, but she could climb like Kat. Or so she thought. Her toe had other ideas and pain shot through her foot. She'd worried the injury would slow her down, but she hadn't dreamed the agony one little toe could cause. She cried out but kept climbing and landed on the other side moments later.

"Let's go!" Andrew ordered as the group scurried to the second, slightly higher wall. He was up and over the wall before the rest of the team approached. Kat attempted the wall next.

"I can't get a grip," she complained. The wall was too tall for her to reach the top.

"Dig your nails in," Megan suggested. Kat's claws ought to be good for something.

"Are you kidding? They'll break off!"

Megan scrunched her face. "I'll go." She backed up a few steps and took a deep breath. She ran at the wall and threw herself at its mercy. *Thud.* The wall unapologetically sent her soundly back to the sand.

"That worked well," she muttered as she rubbed her shoulder.

"Hurry up, guys, they're gaining on us!" Andrew shouted from the other side.

"I'll climb to the top and balance myself there," Grace suggested. "Do you think you can make it up far enough to grab my hand?" She looked from Megan to Kat.

"Let's try." Megan was encouraged by the idea. She watched as Grace flew up the side of the wall as if she was running on flat ground. Once she had found her balance on top, she reached down as far as her arm would go.

"Go ahead." Megan motioned for Kat to give it a try. She needed a break after flattening herself against the wall once already.

Kat nodded, clicked her nails together with a sigh and took a run at the wall. She caught Grace's hand and Megan watched in awe as Grace pulled Kat up and over the wall effortlessly. Megan took a second to take stock of the other team. Leo was having issues, but it looked like Carson was about to get him over the wall. She needed to hurry if they had any hope of winning the reward.

Megan caught a mass of dark curls bobbing behind the cameras. Cane was there. She would do this. He believed in her, and that opened a well of confidence Megan hadn't known she had.

She backed up and ran at the wall. Her toe complained as she hit the board with all her weight, but she strained upward, trying to be as vertically inclined as possible. The tips of her fingers caught Grace's wrist and she grabbed hold of her hand.

"Yes!" Megan shouted as Grace aided her up the wall. She slid down the other side and Grace followed. They jogged as a group to the third and final wall.

"Let's do this one together from the start," Grace suggested as Andrew took a run at the wall.

He stopped halfway up and glanced at the others. *Did he have suction cups on his hands and shoes?* Megan had to give him begrudging respect.

It quickly vanished as he said condescendingly, "Need help, ladies?"

"Go ahead." Grace shooed him away. "We'll be fine."

He shrugged and threw his tie over his shoulder before scaling the rest of the wall and disappearing down the other side.

"Here's what we'll do," Grace said. "Megan, do you think you can help Kat over from the top?"

Megan nodded. She'd certainly try.

"Let's build a pyramid to get you to the top, Megan. Then you can help Kat over like I helped you and I'll climb up last. Ready?"

"Let's do it." Megan didn't know if the plan would work, but it was better than throwing herself at the wall alone and ending up like a bird hitting a window.

Grace knelt in the sand and asked Kat to stand on her shoulders. Kat did as she was told, but didn't look certain about the idea as Grace stood and walked closer to the wall.

"Lean against the wall, Kat. Okay, Megan, climb!"

Megan studied the tower of women against the wall. She hadn't thought this part through. Now she had to climb up and over Grace as well as Kat to get to the top of the slanted board. She was afraid that Grace would be crushed beneath their weight.

"Are you sure this is going to be okay?" she asked.

"Positive. Do it, Megan. Do it!" Grace encouraged.

Megan took a step closer to her friend and surveyed her options. She planted her good foot on Grace's thigh and used it as a ladder. Then she grabbed Kat's leg and hoisted herself onto Grace's shoulders. She glanced down at her friend to make sure she was still holding up.

"Good going, Megan. Keep it up," Grace called. Megan didn't seem to be hurting her, despite her miniscule size.

Megan's eyes moved up Kat's body as she searched for a way to advance up the wall. She wrapped her arms around Kat's waist and her legs around her feet.

"What are you doing?" Kat screamed.

Megan blinked. Kat was right. This wasn't working. She was stuck. Megan inched upward. She could climb Kat this way, but it wasn't going to be pleasant for either of them.

"So sorry." Megan moved her arms around Kat's chest. Kat's

arms were straight above her head and flat against the wall, trying to keep the wobbly pyramid upright. "Sorry again," Megan murmured as she turned her head away from Kat's armpit. The inching was slow, but it was working. Soon, she was level with Kat's disgusted gaze.

"Hurry up," the other woman insisted. "I don't enjoy being climbed like a tree . . . by someone as big as a tree."

Megan wondered why Grace chose her to be first. It didn't matter now—she was almost there. She used Kat's shoulder to help her swing one leg over the top of the wall, and she tried not to pay attention to the way Kat grunted when she pushed off.

"I'm up," Megan announced. "Kat, give me your hand."

Kat placed her hand in Megan's and squeezed as she started to climb off Grace's shoulders and up the wall. Her nails bit into the back of Megan's hand. Megan winced. She might need stitches later, but it would be worth it to eat.

Balancing on top of the wall was harder than Grace had made it look and Megan had to reposition herself several times to stay upright. When Kat surged a final time to reach the top, it was too late for Megan to regain her balance. She followed her leg over the side of the wall and fell to the sand below, taking Kat along with her.

Megan landed with a thud and watched in horror as Kat splayed on top of her. The breath rushed from Megan's lungs as her ribs met the organs beneath them. Megan tried to breathe, but found she could only take small, short breaths of air. She gave Kat a shove. The sooner the woman was off her, the better. They'd been far too close for far too long.

"My nails!" Kat cried as she rolled off Megan and held a hand out in front of her. "Look what you've done to my nails!"

Megan glanced at Kat's hand. All but one of the nails were broken off, but she was still finding it hard to breathe and she wondered what Kat had done to her insides. She sat up and tried to catch her breath as Grace launched over the wall and skidded down the other side.

"We're over!" Andrew called. "We're over and they're not!"

Megan inspected the other group. It was true. Only two of them had made it over the last wall so far. She tried to take a deep breath and failed again.

"Andrew, Kat, Grace, and Megan win the reward!" Wendy screeched into her megaphone.

"Medic!" Grace called. "Over here!" She knelt next to Megan. "Megan, are you okay?"

Megan wanted to answer, but she still couldn't breathe right. Cane appeared at her side and placed his hand on her back.

"Take deep breaths if you can, Megan. As deep and slow as you can," he instructed.

Megan's breaths came in short bursts, but she tried to do as he said. He pushed her back into the sand and felt her rib cage.

"Nothing seems to be broken. You probably just got the wind knocked out of you." Cane's concerned face blocked out the sun. "I think your breathing is slowing down. Are you starting to feel better?"

Megan was able to take a slightly deeper breath. She couldn't speak, but she nodded. After a few more breaths, she turned to Kat. "Sorry . . . about your nails."

Cane chuckled. "I think Kat should be the one apologizing to you. Your hand is a mess." He took her hand into his and opened his medical bag. He cleaned the scrapes on the back of Megan's hand and covered them with a few Band-Aids. "There. All better. Enjoy your reward." Cane ran his thumb across the palm of her hand before he disappeared behind the pit of cameras nearby.

Megan watched him for a bit too long before she remembered the red blinking lights on the cameras all around her, taking in her every expression.

Grace offered her a hand and Megan stood, brushing the sand

from her backside. Her toe ached and the rest of her body didn't feel much better, but they'd won. She joined the celebratory circle and united with her group in a hug. She didn't even mind the rough fabric of Andrew's suit jacket against her bare arm.

"Reward begins immediately. Winners, follow me. The other group can return to the beach." Wendy removed her spiked heels and gingerly stepped from her board. She walked on tiptoes through the sand as the winning group followed.

Megan raised a hand to Leo and Carson. She wished she could trade them for Andrew and Kat. It still would have been hard to choose someone for protection, but at least it would have been someone in their group for sure.

Megan limped behind Wendy through the sand and into the woods. When she stopped, Megan gasped.

"Behold, the grill!" Wendy pressed her hand against its shiny silver cover and ran her fingers over its top like she was a model from *The Price is Right*. "You will have two hours to grill your own burgers and discuss who will receive protection from elimination tonight. After those two hours are up, we will hold a secret vote. If even one of the votes reads a different name than the others, no one from this group will be protected and everyone in the other group is safe. Does everyone understand?"

"Yes." Megan spoke in unison with the others.

"Okay, then. Without further delay, I give you . . . the burgers." Wendy waved her hand as a crewmember appeared with a platter of raw meat. Another staff member had a bag full of buns in one hand and various condiments in the other. "Enjoy. I'll return in two hours." Wendy tiptoed back through the sand.

Megan's stomach echoed several others in the line. "Well," she said, trying to control her watering mouth. "Who's good on the grill?"

Chapter Twenty-Three

Megan wanted to lick the grill, but she knew it would be way too hot. The burgers sizzled and she had to hold herself back from eating one half-cooked. She and Grace took turns on the grill and the group kept the conversation light. Once the burgers were cooked to perfection and Megan's held enough ketchup to satisfy the entire state, they sat on tree stumps.

"Mmm," Megan moaned as she took a bite.

"I second that." Grace opened her mouth wide and did some serious damage to her burger.

Andrew gingerly removed his dirty tie and stuffed it in his pocket.

"Don't you get hot?" Grace asked with her mouth full.

"Sometimes," Andrew admitted. "But I get past it."

"Why do you want to?" Megan asked.

"It pays to look good."

Megan and Grace exchanged a look. Andrew didn't look good in their book. His crumpled suit didn't fit in with the woods and the tie had never been pleasant on the eyes, even when it was clean.

"So, what are we going to do with the protection?" Kat asked, taking a small dainty bite. She chewed thoroughly before swallowing.

Megan stayed silent and let her eyes roam the group. No one looked comfortable with the change of topic except for Andrew.

"Maybe we should take a preliminary vote," Andrew said. He called out their names one by one, and each person stated who they wanted to receive protection. As it turned out, each of them received one vote—Grace and Megan voted for each other and Kat and Andrew voted for themselves.

"Looks like we have a little work to do." Andrew sighed.

"Let me just pose a question." Grace paused between bites. "Andrew, Kat, is there anything that would make you vote for someone other than yourself?"

Megan didn't like taking time away from her burger, but this discussion was important. Grace had asked a poignant question. If they were going to get any further in making a decision, the group needed to know.

Andrew took a bite of his burger and let Kat hem and haw as he used chewing as a stall tactic.

"Well," Kat finally answered. "I guess I wouldn't mind throwing protection to someone else as long as I felt safe myself."

"I think we all feel that way," Grace said. "Is there some kind of deal we can make with each other for this vote only?" She emphasized the last three words as she stared at Andrew.

"What if," Kat broke in, "we agreed not to vote for each other. If all four of us vote for someone else, none of us will go home no matter what the others do."

Megan nodded. She wasn't sure how they would agree on whom to vote out, but she liked the idea that she and Grace would be safe. Even if it meant working with Andrew.

"Anyone have a problem voting for Leo?" Andrew asked.

Megan cleared her throat and both she and Grace raised their hands.

"Leo is a gentleman, and I think we can all admit he's not a threat in challenges. Sure, he's older than the rest of us, but he's a joy to have in camp and when it comes to the end, any of us could probably beat him. I think it would be foolish to get rid of him now." Grace's argument made sense and Megan certainly agreed.

"Carson?" Andrew inspected Grace and Megan.

"No way!" Kat screeched beside him. "He and I are just getting to know one another. Things are getting good, if you know what I mean."

Megan's stomach grumbled at the comment . . . or perhaps from the sudden intake of beef. She didn't know what Kat meant. Carson was letting Kat hang on him and he would occasionally play along and flirt in return or put his arm around her, but that was about as far as their "relationship" went. He only seemed to be acting with Kat in order to please Grace.

"That only leaves Tank and Danae," Andrew stated.

Megan's pulse raced. Two people . . . from the *other* group! It would swing the numbers back to the lean-to crew's favor.

"It's a hard decision to make." Kat took another dainty bite of burger.

Megan wanted to grab it from her hands and show her how it was done. She was down to her last bite. She stuffed the rest of her second burger into her mouth and closed her eyes, trying to enjoy every sensation as she chewed. When she had no choice but to swallow, an idea dawned on her.

"Tank and Danae are both good competitors in their own way," she began. She noticed Andrew lean forward to listen. The advantage of being the quietest in the bunch was that when she spoke, people generally thought she might have something worthwhile to say. "You guys took out Juan and Nathan because you felt like they were trying too hard. What if we did something similar with Tank and Danae?"

Andrew tilted his head. She had his interest.

"Two of us will vote for Tank and the other two Danae. It's up to us to get our groups to conform to the decision. Tell Danae you're voting for Tank and have Tank vote for Danae. The numbers will add up and it'll be a tie again."

"And they'll both go home," Andrew finished with a Cheshire grin. Megan would have thought it was his idea based on his smug expression.

"Exactly. The more of them on the other side, the better, right? There can only be one in the end." Megan waited as Andrew processed her suggestion. It was obvious Kat didn't care who went home as long as it wasn't her or Carson.

"How do Kat and I know your group won't pick the two of us off next?" Andrew asked after a few beats.

Megan shifted on her tree stump. She didn't want to lie. She promised herself she'd play the game as close to the truth as possible. It wasn't what her sister advised, but it lined up with her personality and values. "You don't," she stated.

Grace's eyes widened as the smile slid from Andrew's face. Megan had Andrew on the line and she knew it. Her honest statement could lose him. But if she knew one thing about Andrew, it was that he lived by his ego. "But face it, you're the strongest in the bunch. Chances are you'll win the next protection. Plus, if I ever win, I have to hand it over to you, right?"

Andrew nodded slowly as a smile spread over his face again. "That's right, we still have our deal."

Megan didn't think Andrew realized how little their deal meant to her now. Cane knew about her crush. Her conversation with him post-shot last night had made sure of that. She'd throw the competitions if she had to, just so she wouldn't win protection. She couldn't hand it over to Andrew if she didn't have it!

"It's settled then." Andrew stood and stretched. "Tank and Danae will go home."

"So who are we giving protection to tonight?" Kat asked.

"I have an idea for that too." Megan licked the grease from her fingers, even though they were dirty. "All of us are safe, so when elimination time comes, it doesn't really matter. But I think we should give it to Grace as a symbol of gratitude. I know I never would have made it over two of those three walls without her. Kat, I think you can say the same thing."

Kat nodded reluctantly. "Yeah, I suppose so."

Andrew clapped his hands together. "Grace, is that okay with you?"

Grace shrugged. "I guess I won't turn away protection if you guys are sure that's what you want to do."

"It's settled," Andrew commanded as he stood.

Grace tilted her head toward the tree stump Andrew had occupied. Megan caught her eye and saw what she was looking at. His tie had slipped from his pocket and was lying on the ground between two stumps. Megan gave her a slight nod. They were on the same page. Even if they had to work with Andrew this time, it didn't mean his tie had to make it any further in the game.

"Wendy should be back soon." Andrew paced around the stumps. "I'm ready to get to camp and start working things for tonight."

Megan was glad to be away, but they would have some talking to do in order to get everything lined up for a double surprise elimination. She was overjoyed that Tank and Danae were on the other side of the fence. She wouldn't have to lie to either one of them, yet they would both go home because of her plan.

"Wendy Weathersby, at your service!" The weather girl popped up behind them, her shoes in her hand. The dune buggy was likely parked at the edge of the trees. Megan was surprised she hadn't heard it. "Who's ready to vote?"

The group looked from one to another and nodded. "We all are," Grace said.

"Let's do it!" Wendy's enthusiasm sparked a round of applause and cheers. The food had really done something for team morale. "Now remember, if you don't agree unanimously, the entire opposing team will be protected tonight. We'll vote by secret ballot. Who's first?"

"I'll go." Kat took the piece of paper and pen from Wendy and scribbled a name on it. She handed both items back to Wendy.

The rest of them took turns and Megan waited expectantly. Grace deserved protection more than anyone else on the beach. She could survive much worse conditions completely alone and probably thrive while doing it. Megan was glad to keep her safe that night.

"Wendy Weathersby will read the votes," she chirped. "The first vote goes to . . . Grace!" She waved the slip of paper in Grace's direction. "The second vote, also Grace. Third vote, Grace. I'm seeing a pattern here!" Her smile lit up the woods as excitement radiated from her eyes. "Last vote . . . " Wendy opened the piece of paper and frowned. "Andrew?"

Shock coursed through Megan's body. "What?" she said. "Everyone agreed a moment ago. What happened?"

"I'm sorry, but this means the four people on the beach are safe tonight. Everyone will vote to eliminate one of you. I'd suggest you get back to the beach." Wendy disappeared into the woods, leaving the four of them to figure out what went wrong.

Megan's eyes roamed the trees until they landed on Andrew. "Did you . . ."

"I'm surprised you believed I would vote for anyone else." Andrew shrugged.

"Me too," Megan murmured. So much for voting Tank and Danae out. They were both safe now.

"Walk with me, would you?" Andrew gestured toward the beach, inviting Megan to join him.

She glanced at Grace, who seemed unaffected by missing out on protection. "Go ahead," she said. "Kat and I will follow."

Megan slowly turned to catch up with Andrew, who had already started walking. She spied Grace stuffing his tie into her pocket. Andrew deserved every dirty trick they could pull, but it wasn't enough.

"Ah, Megan." He slung his arm around her shoulders. "You've been holding back on me."

Megan forced herself not to cringe away from him. "I . . . I have?"

"And here I thought we had an understanding."

Megan's mind moved from their agreement to Cane. Did Andrew know more about her and Cane than he should?

"I saw everything I needed to see," Andrew continued. "Did you really think you could hide it from me?"

Megan's heart raced. She didn't want to give anything away until she knew what he was talking about. It could be a trick. "I'm going to need a little more information," she said as she stepped out from under Andrew's arm, turning to face him.

"I hope you don't think I'm nosy, but while you were away in the medic tent and the rest of your group was fishing, I took the liberty of searching your bag."

"My . . . bag?" What would he want with her change of clothes and underwear? Sick!

"You neglected to tell me you found the Protection Piece." Andrew took a step toward her and threw a look over his shoulder to make sure no one was close enough to hear him. "I want it."

Megan frowned, slowly processing this new information. Protection Piece? The item that was supposedly hidden around the taping site somewhere, giving whoever found it a place in the final four? How had it gotten into Megan's bag? She'd never even looked for it.

"I'm not sure I know what you mean." Megan didn't want to shoot Andrew down just yet. She didn't have the Protection Piece, but that didn't mean she couldn't use the situation somehow.

"Oh come on, Megan. You know exactly what I'm talking about. Don't play coy with me. It's a little beaded thing on a chain. Looks like a troll or something."

Megan tried very hard to control the look on her face. "Oh," she said, trying to look disappointed. "You found that in my bag?"

Andrew nodded wisely. "I did and I want it. Or I'm going straight to Cane the minute we get back to the beach."

Megan studied him under the mottled sunlight filtering through the trees. For a moment, she wondered what had happened in his life to make him who he was. He was an arrogant bully, and he needed to be taken down a peg or two. She wanted nothing more than to be the one to do it, but she'd be satisfied simply watching it happen due to his own selfish actions.

"I wasn't trying to hide that from you," Megan stated truthfully.

"It's okay." Andrew used a magnanimous voice. "I understand it's not something you want to just hand over. You had to try."

Megan sighed and played along. "Come with me to the lean-to and it's all yours, okay?"

Andrew smiled and clapped a hand on her shoulder. "I knew you'd see it my way."

Megan spent the rest of the walk to the beach trying to stifle her laughter. When they reached the lean-to, she asked Carson and Leo to give them a minute. Carson gave her a questioning look but accompanied Leo out of the shelter.

Megan dug through her bag and located the beaded item Andrew had brought into question. She held it in the palm of her hand and stroked it a few times with her thumb. Molly would forgive her. In an effort to further herself in the game, her sister would have let Megan give away her engagement ring—or maybe even her firstborn. She certainly would understand why Megan gave away the princess good luck charm Molly had made for her in grade school. It was Megan's luxury item. Looking at it now, she had to admit, it really did look more like a troll than a princess.

She took a final look and held it out to Andrew. "Here," she said. "It's yours." She silently hoped she'd see it again. It didn't look like much to anyone but her, but it had sentimental value.

Andrew wrapped his hand around the beaded creation with a sly smile. "Thank you, Megan. I believe our deal has been fulfilled. It's been nice working with you."

Megan didn't like the sound in his voice as he left the lean-to. He was done with her. He'd allowed her to stay around long enough to get what he wanted from her. And now what? He was going to vote her out? He certainly had the power to do so. She mentally slapped herself. She should have bargained with him, saying she would give it to him after tonight's elimination. Now, she had to do something to stop him.

Chapter Twenty-Four

By the time Grace reached the lean-to, Carson and Leo had returned, and the crew had a quick chat about what went down. Grace filled them in on the discussion they'd had with Kat and Andrew over burgers without dallying on how good the burgers were. Then Megan told them about the vote and how Carson and Leo were now safe because of it.

"Well, I'm sorry for you two that it worked out that way," Leo said. "But it sure was nice of you to let us have protection."

"We didn't exactly let you," Grace corrected.

"Can't an old guy say thank you? Let me have my moment."

They chuckled and then got down to business.

"So, what should we do?" Carson asked.

"I have a feeling Andrew's coming after me." Megan didn't want to reveal the information about the lucky beaded creation Andrew ransacked from her belongings just yet. "He never has liked me."

"Whether it's you or me, we know it's one of us." Grace folded her legs beneath her.

"Is there any way we can get one of them over to our side?" Leo questioned.

Grace stared into the distance. "We should be able to find out for sure who they're voting for. Right, Carson?" She grinned knowingly at the PE teacher.

"I'll ask Kat," he said with a deep sigh.

"Thanks for taking one for the team." Grace clapped a hand on his shoulder and let it linger. "Let's figure out who we're voting for, then leave the rest up to me. I have an idea."

Megan glanced over at her friend. She trusted Grace. If she had a plan, Megan would roll with it, keep her fingers crossed, and hope for the best. Perhaps she could spend the afternoon in the woods searching for the real Protection Piece.

〜〜〜〜

Cane heard the news from the crew. Half the people on the beach were safe from elimination that night, but Megan was not one of them. This could very well be her last evening on the show.

He sighed, running a hand through his hair. After having some time to think, he had decided he had mixed emotions where Megan was concerned. His attraction grew upon every encounter and he found himself falling for her quirks, but starting a relationship surrounded by the reality TV setting was not something he aimed to do a second time, even if he didn't appear on camera nearly as much as before. It had all happened so fast—which he realized was a red flag. Part of him didn't want to see her leave because it would mean the end of their time together . . . at least for now. The other part of him wondered if it might be better for her to go so they could figure out their feelings for each other without one another's constant presence.

Cane shook his head. It was selfish of him to wish for her to stay or to go based on his own reasons.

He peeked out of his tent at the gathering for the elimination ceremony. He wasn't required to go since there were no outright dangers. He only had to be in his tent around the clock in case an injury occurred. But there was nothing prohibiting him from going. He was anxious to see how things turned out and, truth be told, he wanted to see Megan one last time before she left, just in case she happened to get voted out.

Cane took position behind a camera operator. He was far enough in the darkness that the group would never even know he was there. As they slowly filed into the campfire area and took seats around the semi-circle, Wendy Weathersby's short skirt and tight blouse caught his eye. She was something else. Her natural beauty was concealed by her caked-on makeup and overly coiffed hair. While the look might work well for TV cameras, Cane much preferred Megan's comfortable, low-maintenance attitude towards life.

"Welcome, Leftovers," Wendy greeted the group with a plastered-on smile. "It has been an eventful day here at Cove Bay Beach. Congratulations all around. First, to the team that won today's competition and got the barbecue reward. Second, to the opposing team that ultimately received protection from tonight's elimination. Would anyone like to comment on that?"

Danae spoke up first. "We heard the whole story from Andrew, and really, it was gracious of him. I mean, one of them could have had protection tonight, maybe even him. But instead of letting that happen, he decided to throw protection to the four of us."

So that's how he's playing it. The unsung hero. Megan shook her head. Andrew certainly knew what he was doing in making his posse even more loyal to him.

"It just made sense," Andrew piped in. "Why should one person get protection when four people could have it?"

"But that means you're vulnerable to tonight's elimination, right?" Wendy asked.

Andrew reached up to adjust his tie. When he found it missing, a frown started in his eyes and moved down his face. "I'm not concerned about that, Wendy," he said, his voice rising. "Has anyone seen my tie?" He searched the faces around the fire. Cane noticed Grace shifting on her boulder. She could hardly contain her glee, though she kept her eyes on Wendy.

"How did it feel to get your team up and over the walls, Grace?" Wendy changed the subject.

"It was great, Wendy. We worked together to get one another through the competition and we succeeded. Oh, but when I say 'we,' I mean Kat, Megan, and me. Andrew was really no help at all."

Cane wished he could see Wendy's face better. Surely she had shock written all over it at the way Grace threw Andrew to the wolves.

"I mean," Grace continued, "he had a tie on for heaven's sake. He could have taken that off and flung it over the wall to help people up. Then again, it was so ugly it might have blinded us."

Cane stifled a laugh as Andrew's jaw hung open. Grace was usually more reserved with her comments. This change in character was surprising.

"You know where my tie is, don't you?" Andrew leaned across Kat and shot a fiery stare at Grace. "Where is it? What did you do with it?"

Grace shrugged. "It didn't help us in the last competition and I'm afraid it won't be helping in any other competitions."

Andrew lunged at her, but Tank caught his arm and held him back. "Hey, man," Tank said. "She's a lady!"

Andrew brushed the dust from his suit coat. "Where . . . is . . . my . . . tie?"

Cane watched with exuberance as Grace put on a sheepish expression. "Let's just say the fish didn't seem to mind how ugly it was."

Andrew stared first at Grace, then out into the bay. Cane wished the tie would surface. Andrew might just wade out into the water to save it.

"I'm sorry, Andrew. I really am, but the world is a better place without that tie." Grace slapped her knees as Andrew seethed.

"This beach would be a better place without you, Grace." He spoke through clenched teeth.

Wendy's wide eyes took in all the drama and Cane wasn't sure she knew what to do next. "Okay," she said as the group quieted down. "Why don't we vote? Tank, you go first."

Cane observed as each person voted. Grace almost skipped to the box while Andrew stormed over when it was his turn. He scrawled a name on the page so forcefully Cane wondered if he ripped through the paper as he wrote. What was Grace up to? She was normally so congenial—there had to be a reason behind what she was doing.

"Time to count the votes," Wendy sang. She ceremoniously took the box from the voting stand and drew out the first slip of paper. "One vote for . . . Megan."

Cane sucked in a breath. This could be it, but there were still plenty of votes. It was too early to write her off as going home.

"Megan again—that's two votes Megan. Next vote . . . Megan. That's three votes for Megan."

It wasn't looking good.

"The fourth vote goes to . . . Kat." Wendy read. "Another vote for Kat—three votes for Megan, two for Kat."

Cane sensed a change in the tide and a slow smile spread across his face as he crossed his fingers at his side.

"Another vote for Kat, that's three for Kat and three for Megan."

Kat's face was falling fast and Cane knew she didn't understand why she had so many votes.

"Next vote . . . Grace." Wendy held up the sheet of paper. "We have three for Megan, three for Kat, and one for Grace. Only one vote remaining and Wendy Weathersby will read it right now."

She paused as she dug the paper from the box and unfolded it. Cane held his breath.

"The last vote goes to . . . Kat. Kat, I'm sorry, please gather your belongings and head to the parking lot."

Kat stood and wobbled on her feet. "But . . . what . . . I broke all these nails for nothing?" She held her hand up in front of her face.

Cane surveyed the group around the fire. The group from the beach shelter looked shocked, especially Andrew. Cane didn't know if his shock came from the vote or from the loss of his tie. After a few beats to process the vote, Cane thought he had it figured out. Megan's group voted for Kat. Andrew's group was supposed to vote for Megan. When Grace goaded Andrew and pushed him over the edge, he changed his vote to Grace at the last minute, leaving Megan's group in the majority and Kat heading home. Brilliant of the lean-to crew. Completely stupid of Andrew.

Kat wavered and Cane stepped forward. She didn't look right. He rushed in front of the cameras and caught her just before she hit the sand. Danae gasped.

"My bag," he called to the camera operator nearby. He took Kat's pulse. It was racing. He guessed that the heat from the day coupled with the lack of eating followed by a large meal in addition to the stress of the vote had been too much for her. She'd simply fainted. He grabbed smelling salts from his bag once the crewmember delivered it and waved them under her nose.

She stirred. "Am I dreaming? Am I still in the game?"

"I'm afraid not," Cane said. He almost felt sorry for her. She obviously hadn't seen it coming. "Given your current state, it might be for the best anyway. You seem to be in a fragile physical condition. It might be better for you to go home and rest."

Kat sighed and tilted her head up to try and stand. Cane gave her a hand and helped her to her feet where she swayed back and forth.

"I got this." Tank worked his way over to Kat and swept her

off the sand and into his arms like a groom carrying his new bride across the threshold.

"Carson?" she called.

Carson gave her an impish grin and a wave as he leaned toward Grace.

"Oh, I see," she said as another wave of realization hit.

"Who cares about him," Tank said as he carried Kat away from the circle. "You've got me."

Cane raised his eyebrows. There was even more going on around the beach than he thought.

"Oh, and Wendy?" Tank threw the comment over his shoulder. "Tell the producer I'm out."

Silence settled in around the campfire as Tank carried Kat away from the elimination area. By the time they were a dozen steps away, Kat had snuggled into the crook of his neck. So much for Carson. She'd moved on quickly.

Cane turned back to those around the fire as he gathered his medical bag and stood. The group stared at him as if he had answers about what just happened.

"I guess it's down to six," he said with a shrug. "Pardon me." He moved back into the darkness after allowing a lingering gaze to settle on Megan's face. She'd survived the night. And despite his concerns earlier about the confusing course of their relationship, he felt relieved to see her live to spend another day on the beach.

Chapter Twenty-Five

Megan turned over to lay on her other side. She was achy from the physical activities and from sleeping on the ground. *The Leftover* was no joke. She wondered how people on *Survivor* lasted for over a month. She certainly wouldn't be disappointed when the short time on the beach was behind her and she was back in the comfort of her own bed with her fully stocked fridge nearby.

She turned onto her back, looking up at the branches that made the ceiling. She couldn't believe it, but she was actually incredibly glad she had agreed to go on the show. She had made real friends, pushed her body much further than she thought possible, and met Cane. Plus, look how far she'd come. There were only six left. Two more to go before she was in the final four. It was a feat to get this far.

She would trade a bed and food for this any day.

A memory of Andrew's face when he realized his tie was no longer with him—and that it was with the fish in the bay—flashed through her mind. She stifled a giggle. Grace's master plan had worked better than Megan could have hoped.

The wind blew a breeze through the lean-to. They'd been lucky in their shelter so far. The leaf barriers on the outside kept out the bugs. Megan scratched a mosquito bite. *Some* of the bugs. She still had a dozen or more bites.

Megan shifted her position as a light rain began to patter

down on the lean-to. The drops slowed down on the leaves, but soon enough of the water soaked through and dripped onto those beneath it. She shivered. The nights got chilly and rain wouldn't help.

Grace shifted beside her and Carson sat up. "Rain, great," he said groggily.

"My thoughts exactly," Megan agreed. She was getting wet already, so parting the leaves at the side of the shelter to inspect the sky didn't make matters any worse. "Wow." Her eyes widened as the sky lit up with lightning that looked like a spider web.

Thunder rumbled through the lean-to and Grace and Leo awakened. Grace rubbed her eyes. "What's that?"

"A storm." Megan caught another glimpse of lightning. It was much closer. "And it's heading this way."

Grace joined Megan at the side of the lean-to. "By the looks of those clouds, it's a nasty one."

Megan wiped drops of rain from her glasses and squinted into the darkness. When lightning struck again, she could see the bubble-like appearance of the clouds. "What's that?" She pointed to a large mass of clouds across the bay.

Carson joined the girls at the edge of the shelter. "I'm no Wendy Weathersby, but I think that may be a wall cloud."

"You mean . . ." Living in Nebraska, Megan knew pre-tornado weather signs, and Carson's next words confirmed her fears.

"Yeah, watch that thing for rotation. This storm doesn't look good." Carson ran his hand over the back of his neck.

The wind picked up again, making sand swirl through the shelter.

"How do you think they're faring in the other shelter?" Megan wondered.

Leo popped his head out the other side of the lean-to. "Not good considering they're headed this way."

Megan shook her head and moved aside as Andrew and Danae

dove into the lean-to.

"The wind blew one of our walls in," Danae admitted, "and the roof came down with it."

Megan heard a loud crack and a brief glance through the leaves told her the other shelter was now completely dismantled.

Andrew glared at Grace and said nothing.

"The lean-to and the forest oughta give us a bit more shelter." Grace spoke directly to Andrew.

The rain came down in torrents and the lean-to was no longer holding back any of the drops. The group huddled together in the middle as best they could. Andrew had disappeared under his suit jacket.

"This is getting to be too much," Leo announced. "They wouldn't leave us out here in such dangerous conditions, would they?"

As if on cue, Mike, the producer, appeared with a camera operator at the side of the lean-to. The camera was wrapped in a poncho so it would be waterproof, but both men were soaked to the bone.

"I've secured a house to use as shelter for the night." Mike had to shout to be heard over the rain and wind. "We've been keeping tabs on the storm and apparently a tornado touched down a couple of miles from here. It's headed this way. We need to get out of here now."

Megan's blood pressure rose. This wasn't just a bad night on the beach. They were out in the open with a tornado just a few miles from them. She charged out of the tent behind Andrew, only stopping to grab Grace's hand.

"Follow me," Mike ordered. "The house is just around the corner on the beach."

Megan surveyed the group. They had everyone from both shelters as well as Mike and one camera operator. The crew didn't generally stay overnight so they were likely all safe in their beds at home. Or in their basements, as the case may be. Everyone was here . . . but what about Cane?

They raced past the medic tent, following Mike to the safe house. Megan slowed long enough to watch Cane emerge from the tent. His medical bag was slung across his body. He joined the parade of contestants behind Mike. Megan sighed in relief. She didn't want anyone left out here in this, not even Andrew.

Mike led the soaked group up the beach and back into the trees. If they had been inside, Megan would have wanted to marvel at the lightning. Being outside was downright terrifying. The crack of thunder that pierced the darkness immediately after the sky lit told her the storm was too close for comfort.

Cane's medical bag bumped against Megan's side. She caught his gaze and saw that he was frightened as well. His presence made her feel better about their current state. At least they were in it together.

She held tight to Grace's hand and kept her eyes on Andrew's back. Soon, she spied a glowing house before them. They were almost there. Her injured toe throbbed as she pushed herself forward. The wind swirled around her and she felt like it was strong enough to lift her off her feet.

The next bolt of lightning was so close the electrical charge surged through the air. The loud crack caused Grace to pull her hand from Megan's and cover her ears before sprinting on ahead. Megan futilely wiped the rain from her glasses as she saw that she and Cane were bringing up the back of the pack, Andrew right ahead of them. She needed windshield wipers.

Movement in her peripheral caused her eyes to snap to a tree that was . . . moving. The wind or lightning or a combination of the two had freed the tree from its permanent position and it was falling to the earth.

Time slowed as Megan calculated where the tree was in relation to the rest of the group. She was fairly certain everyone was out of harm's way except for the three in the back—her, Andrew, and Cane. Without thinking, she launched herself at Andrew's back, shoving him as hard as she could with both hands.

Andrew grunted and fell to his knees as Megan switched direction in what felt like mid-air and threw herself on top of Cane. She took him down hard and landed soundly on top of him.

The large tree fell with a deafening thud between the two sections of the group. Megan jammed her eyes shut as she waited for the pain. When nothing came, she opened them to assess the damage. She placed her hands against Cane's chest and pushed herself up.

Cane grabbed her wrist and looked into her eyes. She couldn't see well due to the rain running off her glasses and down her nose, but the look he gave her was not something she would soon forget. Megan wanted to stay near the warmth of his body all night, but then again, there was a tornado heading straight for them. She jolted back to her feet and took stock of the large tree that was now in their path.

Cane was up a moment later, pulling her hand. "Let's get to the house." They skirted around the tree and made for the house, Andrew just ahead of them. She squeezed Cane's palm tight as they made up the distance between them and the safe house, where the rest of the group had already taken refuge.

Mike held open the walk-out basement's sliding glass doors as the wet threesome stumbled inside, gasping. Once the door was shut tight behind them, they stood in a bunch, dripping and in dismay.

"You saved Andrew," Grace said as she ran up to Megan and gave her a hug.

"I did?" Megan was trying to find the driest piece of her clothing to dry her glasses on but gave up when she realized she was a soaked mess.

"He would've been right in its path. I looked back when I heard it fall."

Megan shrugged. It had happened so fast she barely had time to think about what she was doing. The tree looked like it was coming down in slow motion and yet her actions took place in a split second.

"Are you getting this?" Mike snapped at the camera operator.

The operator held a thumb up toward Mike. The red light blinked on the camera. It was a wonder the electronic device was still working.

Andrew wrung his suit jacket out on the tile floor near the door and slung it around his shoulders. Megan hadn't let go of Cane's hand. They were inside, but the storm still raged on the other side of the wall. Megan stared at Mike, awaiting further instructions when Andrew appeared before her. He put one hand on each of her shoulders, bent over, and placed his wet lips on her forehead.

"I saw my life flash before my eyes, Megan," Andrew said. "You pushed me out of the way. If you hadn't, I might be beneath that tree right now."

Megan shifted her feet uncomfortably. "I . . . you're welcome."

"I won't forget this." Andrew retracted his hands and plopped down on the couch in the corner of the room.

"The homeowners are away for the summer." Mike said, drawing the attention of the contestants. "The studio made arrangements with them in the off chance we needed refuge. We are not allowed to go upstairs, but the basement is ours for the night. I'm going to check on the storm's progress. In the meantime, make yourselves comfortable."

Megan shot a look at Andrew on the couch. It seemed like he'd already acted on that advice. She had almost forgotten Cane's hand sitting in her own until his thumb moved across her palm.

Megan removed her glasses, squinting at her surroundings.

She was having trouble seeing clearly around the drops of rain on the lenses, but everything she normally would use to absorb the water—shirt, pants—was fully saturated. Maybe she could use the carpet . . .

"Here, let me." Cane dug inside his medical bag and produced a clean cloth. He gingerly removed his hand from hers and grabbed the frames. He wiped them dry and placed them back on her face. "Better?"

Megan noticed his hands lingered near her cheeks. She might have been delirious from hunger and fear, but she thought he tucked her wet hair behind her ears before he lowered his arms.

"Okay." Mike returned to the group with news. "The storm is weakening and the tornado has gone back up into the clouds. That being said, it's still very dangerous outside. It would be a good idea to stay away from the windows. There have been reports of hail."

As if on cue, the noise of the rain increased ten-fold and Megan noticed large ice chunks hitting the ground outside the door. "Holy mackerel," she whispered. She tilted her head at Cane and led him to a spot along the wall farthest away from the windows. She leaned up against the wall and slid down into a sitting position. Grace and Carson were huddled a few feet down and Danae and Andrew sat on the couch across the room. Leo looked to be asleep on the floor already.

"Have you ever seen a storm like this?" Megan asked as lightning struck again and thunder shook the windows.

"Just once," Cane answered. He placed his medical bag on the floor between them and sank to the tiles beside her. "I was five and even semi-dark clouds terrified me for years after."

"I can see why," Megan admitted.

"Can I ask you something?"

"Sure." Megan couldn't take her eyes off the hail falling to the ground. It was starting to pile up like snow.

"Why did you throw yourself at me?"

Megan frowned. He *had* to bring up the incident after she broke her toe? She was medicated! She didn't know *what* she was doing. And it wasn't like she had tackled and held him down or anything. She just made some inappropriate comments, right?

"Outside," Cane continued. "When that tree was falling. You were close to everyone in the group. You could have protected any of them, but you chose me."

And Andrew. Megan exhaled. He wasn't talking about the broken toe debacle. She glimpsed his eyes resting on her out of the corner of her eye. Her wet hair hung in front of her face and created a shield between them.

"I . . . I guess I'm not really sure." Her quick calculations had told her Cane and Andrew were in the most danger. But her body had flung itself into action before she had been able to think anything all the way through. Everything happened so fast, and she had just reacted. She certainly hadn't planned anything. And if anyone had told her that she would think to push Andrew out of the way of a falling tree, she never would have believed it.

Cane rested his elbow on his bag and reached for her hand. Once his fingers were woven between hers, he sighed. "You chose me," he said softly, "over everyone else. I was the one."

Megan wasn't sure if his quiet words were meant for her or if he was talking to himself. She tightened her grip on his hand.

She didn't know what she was doing when it came to relationships, but the more she was around Cane, the more she understood what she wanted. She felt like he saw her—and not just her messy hair and wire-rimmed glasses. He saw her personality, and more importantly, her potential. He encouraged her to do her best on the show and supported her when things went wrong. For her whole life, she had avoided men and the dating scene—but Cane made her want to try. It was more than a crush on a TV personality. Cane was real and he was here and she felt more drawn to him than she ever imagined possible. He was the cute medic from *Accept this Dandelion*, but he was so much more.

Bolstering her courage, she pushed her wet hair behind her ear and turned to face him. She let herself get lost in his eyes for a moment before speaking.

"I'd do it a hundred more times for you, Cane."

Chapter Twenty-Six

The storm raged on through half the night. Cane held Megan's hand and watched as the hail slowed and then stopped. The lightning moved away and the thunder lessened. It was almost over. During the scary parts of the storm, they had settled into an easy conversation, neither wanting to sleep. Cane enjoyed hearing her talk, but he felt conflicted. He'd just finished telling himself there was no way he was going to get serious about Megan for the duration of the show. And yet when she had risked her own safety to save him, he realized he might be making a mistake to delay things. Here was this unique, phenomenal girl willing to sacrifice herself for him and he was going to push her away? It was insanity, no matter what their current circumstances.

In the early morning hours, their conversation dwindled, and he watched her head sag in his direction. His shoulder gladly accepted its weight and he settled his temple against her hair. Her even breathing told him she was asleep. He wanted to move so he could see her. The peace on her face would be like that of an angel. Given how they were positioned, he had to make do with holding her hand and marveling at the feel of her shoulder next to his.

All the promises he made to himself aside, he was doomed. Downright doomed. Whether she realized it or not, Megan Malone was taking his heart and there wasn't anything he could do about it.

Megan woke with a distinct crick in her neck. She cursed the rock that had made its way beneath her head as she slowly opened her eyes. The darkness confused her for a moment as her eyes adjusted. The rain was still coming down, but they weren't in the open anymore. All of the contestants were in the basement of a house.

Megan moved her eyes down her arm and found her fingers intertwined with Cane's. Her heart skipped a beat as she realized the weight on the side of her head was his cheek. And the hard rock she thought she was laying on outside was actually his shoulder. She smiled, heart thudding in her chest.

Their conversation had stretched well into the night. She'd watched Grace and Carson fall asleep against the wall. Andrew and Danae had crumpled on the couch. Mike finally let the camera operator stop filming when the storm let up, and the two of them had stretched out on the floor as well. They'd gotten all the excitement that occurred outside and after a while, they got bored of the contestants rehashing things and drifting off to sleep. It was once the camera lights turned off that Megan enjoyed the conversation with Cane. She was the only one awake now, and honestly, she wasn't sure why. She couldn't have gotten more than a couple hours of rest.

She reached her free hand up and over her head. She could no longer resist. Cane's hair was slightly damp and felt like heaven to her touch. She gently patted it before threading her fingers through the soft curls. She allowed them to run through her hand before she singled out one curl and twirled it around her index finger. What a beautiful man. How was he still single? Any woman would be lucky to have him. And he was holding *her* hand.

She smoothed the curl back onto his head and threaded her

fingers through the mass. She wasn't sure she could stop. It was the softest thing she'd ever felt.

"Mmm," Cane mumbled into her ear.

Megan's hand froze as her body stiffened. She hadn't meant to wake him.

Cane nestled against her and smacked his lips. "Eva," he whispered.

Megan's eyes widened as she fully awoke. Had he just said Eva? He had admitted he was trying to get over her, but he shouldn't be holding Megan's hand if he still wanted to be with Eva. Why was he flirting with her? Why had he laid his soft, curly, perfect head of hair on her shoulder?

Megan drew her hand back and stuffed it under her leg. Suddenly, she was uncomfortable in her seated position. A moment ago she thought she could stay this way forever, but now she had to move. She pulled her other hand out from Cane's fingers and placed it under her knee. Her head was still on his shoulder and his head was on hers, but she wasn't going to allow any further connection.

As she stared into the night sky outside the basement windows, she felt like she was falling into a deep chasm. Here she thought she had a chance with a man like Cane. What an idiot she'd been. He was still hung up on Eva. Of course he was. She was petite, gorgeous, every man's dream. And what was Megan? Megan was awkward, poorly dressed, and . . . well, Megan. That was enough to scare most guys away.

Megan spent the next hour watching the sunrise over the horizon, holding back tears, and building a sound, solid wall around her heart.

The muscles in Cane's shoulders ached as he awoke and lifted his head. He noticed his hand was cold, but Megan was still close. The moment he removed his head, she scooted away.

"Good morning." He smiled. He didn't want her to move, but he did want to look into her eyes and see how she was reacting to the change he felt between them.

"Yep, it's morning," Megan muttered.

Cane rubbed his eyes, recalling the conversation they'd had the night before. Everything had fallen into place where Megan was concerned. He was still worried about getting hurt, but he believed she was worth the risk.

"I had a dream last night." Cane turned to shift the bag he'd used to prop himself up, and when he turned back around, Megan had scooted ten feet away.

"I gathered that." She wasn't looking at him.

Cane frowned. Where was she going? He wanted to tell her about his dream. It was further proof he was headed in the right direction. In the dream, he'd seen Eva out on the street. He'd said hello and that it was nice to see her. Then, he shocked himself by saying, "Eva, I'd like you to meet my girlfriend. This is Megan." He'd turned to the woman beside him and wrapped his arm around her shoulders. Eva looked happy for him as she smiled and greeted Megan. Normally, when he thought of Eva, his heart ached. But when he saw her in the dream, his heart was tugging him in another direction. One that led him toward Megan.

"Oh good, everyone's awake." Mike interrupted the conversation Cane so badly wanted to have, though Megan seemed to be moving farther away by the second. "I've spoken with the Cove Bay Beach authorities. Apparently the beach sustained quite a bit of damage and the bay was struck by lightning. To make a long story short, you won't be allowed to stay on the beach until cleanup is complete. Given what I heard about the storm's affects, that could be weeks."

Cane rose to his knees and stretched his back. What would this mean for the show?

"Obviously, since *The Leftover* is set to air next month, we don't have that kind of time. I've decided to speed up the game rather than find a new location. The authorities are allowing us to film one more challenge today and then we are to vacate the premises for the cleanup crew. Take a few moments to wake up and we'll all head back to the beach. The rest of the camera crew was called in an hour ago and will meet us there to get started."

Cane watched the contestants react to the news. Everyone looked shocked and confused as to what this would mean for the game.

"We'll have Wendy explain everything when the time comes." Mike shook his head. "Would have been nice of Mother Nature to hold off, but what do you do? The show must go on."

Cane noticed that Megan was now standing next to Grace and Carson. He wasn't going to get a chance to tell her about his dream this morning. Why had she seemed to shrink away from him? His positivity and confidence plunged, but he tried to shrug it off. The conversation would have to wait. If his emotions held any truth, they would have plenty of time to discuss that and many other things. Maybe even a lifetime.

He tried to catch her eye again, but she resolutely examined her sandals. A bad feeling was growing inside him. Was he reading things between them all wrong?

Chapter Twenty-Seven

Megan kept her eyes on the sand surrounding her sandals. Her clothes were finally dry, but the humidity after the storm made them stick to her body. She shuffled her feet and tried to shake off the horror that rose within. She had let Cane into her heart, bit by bit. And he still had Eva in his.

When she arrived on the beach, all thoughts of Cane flew from her mind. Her jaw dropped as she surveyed the damage. Branches lay haphazardly here and there. She couldn't believe how many dead fish floated in the bay. The lightning strike had done a number on the water. Who knew if there were any fish alive or how contaminated the water was. That was probably a big part of why the show was moving at a rapid pace. They needed to vacate the beach for their own safety.

Wendy was standing on her board near logs placed upright in the sand. "Welcome back to Cove Bay Beach." She drew their attention away from the wreckage. "As you can see, the bay took a beating last night."

Megan inspected Wendy's face. Her makeup was heavier than normal and she wondered if she was trying to cover bags under her eyes from a long night. She had a home and a bed, but she had experienced the storm as well.

"Today, we're speeding up the contest. The remaining six contestants will stand on top of these logs."

Megan stared at the logs behind Wendy. They did not look very large, maybe six inches in diameter and three feet high. She was going to have to balance up there?

"In order to whittle the group down to four, we need to eliminate two people with the competition. The first two that come down from their logs are off the show. The rest of you will still want to remain up there as long as possible. The last one standing will receive protection from the vote, which will take place immediately after the competition."

Megan did some math in her head. When two people left the logs, they would be down to the final four. The four would then eliminate one more person. That would leave the group open for someone to rejoin the ranks if anyone had found the Protection Piece.

"The sun will be hot soon and the logs are not comfortable. Wendy Weathersby wishes you luck." Wendy smiled, but it looked forced. "Leftovers, choose your logs."

Megan walked to a log in the center of the group.

"Take your positions," Wendy ordered.

Megan placed one foot on the log and hoisted herself up. She couldn't fit one entire foot on the log, much less both feet. It was highly uncomfortable and it would become painful very quickly. She envied Grace's smaller feet but hoped that Andrew would feel the pain faster than she would. She glanced down the row of logs. Leo, Carson, Grace, Danae, and Andrew were all in position atop their own uncomfortable logs.

"Everyone's ready. The competition begins now." Wendy shifted her feet on her board. Megan wondered if Wendy Weathersby felt more out of place on the beach than normal. The dead fish didn't give off a pleasant odor and the fallen branches were a reminder of how scary the storm had been.

Megan took a deep breath and tried to remind herself how

lucky they were. The storm could have hurt or injured any of them, but they'd escaped with just one close call.

Out of habit, her eyes roamed the beach until they landed on Cane—but the memory of him murmuring Eva's name came flooding back, and she quickly shifted her gaze. She needed to concentrate. No distractions. Her foot ached so she shifted her weight and placed the other foot on the log to give the first one a break. Her toes curled over the edge of the log. The injured toe did not appreciate being bent in this manner and sent waves of pain up her leg. She wouldn't be able to use her bad foot for long.

She glanced down the row. Grace looked completely comfortable and at peace. Her eyes were closed and she had a slight smile on her face. She'd do well. Danae wavered a bit. Megan watched as she swayed and switched feet to regain her equilibrium. Leo wasn't faring well either and Megan was certain he wouldn't last long. The time on the beach had weakened all of them, making a relatively simple task much more difficult. She had no illusions of gaining protection, but if she could outlast two of them, she could at least get to the final four.

A sudden motion caught Megan's eye and she swiveled her head to the right.

"Enough of that." Andrew stepped from his log and sat in the sand, rubbing his foot. He stood and brushed the sand from his suit pants. Megan's eyes widened. Andrew was giving up? He was out! He walked past her log and caught her eye.

"See you in the finals, sweetheart." He winked.

A slow smile spread across Megan's face. Of course. He thought he was in the final four because of the beaded creation he found in her bag. Boy did he have a rude awakening coming. His ego didn't allow him to play fair and square. He wanted to rub it in their faces that he'd found the Protection Piece. Megan took a deep breath and steeled herself against what was to come. Andrew would not appreciate her in any way, shape or form very soon.

The breeze blew against her shoulders as she switched back to her other foot. She imagined her sister's face when she found out Megan had made it to the final five. It was astounding. She wasn't sure she would last through the first vote and yet here she was.

Megan reviewed the past few days in her mind to keep her thoughts as far away from the pain in her foot as possible. Some of it had been pure luck, but there were parts that Megan played intentionally. She'd had a hand in getting several dangerous players voted out while keeping the lean-to crew safe. Her group surrounded her now on individual logs with Grace on her left and Carson next to her. Leo was on her right. They'd made it this far together.

"We're at the ten-minute mark." Wendy held her hair up off her neck and fanned herself.

Megan sighed. Ten minutes? That was all? It'd felt like an hour. Her foot was screaming and she wasn't sure she'd be able to shift back onto the other one. Her injury could cause her to falter sooner.

"Whoa!" Leo called from the end of the log line next to Megan. One moment after he cried out, he hit the sand. He stood and brushed himself off. "Got off balance," he explained. "I guess that's it for me." He hung his head as he joined Andrew on the patch of sand next to Wendy.

The log was starting to cause pain to radiate up Megan's leg and into her hip. As much as it hurt, she knew switching to her other foot would be infinitely worse. If she hadn't stubbed that baby toe, she'd be able to last longer by going back and forth.

"Twenty minutes." Wendy gave the competitors a sympathetic smile.

Carson dropped to the sand just after the pronouncement. "My feet are too big for this," he announced. "Besides, Grace could be here all night."

Megan shot a glance at her friend on the next log. She hadn't moved. Her eyes were still closed and she looked perfectly at ease. Carson was right and Megan wasn't going to last much longer. She tried Grace's tactic and closed her eyes. Her sister and the fast-paced training session she'd put her through flooded her memory.

Megan remembered how her legs had burned after all the stairs Molly made her run. She hadn't thought it would make a difference, but here she was, mentally forcing her body to stay on this log, just like she had forced her way up the stairs. And she had watched the *Survivor* marathon just to humor Molly—but that too had come in handy, cluing her in on using her glasses to start the fire. Molly had pushed her through those experiences because she seemed to think more of Megan's skills than Megan did. But now, Megan realized, she was doing this by herself.

"Danae, you're out," Wendy called.

Megan opened her eyes. It looked like one of Danae's feet had hit the sand. She tried to cover it up by jumping back on the log, but Wendy caught her.

She shuffled past the remaining two contestants. "Hey, final four works." Danae shrugged. She wasn't safe past that, but she seemed to be happy with that outcome. It was more than Leo could say. Unless he had the Protection Piece, he was out.

Megan closed her eyes again and remembered the conversations she and her sister had about the show. Her sister promised to let Megan name her child if Megan won the show. Megan ran a few names through her mind. Evan. Sadie. Jordan. Kaelyn. She wasn't sure what she would choose. And it probably didn't matter.

Her lower back began to ache. She was going to feel that log sticking into her foot for days. She opened her eyes and cast a glance at Grace. Grace was staring back at her.

"How are you doing?" Grace asked.

"I've been better, you?"

Grace laughed. "Remember when our team won the wall contest and you talked everyone into giving me protection? Well, almost everyone." Grace narrowed her eyes in Andrew's direction.

Megan frowned. "You deserved it."

Grace rolled her eyes. "You deserve this." She kissed the tips of her fingertips, placed her hand over her heart, and jumped from her log.

Megan watched in astonished silence as Grace landed like a cat in the sand below. She rebounded quickly and took her position next to Wendy and the others.

"Congratulations, Megan, you withstood the log for over half an hour . . . and you've won protection from today's elimination! You may get down now."

Easier said than done. Megan concentrated all her efforts on gingerly placing her bad foot on the sand. The leg that suspended her on the log shook beneath her. She crumpled to the sand. It would take a few minutes to regain feeling in her extremities. She held up a hand. "I'm okay." The last thing she wanted was for Cane to rush to her aid. She needed distance from him. And a moment to revel in the fact that she'd done it. She made the final four and, because of Grace, was guaranteed a spot in the final three. Maybe her confidence was often missing, but standing on a log, she'd discovered it again—maybe for good.

Chapter Twenty-Eight

Megan situated herself on a large boulder beside Grace. It was strange having an elimination ceremony in broad daylight, but the crew managed to get a fire going in the center of the circle to set the mood. Not that they needed it—the warm, damp air was oppressive.

It felt good to sit down and Megan wondered how long her foot would feel the dent of the log protruding into its center.

"Congratulations Megan, Danae, Carson, and Grace. You made it to the final four! Unfortunately, one of you has to go home immediately. Then, if anyone has found the Protection Piece, that person will come back into the game. They will not only have the power to return, but also the ability to remove one of the remaining players and take their place. If no one has the Piece, we will proceed with the three remaining players. Does everyone understand?"

Megan nodded along with the group. Grace caught her attention as Wendy took a breath. "Vote Carson," she muttered out of the side of her mouth.

Megan furrowed her brow and leaned toward Grace for an explanation.

"Trust me," Grace whispered.

"Megan, you earned protection from today's elimination. No

one can vote for you. The rest of you are at risk. Carson, start the voting."

Carson stood, winked at Grace and Megan, and cast his vote. The rest of the group followed. Megan had to limp to and from the voting box, but she made it. It felt weird writing down Carson's name and revealing it for the camera. She didn't know what to say when she held up her vote so she simply shrugged. She knew the worried look her on face would tell the story. She assumed they'd vote for Danae and she didn't know what Grace had in mind.

"I'll read the votes." Wendy grabbed the box and pulled the first paper from its center. "Carson, you have one vote." She pulled another paper and unfolded it. "Grace, that's one vote for you." The third paper read Carson as well. Wendy unfolded the final ballot and gave the group a summary. "Two votes for Carson, one for Grace and . . . Carson, that's three votes. I'm sorry, you've been eliminated from the game."

Carson stood and shrugged. He bent over and kissed Grace on the cheek. She blushed while Carson gave Megan a tight hug. Based on the confused look on Danae's face, Megan bet Carson voted for himself. Danae had cast the only vote for Grace. What was their master plan?

Wendy stood a little taller. "Congratulations to the three of you. You *may* be the final three in the game. But first, we need to find out if anyone has the Protection Piece. I've heard from our producer that no one who was eliminated prior to today found the Piece. That leaves Andrew, Leo, and Carson." Wendy turned to the competitors who remained next to her on the beach. "Do any of you have the Protection Piece?"

Megan held her breath as Andrew stepped forward with a cocky grin on his face. "That'd be me." He dug into his pocket.

Megan registered the surprise on Carson's face. His skin paled as Andrew exposed the beaded creation Megan's sister made so many years ago. He held it up for the group to see and began moving toward the boulders. Andrew eyed each of the remaining contestants as if trying to decide whom he would replace.

"Uh . . ." Wendy came up behind him and tapped him on the shoulder. "I'm sorry, Andrew. I have no idea what that thing is, but it's not the Protection Piece."

Megan exhaled as rage filled Andrew's eyes. They focused on her and he took a step in her direction. "Not . . . the . . . Protection . . . Piece?"

"May I ask where you got it?" Wendy prodded.

Andrew stared daggers at Megan. He tossed the piece to the sand by her feet. "Worthless. I should have known better than to believe you."

"Not to make matters worse," Megan's voice rose from her throat, "but I never told you that was the Protection Piece. You simply said you wanted it and I agreed you could have it. But thanks for giving it back." Megan leaned over and picked up the beaded good luck charm. "My sister made this when we were little, and it's pretty special to me."

Andrew sucked his bottom lip in between his teeth.

"I'm sorry, Andrew. Since you have not produced the Protection Piece, you are out of the game. You may stay and observe until we are done with the eliminations." Wendy waited until Andrew stomped back to stand with Leo and Carson.

"Leo, Carson, do either of you have the Protection Piece?" Wendy asked.

Carson and Leo looked at one another. Leo shrugged and held up his empty hands. Carson fished around in his pocket and brought out a palm-sized rock with PP carved in its center. "Is that what you're looking for?"

The smile on Wendy's face grew. "That is indeed the Protection Piece. Carson, how did you find it?"

Carson stared at Grace. "Grace and I got a clue to its location after one competition. I didn't have any idea where to start, but she found it with ease. She insisted I keep it. I wanted her to have it, but she convinced me I was a lot more likely to need it than her." He smiled, eyes twinkling in the sunlight. "She's amazing in every way."

Megan's heart danced in her chest. She knew Carson had a thing for Grace and based on the sparkle in Grace's eye, she guessed the feeling was mutual. When she'd broached the subject of Carson in order to put in a good word for him, Grace had told her there would be time for that later. Megan hoped a relationship would blossom between the two of them. It couldn't happen to two better people.

"Carson, this earns you a spot on the boulder with the others. But who will you replace?"

Carson stroked his chin. "It would be smart of me to take out Megan or Grace, but they got me through this game with their wit and wisdom. There's no way I would remove them now. I'm sorry, Danae, it has to be you."

Danae's face fell as she stood in resignation and swapped places with Carson.

"Carson, Megan, Grace, you are the final three Leftovers. As you know, our taping sessions at the beach are complete, thanks to last night's storm. We were forced to speed up the process in order to get to the final three contestants, but now that we're there, we will resume the game as planned. Each of you will go home and have the next few weeks to think about your end game. No one can talk about the show to family members or friends. It will begin airing in a week and on the final night, we will gather in the studio for the live finale. We'll bring back all of the contestants and they will vote on who the final Leftover will be. Wendy Weathersby encourages you to use your time wisely to think about what you want to say to those you had a hand in voting out. Until then, enjoy your beds, your home-cooked meals, and real floors beneath your feet." Her eyes roamed the sand and she crinkled her nose at the dead fish strewn across the sand.

"And cut!" Mike shouted from behind the cameras. "Okay, everyone, that's a wrap. Like Wendy said, you'll all go home, but you can't talk about the outcome of the game and you cannot contact one another. I'll send you details on the live taping. Until then, nothing—and I mean *nothing*—about the show can leak. Got it?"

Megan nodded. She wanted nothing more than to go home and spill everything to Molly. Keeping it from her sister would be next to impossible. But watching the episodes with Molly and seeing her reaction to Megan's triumphs and failures would be worth it.

Megan stood as the crewmembers began tearing down equipment and tossing the logs they'd used in the final competition back into the forest. Was it really over? Was she in the finals? Megan hardly believed it.

She searched the edge of the crowd for Cane. He was kneeling next to Danae, who seemed to be showing him a cut on her foot. She must have sustained it during the competition. Part of Megan wanted to catch his gaze one last time. But her heart told her that remembering the feel of his head against hers would have to be enough. He was in love with someone else.

"You should be all set, Danae." Cane finished wrapping a bandage around her foot. "Just clean the area twice a day and it will heal in no time."

"Thanks."

Cane could see the disappointment etched in her features, but he didn't comment on the game. It was just a show after all, and she'd played well enough to get to the final four. She should be proud.

He stood and shoved his gear back in the medical bag. He needed to find Megan before she disappeared. He wanted to make sure things were okay between them before they left the beach. He'd stalled long enough. It was time to cement their relationship.

Cane spotted her ponytail swinging back and forth near the edge of the woods and he jogged to catch up to her. He was still twenty feet back when Andrew appeared next to her. Cane watched as he grabbed Megan by the elbow and pulled her off the path. Cane quickened his pace, but then slowed as he noticed how close the two of them stood.

Cane surveyed his status. He was out in the open. He darted behind a tree and strained to hear their conversation. Their voices were too hushed. He couldn't hear a thing.

Andrew leaned over and closed his eyes. Cane waited for Megan to slap him across the face, but she didn't. Instead, Andrew pressed his lips against hers. Cane's heart dropped into his feet. Megan hadn't thrown her arms around Andrew, but she was allowing him to kiss her. Cane turned away. He'd seen enough.

He made his way back through the trees to the beach as fear settled into his bones and caused his hands to shake. His past was coming back to bite him. Ever since his time with Eva ended, he'd dreaded repeating such heartbreak. He never wanted to be second in any woman's life ever again. Yet, it was happening again now. A woman he fell for had picked someone else. Maybe she'd wanted that guy all along. Sure, Andrew had been a jerk to Megan, but didn't women go for men like that? The ones who strung them along, and played hard to get? Maybe Megan liked a challenge and found it in Andrew.

He shook his head. It was his fault for letting his heart get ahead of his head on a regular basis. First Eva, now Megan. He was never going to fall for another woman again. He steeled his heart against females everywhere. He'd become a hermit, do his job, and live out his life alone.

Andrew pulled back and let go of Megan's arms. He studied the trees over her head. Cane was gone, but he'd gotten an eyeful . . . Andrew had made sure of that.

"Like I was saying," Andrew continued as if the kiss hadn't happened, "I'm really grateful for what you did for me during the storm."

Megan wiped her mouth with the back of her hand. "You already thanked me, Andrew. You didn't have to do . . . *that*. Pushing you out of the way was an instinct. Even if we didn't get along, I didn't want you to get hurt."

He dropped her arms and took a step back. "Yeah, well, forget it then." He turned on his heels and stomped through the woods to the parking lot, a sly smile spreading across his face.

Was he grateful to Megan? Sure, maybe a little. Was he angry about the Protection Piece? You better believe it. No one got the best of him. And in the end, he got even. Whether Megan realized it or not.

Chapter Twenty-Nine

Megan enjoyed her first shower at home more than she could have imagined. After nearly a week on the beach, she had sand in unmentionable places. The smell of soap and the feel of fresh water trickling down her back was simply amazing. She shuddered to think what condition she would have been in had the taping lasted its full term.

Her second task was a meal. Anything other than fish. She searched her fridge and managed to put together a ham and cheese sandwich with plans to stick a roast in the Crock-Pot for a feast later.

She had put off calling Molly for as long as she could. As the phone rang, she steeled herself against the questions her sister would ask.

"Hello?" The voice on the other end was breathless.

"Molly, it's me."

"Oh no! I was hoping you wouldn't call for another few days. You got kicked off, didn't you?"

"You know I can't say anything about the show. They actually had to wrap taping because of the storm."

"Gosh, that was something, wasn't it? The oak in the corner of our yard fell on our house."

"Is everyone okay?" Megan pictured the side of the roof caved in as her sister lay trapped beneath it in her bed.

"We're fine. We were in the basement. The roof is damaged, but Derek has some people coming out today to get an estimate on the repairs. It's all good."

Megan took a deep breath. "Good."

"And you were stuck out on the beach during that. I was so worried!"

"The producer got us a house for shelter that night. We were just as safe as anyone else in the city."

"I'm so relieved to hear your voice, Megan. I didn't want you to come home this early, but I'm glad to talk to you."

"I'm not home early," Megan insisted as she made a face. She didn't want Molly to know the details. She had to be careful. "The show is over. The beach was damaged and they couldn't allow taping because of the cleanup efforts."

"Does that mean you made it to the end?" Molly prodded.

"I'm not saying another word. I just wanted to call and let you know I was home."

"You better believe I'm coming over to watch the show with you. Every single second that airs, I'm by your side, you got it? And don't think I'm going to let you get away with keeping everything quiet in the meantime."

Megan laughed as she heard a doorbell ring through the phone.

"That's the guy about the estimate. I gotta run. I'll call you later, okay? Be prepared to spill details."

"Bye, Molly." Megan flopped backward onto her couch into her favorite position. She sighed. She had a warm towel wrapped around her wet hair, a soft robe wrapped around her body, and a delicious sandwich in her hand. Life was good.

The week after the taping wrapped did not go as Cane anticipated. He had visions of spending time with Megan, talking and laughing and enjoying the warm summer weather. Since the show completed taping early, he was still free from his regular job and left with nothing to do. That just gave him even more time to agonize.

How could she do it? Lead him on while she had another man on the line? And a jerk at that! He hadn't thought Megan capable of being so two-faced. They'd had long talks and she knew his history with women. She knew how he felt when women strung him along, and she knew how heartbroken he was when Eva chose someone else over him. In fact, she knew a lot of things about him. Things he hadn't brought himself to tell anyone in years. He had allowed things he had buried deep to rise to the surface during their talks in the dark. But did he know her at all? Apparently not.

It wasn't all Megan's fault. He was more furious with himself. He'd laid his heart on the line again despite his best efforts to shield himself and it got trampled. And now he was stuck mending the pieces, just like always. Every time he looked at the phone and thought about calling Megan, he put another brick into the wall around his heart. Eva was behind him. Megan was a brief, delightful blip. He was alone, and that's the way it would stay.

*****

Molly sank into the couch next to Megan with a bowl of popcorn on her lap.

"Shouldn't you have a belly by now?" Megan asked. Her sister was going to be an annoying svelte pregnant woman. She'd only show at the last minute and only from the side.

"I'm not *that* pregnant and I feel pretty good. I can't stop eating, though." Molly shoved a handful of popcorn into her mouth.

"The baby likes popcorn, I see."

"We'll have months to talk about the baby. Now that we're about to watch the show, can you just tell me how you did? Come on, Megan, I need details! You've given me hardly anything in the week you've been home."

"It was quite an experience."

"I figured that. I want more! How'd you do?"

"Better than I thought. I'm pretty surprised I survived the first afternoon."

"Does that mean you got kicked out the first night and you've been hiding here ever since? Or did you win? Tell me, Megan!"

"It's starting. See for yourself." Megan unmuted the TV and sat beside her sister, watching Wendy Weathersby describe the show and introduce the contestants. When Megan's face filled the screen, Megan covered her eyes. "Is that what I really look like?" she asked. "I'm a mess and it's only the first day."

"You're cute," Molly affirmed.

Megan peeked at the screen from between her fingers. No wonder Cane still had a thing for Eva. Why had Megan thought her flyaway ponytail and crooked glasses would ever catch his eye? She glanced at the phone. Part of her wanted to have Cane next to her watching the show with them. When she'd woken up with her head on his shoulder and she'd wrapped her finger around a curl in his hair, she'd allowed herself to take what they had out of the show and place it into the real world. She thought they might have a chance—she knew she wanted one. But it was impossible. He hadn't called, and why would he? He was probably off chasing Eva, trying to get her to change her mind about the man she chose over him.

Megan sighed. Her heart ached as she thought of the soft tendril of hair between her fingertips. Cane was the closest she'd ever come to having a boyfriend. Kissing him had made her melt into the sand where she stood. But the few kisses they'd shared would have to tide her over until she met someone else. He was in love with another and there was nothing she could do to make him forget the other woman. Megan shook Cane from her mind. *The Leftover* was on and she wanted to enjoy every moment of the present.

As the show ramped up and the competition began, Megan

enjoyed watching Molly more than the screen. She'd been on the beach so she knew what happened there, but Molly's reactions were priceless.

"That log almost took you out!"

"Ooh, Megan, you are playing a serious social game!"

Molly's proclamations were frequent and the smile on Megan's face grew with each one. Her sister approved. She was clumsy and didn't look nice on screen, but her sister was happy about the results of the first show.

"Megan, I simply cannot wait. You have to tell me what happens next," Molly begged.

Megan searched her sister's face. She was desperate to talk to someone. She knew she shouldn't say much, but there was one thing she could admit and not get into trouble with the station. Her so-called relationship wouldn't show up on screen.

"I met someone." Megan tested the waters. The surprised look on Molly's face told her to continue. "Don't get too excited. It didn't work out. But oh, Molly, I wanted it to so badly."

Molly extended her hand and wrapped her fingers around Megan's palm. "Tell me, Megan. Tell me."

Megan spent the next hour detailing her crush on Cane. She told Molly about their long conversations, the way they'd fallen asleep beside each other several times, and even about the dare when she kissed him.

"And then he pulled me into the tent and kissed me for real. Molly, I swear, I felt that kiss down to my toes."

"Wait a minute, there's something I don't understand," Molly interrupted. "You said it didn't work out between you. Why? He was a real sweetheart on *Accept this Dandelion* and it sounds like he was Prince Charming on *The Leftover.* Granted, I wasn't there, but from the outside looking in, he seemed totally into you. What went wrong?"

Megan shrugged. "He's still hung up on his ex." Her eyes

watered. "He's not ready to move on and I can't imagine competing with her." Megan dropped her head onto Molly's shoulder as her sister stroked her hair.

"You're talking about Eva, aren't you?

Megan nodded against her sister's textured shirt.

"When will you learn, Megan? You don't give yourself enough credit. Forget about Cane Trevino. You want a guy who wants you and the one who does will be the luckiest man in the world. You don't realize it, but any man would be lucky to have you. You can compete with anyone. But when the right guy comes along, you won't have to. You'll be the only woman he sees."

Chapter Thirty

Megan smoothed her hand over the dress her sister had forced her to wear. Molly had even curled her hair and nearly poked her eye out with a mascara wand. Megan felt more in her element on the beach with sand between her toes than in the wedge heel platform shoes Molly had shoved onto her feet. But when she'd seen the finished product, she had to admit, she didn't look half bad.

The contestants were back together again in the studio in front of a small live audience. They weren't allowed to talk under order of Mike, the producer, so Megan had some time to work up a good panic. She was thrilled to see Carson and Grace and less than thrilled to see Andrew and Kat. Megan made it a point to connect with each of the contestants with eye contact, a smile, or a small wave. They couldn't speak, but she wanted to greet them all in some manner. She was surprised by how quickly the weeks had passed and she reveled in watching the show with her sister. But even though she'd done a passable job on the TV show, she now had to face a live audience plus all the people watching at home. She was bound to do something outlandish.

Megan had spent the time between the taping and the finale holed up in her home, returning to her old habits. She caught up on work, paced around her couch, and flopped over to relax. But no matter what she did, she couldn't keep her mind off Cane. From her small-time crush after watching him on *Accept this Dandelion*, she'd developed real feelings for him. He had paid attention to her and made her feel like she mattered. Coupled with his natural good looks, his big heart, and his willingness to help anyone in need, he had turned into her ideal man. That was probably why his curly hair and sparkling eyes kept creeping into her mind every time she tried to shove thoughts of him away.

As much as she tried to stop herself, she wondered if he would be there to watch the finale. His part of the show was over. There would be no medical emergencies to tend during a studio taping. He didn't need to be around, so why would he come?

Megan had almost convinced herself that Cane would be nowhere near KETO when she saw a head of dark hair catch the light just off to the side. She squinted. She and the other contestants were sitting under bright lights and the rest of the room was completely dark. It was hard to tell who was who outside of the staging area.

She shook the thought from her head. It was better to concentrate on the task at hand . . . to not be humiliated on live TV. She could worry about whether or not Cane was there later. And really, what did it matter if he was? He'd probably brought Eva as a date anyway.

"Places!" Mike shouted from the center of the room. "Quiet on the set."

Megan watched as camera operators scurried behind their equipment and the small live audience fell silent. Her hands began to sweat.

"We're live in three . . . two . . . one . . ." Mike pointed at Wendy.

"Good evening, KETO audience!" She paused for applause. "For the past few weeks, we have all enjoyed watching *The Leftover* on KETO and tonight, we re-unite the cast of the show. We'll get insider details and see some behind-the-scenes footage. We will also find out who *The Leftover* will be. First, let's welcome our final three. Grace, Megan, and Carson . . . congratulations again to all three of you."

"Thanks, Wendy," Megan muttered along with the others. She wished she'd been able to talk to Grace and Carson before the show began. She didn't want them to feel like competitors. They were her friends.

"We're going to let each of the eliminated contestants ask questions tonight. It should be an interesting evening. But first, you each have thirty seconds to state your case. Remember, the nine people sitting over there will be voting for who they think should win."

Megan swallowed the lump in her throat. She listened as Carson eloquently talked about his athletic nature and his hand in building the lean-to shelter and cleaning fish for everyone to eat. His points were valid and Megan found herself on his side. His looked like a true PE teacher with his tanned skin, tight polo shirt, and jeans.

Then Grace talked about how she felt at home in the woods and beach and how she fit right into the environment. It was hard to believe Grace was the same person Megan knew on the beach. She recognized her short, dark hair, but instead of shorts and tank tops, she wore a bright yellow sundress. She didn't overdo it on the makeup, but she definitely wore tinted lip gloss and mascara. She was lovely. Megan was impressed when Grace didn't brag about catching fish left and right or helping her group make it over the wall or any of the other amazing feats she had pulled off. She simply acted like Grace—humble, but as if she could do anything with one arm tied behind her back. And she probably could.

When Grace finished her short speech, Megan cleared her throat and sat up straight. Wendy was staring at her. Was it her turn?

"Um, I don't have any of the skills Grace and Carson have."

Good start, Megan. "And I never pretended to feel comfortable in those woods or on the beach." *Even better.* "In fact, I was totally and completely out of my element." *Perfect, why not just let them kick you to the curb now.* "And maybe that's why I should make it even farther than I already have." *That's it, getting warmer.*

"Let's face it, I had no business being out there. Sure, I helped start the first fire, but I didn't want to have anything to do with the fish and I didn't help myself or anyone else in most of the competitions. And yet here I am. A normal, everyday girl, sitting beside two extraordinary people." Megan nodded as her eyes roamed from one eliminated contestant to another. That wasn't so bad. She'd made herself sound like she might at least deserve to be in the final three. It was hard to tell what anyone thought of her speech compared to the others. No one on the other side was showing much emotion in their expressions. They'd all be very good at poker.

Wendy Weathersby clicked her tongue. "And now we'll turn the mic over to the other contestants. We'll start with the first contestant voted out and move on from there. Lucy?"

Megan tapped her shoe against the concrete floor, but stopped when it echoed in the still room. She was nervous, but she felt more comfortable around these individuals after their time on the beach than she thought possible. She wasn't going to keep in contact with them all, but she knew if she ran into any of them on the street, she'd be able to have a conversation with them without ducking into a shadow and avoiding them altogether. She'd come a long way as a person and she felt she owed the show a lot.

Megan wasn't worried about most of the contestants on the other side. She didn't know Lucy that well and she hadn't had much to do with her demise. Lucy asked about competitions and Carson answered well enough for all of them, so Grace and Megan sat back and let the next contestant approach. Sabrina touched on survival abilities and Grace crushed the question. Carson cleaned the fish, but everyone who had been on the beach knew no one could touch Grace in that department. It was better to stay quiet than point out her own inadequacies.

When Nathan and Juan approached the mic together, Megan began to sweat. The two strangers had become inseparable on the show and when they were eliminated at the same time, their bond was further cemented.

"We saw the show," Nathan said, looping his fingers beneath a different belt buckle than he wore on the beach. "We know what happened. Megan, what can you tell us about our elimination?"

Juan nodded along with his friend. His short hair was pressed to his head as if he had just removed his Cardinals hat before the taping. "We want details."

Megan shrugged. "I made it my goal not to lie during the game and I plan to continue along that path tonight. I think all of you can agree that I didn't break that promise. I never told the two of you I was voting for you, but I didn't tell you I was voting for anyone else either. Really, I think you can blame your elimination on ego."

"Ego?" Juan asked.

"Oh, not yours." Megan waved her hand. "His." She pointed at Andrew, who sneered at her in return. She was going to regret this later. "I told Andrew that the two of you were looking for the Protection Piece. He took that as a personal attack on his game and, well, you know the rest. I can't really say I'm sorry, guys. You were strong players and to get where I am, you had to go."

Nathan nodded and Juan clapped a hand onto his shoulder. They looked satisfied. Megan sighed in relief. This inquisition was getting tougher by the minute, but she'd gotten through it so far.

Cane could hardly blink. He didn't want to take his eyes off her for a single second. Every time he'd seen her on TV when the show aired, he'd wanted to call. But then Andrew would come onto the screen and prevent him from picking up the phone. He kept picturing the two of them together, whispering in the woods. If Megan wanted to talk to him, she could have called him. She and Andrew were probably cavorting around town together. He hadn't noticed them making eyes at each other on set, but they likely wanted to play it cool for the cameras, like Grace and Carson had.

She looked so beautiful and completely different. Her hair was down and curled, she wore a dress, and even had on real shoes instead of sandals. He noticed polish on her toes and wondered if her injured toe had given her any further problems. He liked seeing Megan dressed up, but if he was honest, he liked her just as much in a ponytail and old shorts. If he was truly being honest, he liked everything about her in any form she appeared.

He'd seen Molly come in and sit down in the audience to view the taping. She'd looked at him but only gave a brief wave. She probably knew all the gritty details and didn't want to approach him. She felt sorry for him. He had come in second place with a woman . . . again.

Cane was surprised at how different Megan looked, but it wasn't the hair, makeup, or even the clothes. It was something about her demeanor. She sat taller perhaps. Or maybe it was the way she focused her eyes on the other contestants when she spoke to them instead of staring at her feet. She had a new air of confidence, which he was finding highly attractive. She'd never seemed all that comfortable in her own skin before but now, she looked happy with herself. He was going to have to stay in the shadows or she would be impossible to resist.

Chapter Thirty-One

Tank ambled to the microphone wearing a black T-shirt stretched across his chest and biceps. Megan remembered her first impression of him and the nickname she'd given him. Skyscraper. It still fit him well.

"Hey everyone." He waved. "I left the show on my own to be with this beautiful woman." He took a few steps towards Kat, grabbed her hand from her lap, and kissed her palm. "So I don't have any grudges against any of you. I have one question and the person who answers it best gets my vote." Tank extended both arms and flexed his biceps. "What do you think of the gun show?" He grinned and raised his eyebrows as the audience tittered behind him.

Carson slapped his forehead. "I think I've got a couple of hand pistols and you have machine guns."

Grace tucked a strand of her short hair behind her ear. "I have to admit, Tank, I've been around a lot of strong men in my Army career, but I've never met anyone quite like you."

Megan hadn't planned on revealing this private fact to any of them, but when it was her turn, it was all she could think to say. "I nicknamed each of the contestants the very first time I saw them and the name I gave you stands true today." She held an imaginary sword out to his shoulder. "I dub thee 'Skyscraper.'"

Tank put his "guns" away with a grin on his face. He looked

pleased with each of the answers. His biceps had gotten the attention they deserved, at long last.

"One quick question while we have you, Tank…or should I say Skyscraper," Wendy broke in. "Whatever happened with you and Kat?"

Tank flexed his eyebrows as he made his pecs dance back and forth. "It was good while it lasted."

Megan stole a glance at Kat, who was rolling her eyes. She took that to mean their relationship hadn't gone the distance. One week? Two weeks, tops? Whatever the end date, they weren't a couple now.

"Let's see what Kat has to say to the contestants," Wendy segued to the next eliminated contender.

Megan's temperature rose as Kat approached the microphone. All of them had a hand in her elimination, but she was nervous for Carson's sake because of the way he played into her interest in him.

"Carson," Kat called out, just as Megan suspected. "I have a question for you, but first, Megan, what was my nickname?"

Megan swallowed. Who else was going to ask? *Here goes nothing.* "Er, Talons."

Kat held her manicured nails out in front of her and tilted her head as the audience chuckled. "Okaaay. Now Carson, back to you. What is it about me that made you think I could be used?"

"I'm sorry?" Carson leaned forward. "Used?"

Kat nodded. "That's right. You knew I liked you and you used that to your advantage. How many times did you put your arm around me and let me tell you about the dates I wanted you to take me on?"

Carson shook his head. "I apologize, Kat. I did what I had to do. I didn't mean to take advantage of your affections, but my alliance was in a precarious position and we were looking for a way to chip through the armor in your group. The fact that you had a crush on me was the break we needed."

Kat tilted her head. "So, you weren't alone in this venture, is that what you mean? They were all in on it?"

Uh-oh. Megan shrank in her seat, trying to disappear.

"I was the one who suggested he use your crush to get to you." Grace's voice came through loud and clear. "It was the only way I could see that we could survive. And, Kat, I'm not sorry for it. It worked."

Kat glared at Grace. Megan held back a smile. She was proud of her friend. She'd owned up to her part in the situation and didn't lie to make herself look better. That took guts.

"Honestly, it may have been harder on me than you—no offense." Megan watched Grace slip her hand into Carson's. "My feelings for Carson were growing too, and it was tough to watch you hang on him while he pretended to like it."

"Humph!" Kat crossed her arms over her chest and tapped her foot on the concrete floor. If Megan had to guess, Grace would not be getting Kat's vote.

"In that way, I think I owe Carson an apology." Grace turned to Carson. "Carson, I'm sorry for denying my growing feelings for you and asking you to take advantage of Kat. I should have just told you I liked you and let the chips fall where they may."

Carson grinned. "It's okay, Grace. I would do anything for you."

A sweet smile spread across Megan's face as Carson and Grace moved closer. When their lips met, the studio audience went wild with applause and cheers. The sparks between Grace and Carson didn't show much on the episodes that had already aired, but the audience was getting a live show-mance now.

Wendy allowed the new couple to enjoy their moment for a few beats before she broke in. "Thank you, Kat."

Kat stormed back to her seat. She hadn't gotten what she wanted, that was for sure.

"Leo, you're next." Wendy raised her chin in his direction.

Megan smiled as Leo approached the microphone. He wore a white button down shirt and black slacks. His slick hair was neatly combed to one side. His shaven face was clean and shiny.

"I became fond of each and every one of you on the beach. You took an old guy like me under your wings and made me feel like one of the group. I'm going to have a hard time voting for any of you over the others. What I want from each of you is to answer this question. Who do you think should win and why? You can't include yourself in the answer. You have to vote for one of the other two."

Megan's fingers tingled. Leo's question was hard to answer.

"Grace?" Leo put one hand in his pants pocket.

"That's a tough one, Leo. I feel like both of these two deserve to be here. But if I had to choose, I'd vote for Megan if I were on the other side."

A small tear formed in Megan's eye. Grace was so sweet and it meant the world to her to hear her friend would vote for her.

"Megan triumphed over a lot of obstacles and she outsmarted a lot of people. All of the eliminated contestants know it now, but when we were on the show, most of the plans we used to get people out were hers. We were a small alliance and we came out on top, all thanks to her."

Megan hugged Grace and when she leaned back, they exchanged a fond look. She mouthed 'thank you' and turned back to Leo.

"Megan? What do you say?" Leo asked.

Megan wiped the tear from the corner of her eye. "I second what Grace said in that it's hard to choose between her and Carson. They're both amazing human beings and they showed huge strength out there on the beach." Megan tugged on her ear. "But I'd have to pick Grace. And not because she chose me just now. She has a knack for being out there in the elements, and she's small but mighty. Grace is the type of person who could fit in just about anywhere and do just about anything. If I were stranded on a desert island, I couldn't think of a better person to take along."

Grace squeezed Megan's elbow and laid her head on Megan's shoulder for a moment.

"That leaves you, Carson." Leo adjusted the microphone.

Carson ran a hand through this hair and a small tuft stood up on one side. "Megan certainly did a lot for our alliance, even though it was done under the radar. But I don't think I can choose anyone but Grace."

Carson didn't elaborate, but the look in Carson's eyes told Megan the full story. His feelings for Grace didn't allow him to vote for Megan and she understood that. She also agreed with him. Grace was the obvious choice to make between the two of them.

Leo bit his lower lip. "Thank you to all three of you. For your answers and for letting some old guy be part of the lean-to crew." He walked back to his seat. Megan couldn't wait to give him a hug after the show. She wanted to tell him he wasn't just some old guy. He was a part of their group . . . an important part.

"Danae, you're up." Wendy extended a hand toward the final three.

Megan noted Danae's asymmetrical haircut. She was The Wedge once again.

"I was wondering what each of you would do differently in the game if you had to go back and change something. Megan?" Danae pursed her lips.

Megan would have liked more time to think about her answer, but she didn't have the luxury this time. She didn't want to highlight her weaknesses too much, but she hoped self-deprecation would make her more relatable. "I think I'd take a few extra swimming lessons before the taping." The audience tittered as Megan made a face. "I've never been a strong swimmer, but I think I would win the Most Likely to Drown Award if the show decided to give that out." Megan shrugged and sat back to let the other finalists take over.

"I would start catching fish earlier," Grace admitted. "I didn't want to come on too strong and put a target on my back, but Tank had a serious medical episode that could have been avoided had he been able to eat sooner. I felt partly responsible for that."

Megan smiled at her friend. She didn't wish a medical emergency on anyone, but she'd never regret her night in the beach shelter with Cane. And she'd never forget the look on his face when he awoke with his head on Tank's chest.

"Honestly, Danae, I don't think I'd change a thing," Carson admitted. "I don't like looking to the past, I prefer to look forward to the future. The way things went down got us to where we are today and I'm pretty happy with the turn out."

Megan noticed the look Carson and Grace exchanged and she knew he referred to their relationship as much as being in the final three. She turned her attention back to Wendy, with a sinking sense of foreboding.

"Andrew, it's your turn to question the contestants." Wendy nodded at the man in the suit.

Megan fiddled with the hem of her dress, but when Andrew stood behind the microphone and glared at her, she raised her eyes and met his stare.

"Congratulations to all of you," he said in a menacing voice. "I would have thought I'd be sitting over there and one of you over here."

Megan rolled her eyes. His ego was still intact.

"Grace, I admired your tactics and I ate the fish you caught. I appreciate that you made it to the end and wish you luck. Carson, though I felt I was a stronger player than you, it was smart of you to attach yourself to someone like Grace and ride her coattails to the end."

Megan frowned. He certainly wasn't giving Carson enough

credit, but the focus was off her for another moment so she wasn't going to complain.

"That leaves you, Megan."

Megan squirmed in her seat. She knew this was coming. She'd wondered for hours on end exactly what he would say and how she would respond. Andrew was a firecracker, waiting to explode. But there was no way to predict how the sparks would fly.

"You want to pass yourself off as an everyday, normal girl, but that's not who you are at all. You're a villain."

What?

"You're a sly, conniving villain," Andrew continued. "You hooked me on the lip when I was just trying to help the group get food. You made me believe I was safe when I found the Protection Piece in your bag. You let me have it and didn't think to mention it was some kind of trinket your sister made and not the real piece. You let Grace take my tie and mutilate it when you knew how much it meant to me. And then, to confuse matters more, you threw yourself at me and kissed me right before we all left the beach."

The audience gasped and Grace gave Megan a questioning look.

"My question is rather open-ended, Megan. All I want to ask is this—what do you have to say for yourself?"

Megan blinked into the bright lights as the audience settled down. Her eyes darted around as she tried to compose herself. There were so many things she wanted to say to Andrew, but she didn't know if she could find her voice. Where should she start? How could she get it all straight and out in a manner that the group would understand? As she opened her mouth to begin, she swore a head of curly dark hair appeared at the edge of the set, next to the camera operator on the left. Megan smiled. Andrew's comments shook her, but she felt her courage returning.

"Andrew." Megan straightened her back and met his gaze.

"You're nothing but a bully and a mean-spirited excuse of a man who puts other people down to make himself feel better. You mention nothing about stealing my clothes when we won the shower reward. You don't bring up the dozens of times you cornered me and made me feel about this tall." Megan held her thumb and forefinger close together. "Honestly, if you were sitting here and me over there, I don't think there's any chance you would win this contest."

Andrew took a step back and frowned. She knew he had thought she wasn't capable of standing up for herself.

She stood up and continued. "Before we talk about the kiss, why don't we talk about the storm? There was a tornado and the wind was ripping the trees apart. So much so that one actually fell right in the middle of our group. Despite everything you did and said to me, who pushed you out of the way, Andrew?" Megan pushed her finger into her chest. "Me. I'm not sure many people in my position would have done that, but I did. You know why? Because I know there has to be more to you. There has to be a *real* man beneath the facade. Someone who cares about other people more than himself. Someone who was so hurt in the past, he put on a fancy suit and an attitude to shelter his fragile ego from the storm of life."

Megan took a breath. "As for the kiss, the cameras didn't see it so let's tell the whole story and set the record straight. You brought it up so you must be comfortable letting the audience in on that moment. I appreciate that you thanked me for saving you from the falling tree in the woods before we left. You finally came off as vulnerable, and I wish the cameras had caught it—I think the audience would have liked that side of you. But no part of me wanted the kiss you laid on me. It was inappropriate and uncalled for and I think you owe me an apology."

Megan held her hands up in front of her to indicate she was through and sat down. The stunned silence broke as the audience cheered. Grace leaned over and whispered, "Way to go!" Megan shrugged sheepishly as she shot a glance at the dark curls she had focused on between breaths. Even if it wasn't Cane, the idea that he might be there gave her the extra bit of courage she needed to stand up to Andrew once and for all.

When the audience quieted, Andrew remained at the microphone in shock. His mouth hung slightly open and Megan wondered if he felt how she often did—unable to form the right words.

"Wow." He ran a hand down his cheek. "I underestimated you."

She could tell he wasn't doing well under the pressure she'd placed on his shoulders.

"I . . . I'm sorry, Megan." And with that brief statement, he turned and briskly made his way back to his seat.

The audience clapped and Megan sat taller in her seat. She'd done it. She didn't even care what resulted from the game now. She'd stood up to Andrew. In some ways, he was like all of the bullies she'd come across in her lifetime wrapped up in one. And she'd finally found her voice . . . and her self-worth.

"On that note, it's time to vote. The contestants who left the show will cast a vote for the person they think should win the contest. The one with the most votes wins!" Wendy tapped her nails on the podium in front of her. "Who's ready to meet *The Leftover?*"

Cheering picked up on the set again and Megan folded her hands in her lap. The ordeal was almost over and she was anxious for the bright lights to shut down. She hoped to get one last look at Cane before she walked away from him and the show for good. He'd managed to boost her confidence when she needed it during the taping, but now, she could do that herself.

Cane wanted to get up and close the distance between him and

Megan. He couldn't believe he'd been so wrong about her. When he'd seen her kissing Andrew, he'd jumped to conclusions. Looking back on it now, it made sense. Though he was finally over Eva, Cane still had a scar on his heart from when she abandoned him to be with someone else. Part of him had thought he'd always come in second place. Megan and Andrew together hadn't made sense, but he'd let himself believe it anyway. Of course she hadn't fallen for Andrew! Why would she? He was a bully and a jerk, just like she said. There was no way she'd willingly kiss her tormenter.

He shook his head. He was such a fool. He'd wasted weeks stewing over losing her instead of reaching out to her. And now he had the girl of his dreams right in front of him, but it felt like she was miles away. He couldn't interrupt the live TV program to talk to her. He would have to wait . . . again.

He was anxious to get the vote over with. He hoped Megan would win, but he didn't even care about that. He just wanted to go to her. He wanted to feel her in his arms and explain why he hadn't called. Surely she'd understand what he'd thought, given his history, right? She'd forgive him and they'd ride off into the sunset together. It had to be a happy ending. Nothing else would fit.

Chapter Thirty-Two

After a commercial break, Wendy stood before the group for the final time. "I have the results!" She waved her hand in excitement. "Wendy Weathersby will now read the votes."

Megan slid her arm through the crook of Grace's elbow and Grace still held Carson's hand. The three were connected, as they had been throughout much of the game. The only one missing was Leo, but he was just across the room and they felt his support.

"The first vote goes to . . . Grace!"

The audience clapped and cheered.

"Vote two . . . Megan!"

Megan's heart pounded as applause took over the room.

"Third vote is for . . . Carson!"

Everyone cheered again as Megan exchanged looks with her friends. They were tied!

"That's one vote for each of you." Wendy paused. "Vote four . . . Grace!"

Once the audience calmed, Wendy continued. "The fifth vote goes to . . . Megan! That's two for Megan, two for Grace, one for Carson." Wendy looked at each of the final three in turn. "Vote six is for . . . Grace!"

Megan couldn't believe she'd already gotten two votes. She examined the other contestants, wondering who had voted for her and grateful anyone had at all.

"Seventh vote . . . Megan!"

Megan's eyes widened. She and Grace were tied again. It was some kind of miracle that they remained that close in the ranks, but Carson was falling behind.

"The eighth vote reads . . . Grace! Let's review." Wendy paused to count on her fingers. "Carson, you have one vote; Megan, you have three; and Grace, you have four. We have one vote left to read."

The tension mounted as Megan squeezed Grace's arm against her rib cage. She could barely breathe and willed Wendy to read that final vote . . . fast! The anticipation was killing her.

"Our last and final vote for the first season of *The Leftover* goes to . . . Megan! We have a tie! We have two Leftovers!" Wendy jumped up and down as she announced the final result to the group.

Megan looked at Grace who rested her forehead against Megan's cheek. "We did it, girl," Grace proclaimed. "You deserve this."

"I never would have made it past day one without you," Megan said in shock. *She and Grace tied?* The group put her on the same level as Grace? A woman who could do anything, anywhere? She was flabbergasted and incredibly flattered.

Megan felt people hugging her and patting her on the back as the contestants gathered around them. It was a surreal, almost out-of-body experience.

"Congratulations," Andrew muttered as he clapped a hand on her shoulder. "I voted for Carson."

Megan smiled as he walked away. She couldn't expect him to change overnight, but she hoped something she'd said got past his facade. Wendy wrapped up the show off to the side, but Megan couldn't hear what she said. The buzz around her was too loud. She'd lost track of the head of dark hair and she no longer searched for it. She didn't need Cane to help her through this moment. She'd found her confidence and she didn't plan to let it go again.

Cane couldn't push his way through all the people that surrounded Megan and Grace. After ten minutes of trying, he gave up. This was her moment in the spotlight. He'd let her enjoy it.

"I need to get in there," a voice next to him said.

"Hey, Molly." Cane recognized the bright eyes and the familiar features. She wasn't identical to Megan, but they had similarities.

"Hey," she glanced at him briefly before concentrating on the task at hand. "I really need to get in there." She stood on her toes to try to see over the others.

"I know. I was hoping to congratulate her myself."

"You?"

Was that a hint of disgust in her voice?

"Why would you want to talk to Megan?" Molly asked.

"To tell her I'm happy for her. And to clear some things up."

"I think things are pretty clear." Molly took a step in front of Cane as if to protect Megan from him. "You're in love with someone else and Megan's moving on. Let her enjoy this."

Molly threw an elbow out to one side and moved through the group. She'd get her way and make it to Megan's side. There was no stopping her.

Cane took a step back. *What had she meant?* Megan thought he was in love with someone else? Why?

He knew he'd spent a lot of their time together lamenting his relationship with Eva, but he'd told her he was getting over it, not that he was still in love with her. Confusion settled in. If what her sister said was true, Megan didn't want to see him. If he burst through the crowd, she'd turn him away and that would not only be embarrassing, but also heartbreaking.

Cane broke free from his position and moved back into the darkness.

Chapter Thirty-Three

In the few days after Megan tied for first on *The Leftover*, she couldn't believe how her life had changed. People recognized her all over the city, no matter where she went. And KETO even offered her a contract to do the voice-overs for their news promos. It meant daily trips to the studio and she found having a professional reason to be around people helped her feel more comfortable around them. Small talk was another story.

Brian Schaffer was a charismatic news anchor and she enjoyed watching him on the morning news as he wrapped up the program every day when she arrived at the studio. However, she was a bit shocked by what she encountered upon entering the newsroom a few days after starting her new job. Brian had a guest on camera, as he often did in the last segment of the morning news. Only this time, it was Cane.

Cane sat hunched over in his chair, reciting answers in a monotone as Brian questioned him about what to do in various types of emergency situations.

The interview wrapped and Brian stood to shake Cane's hand. Cane took a step down from the news desk and Megan hid herself in the shadows. She wasn't sure if she was ready to see Cane. Her heart was beating hard in her chest from the mere thought of speaking to him. She may have found her inner confidence, but she still felt like a schoolgirl at the sight of him.

"Hey, Megan, there you are!"

So much for hiding out. Megan put on a smile and stepped out of the shadows as the promo writer she worked with called out to her from across the room.

"Hi," she greeted in return, offering a fleeting glance to Cane, who stood statue-still next to the news desk.

Megan tried to listen as the writer talked about her script for the day, but the woman entering the studio through the doors behind him caught her attention. Her hair glittered around her and her smile lit up the room. She was stark raving gorgeous. Megan blinked as Brian approached the woman with open arms.

"There's my love." He planted a kiss on her cheek. The woman wrapped her arms around Brian's neck and nuzzled his cheek. The studio light glinted off the diamond ring she wore on her finger.

"Is that Brian's . . ." Megan began.

The writer turned his head. "Fiancée? Yeah, that's Eva."

Megan's eyes widened. That was Eva. And she was attached to Brian. Megan turned and caught Cane's eye and then glanced back at Eva. He was definitely staring, but not at Eva. He didn't look as if he even knew Eva was in the room. No, his eyes were firmly planted . . . on her.

❧❧❧❧

The shock of seeing Megan froze Cane in place, but eventually, he was able to put one foot in front of the other. She was talking to a writer, but it didn't matter. After the finale, he'd stewed over what Molly said. Megan believed he was in love with someone else. He didn't want to take away from her moment by pulling her aside at the taping in order to lay it all on the line. She had enough to deal with when everyone was congratulating her.

In the days after the finale, he had convinced himself she was busy, her days packed with interviews. Truth be told, he was still scared. Megan wasn't with Andrew, he knew that much, but what if she didn't want to be with him either? There was no way to know for sure until he asked.

And now, seeing her, he knew he'd waited long enough—too long, even. It was his turn.

Cane couldn't get across the room fast enough. His interview with Brian had been a disaster and now that he saw Megan, he was certain that had she been here earlier it would have gone swimmingly. She was what he needed. She was what he was missing in his life, and he wasn't going to delay telling her any longer.

"Excuse me." He gave the writer a small smile as he interrupted their discussion. "Could I have a moment with Megan?"

"Sure." The writer stuffed the script into Megan's hand and walked away. "See you in a bit."

Cane shifted his feet, wondering where to start.

"Megan," he whispered. She was adorable. She wore ripped jeans and a sweatshirt with a hole in the elbow. Her hair was in its regular ponytail and her glasses were sliding down her nose. She was perfection.

Before he could continue, she placed a finger over his lips. "I'm sorry, Cane," she said.

He frowned. "What are you sorry for?"

"A lot of things." She glanced over her shoulder.

Cane watched her line of vision and noticed Eva across the room for the first time, chatting with Brian and holding his hand. Cane put his hands around Megan's waist and pulled her closer.

"You have nothing to be sorry for. I'm the one who's sorry. I saw you with Andrew and I panicked. You know my history and how I felt about coming in second place. I let myself believe it was happening again."

Megan made a face, and Cane chuckled, tucking a stray lock of hair behind her ear.

"Exactly. Looking back now, I know you would never have anything to do with him."

"Of course I wouldn't. I was too in love with you." Megan placed her hands on Cane's arms.

Did she just say love?

"I was such a fool," he continued, knowing he had to fully explain himself to her. "I think my heart was still broken from before. Not because I really loved Eva, but because I was infatuated with the idea of her and mad at myself for letting my guard down with the wrong person."

"She's . . . the wrong person?"

Cane lowered his head until their foreheads touched. "Of course she is. I should have seen it a lot sooner than I did." He shrugged. "I guess I didn't know who the right person was until I met you."

Cane pulled Megan closer until only inches separated them. He was vaguely aware of the reporters bustling around them, but the couple was in their own little world.

"Megan, everything changed when I met you. You gave me something no one else in the world ever has. When you're around, I feel like the piece of me that's always been missing is finally in place."

He saw tears glinting in her eyes.

"You make me feel like I matter." She spoke in a soft voice. "When you were around, I could stand on my own two feet and hold my own."

"No." Cane shook his head. "That's all you. Maybe I gave you the strength to find yourself, but it's you in there, coming out for the world to see."

Megan smiled. "I'm different now." She pulled back an inch.

Cane nodded. "I know. I liked you before, when you wouldn't meet my eyes and blushed every time I looked in your direction." He leaned over and closed the space she'd put between them. "But Megan, now I'm pretty sure I love you."

"Wow." Megan stared into his eyes.

Cane wiped the tear that trickled down her face. "Can I be your Leftover?" he asked.

Megan giggled. "Did you really just say that?"

"I did and I mean it."

Megan stood on her toes and planted her lips on his. Cane remembered the first time they kissed, when she was dared to approach him and lay one on him. And he remembered dragging her into his tent. He'd felt something then, but now, the whole world was spinning because the two of them were together.

"Yes, Cane. You can be my Leftover. But you're not a Leftover at all. You're my first and only choice."

Cane smiled against her cheek as he picked her up and twirled her around. The newsroom had taken notice of what was going on and someone in the corner began clapping. Cane's eyes searched the darkness around them. Eva and Brian stood in the middle of the room, clapping along with the rest of the group. Cane gave Eva a slight nod. She had been right all along. They weren't right for one another. He was sorry he'd lost so much time thinking she was mistaken. But now, he was glad for everything he'd been through. In his arms, he held the only woman in the world that was right for him. And he had no plans of letting go.

All thanks to a show called *The Leftover*.